THEODOSIA
and the
SERPENTS of
CHAOS

THEODOSIA
—— and the ——
SERPENTS of
CHAOS

R. L. LaFevers

illustrated by Yoko Tanaka

HOUGHTON MIFFLIN COMPANY BOSTON
2007

The text of this book is set in Minister Book.
The illustrations are acrylic on board.
Map of 1905 London used courtesy of the Harvard Map Collection.

Library of Congress Control Number 2006034284

ISBN-13: 978-0-618-75638-4

Manufactured in the United States of America
MP 10 9 8 7 6 5 4 3 2 1

To clever girls everywhere
who get tired of feeling like
no one's listening.

And to Kate O'Sullivan,
who is very, very clever
and not the least bit bossy.

PART ONE

MOTHER SENDS A SURPRISE

DECEMBER 17, 1906

I DON'T TRUST CLIVE FAGENBUSH.

How can you trust a person who has eyebrows as thick and black as hairbrushes and smells of boiled cabbage and pickled onions? Besides, I'm beginning to suspect he's up to something. What's worse, I think he suspects *I'm* up to something. Which I usually am.

Not that anyone would take the word of an eleven-year-old girl against that of the Second Assistant Curator—even if that girl just happens to be the daughter of the Head Curator of the museum and is rather cleverer than most (or so I've been told; oddly, I don't think they meant it as a compliment). As far as I can tell, it doesn't make any difference to adults how clever children are. They always stick together. Unless you are sick or dying or mortally wounded, they will always side with the other adult.

That's certainly the case here, anyway. My father oversees the Museum of Legends and Antiquities, the second largest museum in London. As a result, I spend most of my time clattering around this old place. I don't mind. Really. Well, not much anyway. Though it would be nice if Father remembered I was here once in a while . . . However, I've got plenty to do. The museum's got loads of secrets, and I've discovered I'm very good at ferreting out secrets. And curses. You'd be surprised at how many things come into the museum loaded with curses—bad ones. Ancient, dark, Egyptian-magic ones.

Take this morning, for example, when a crate arrived from Mum.

At the sound of the buzzer, I hurried down to Receiving. Dolge and Sweeny, the museum's two hired hands, were just opening the doors to the loading area. Yellow fog began oozing into the room like a runny pudding. Outside, I could make out the drayman, blowing on his fingers and stamping his feet, trying to stay warm as he waited next to his cart. His carriage lanterns were lit and looked like two fuzzy halos in the thick fog. Sweeny hopped off the dock and together they lifted a crate from the back of the cart and carried it inside. As they made their way past me, I

4

craned forward to read the label. It was from Thebes! Which meant it had to be from Mum. Her first shipment from the Valley of the Kings! The first of many, most likely.

Once they'd placed the crate on an empty worktable, the drayman tipped his cap and hurried back to his cart, anxious to be on his way. Dolge closed the door behind him with a resounding clang.

By this time, the curators had arrived, and we all gathered round to watch Father open the crate. As I inched closer, I saw that, once again, he wasn't wearing any gloves. My own gloved fingers twitched in dismay.

"Um, Father?"

He paused, his hands hovering over the crate. "Yes, Theodosia?"

"Aren't you afraid you'll get splinters?" Everyone turned to stare at me oddly.

"Nonsense," he said.

Of course, I didn't give a fig about splinters. They were the least of my worries. But I didn't dare tell him that.

With everyone's attention once again focused on the crate, I shuffled closer to Father's side, trying to reach him before he actually touched whatever it was that Mum had sent. I made it past Dolge and Sweeny with no problem, but I had to hold my breath as I sidled past Fagenbush. He glared at me, and I glared back.

When I reached Father's side, I dipped my hand into the

pocket of my pinafore just as he plunged his hands into the crate. As unobtrusively as possible, I slipped a small amulet of protection out of my pocket and into his. Unfortunately, my action did not go unnoticed. He paused and scowled at me. "What on earth are you doing?"

"I just wanted to get a good look, Father. I am the shortest one in the room, you know." To turn his attention from me back to the crate, I leaned forward and peered in. "What do you think she's sent us this time?"

"Well, that's what I'm trying to find out." His voice was tinged with exasperation. Then luckily he forgot all about me as, with great ceremony, he reached into the crate and lifted out an absolutely fetching black statue of a cat: Bastet, the Egyptian fertility goddess.

The moment I laid eyes on it, I felt as if a parade of icy-footed beetles were marching down my spine. My cat, Isis, who'd been skulking under the workmen's bench, took one look at the statue, meowed loudly, then streaked off for parts unknown. I shuddered. Once again Mother had sent us an artifact positively dripping with ancient, evil curses.

"Are you all right, Theo?" Nigel Bollingsworth, the First Assistant Curator, asked. "You're not taking a chill, are you?"

He studied me in concern. Next to him, Fagenbush stared at me as if I were something nasty that Isis had dragged in. "No, Mr. Bollingsworth. I'm fine."

Well, except for the black magic rolling off the new cursed object.

Of course, Mother never realized it was cursed. Nor did Father. Neither one of them ever seemed able to tell.

None of the assistant curators seemed to notice anything, either. Except for that rat Fagenbush. He eyed the statue with his face aglow and his long, bony fingers twitching. The problem was, he looked like that half the time, so it was hard to know if it was his reaction to the artifact or he was just being his own horrid self.

As far as I knew, I was the only one able to detect the black magic still clinging to the ancient objects. Therefore, it was up to me to discover the nature of this statue's curse and how to remove it.

Quickly.

When Mother arrived tomorrow, she was sure to have loads of new artifacts with her. Even more crates would trickle in over the next few weeks. Who knew how many of those items would be cursed? I could be busy for months! The only good thing was that it would keep me out of Mother and Father's way. They tend to get annoyed when I'm underfoot, and then begin talking of sending me off to school. This way, at least I'd be able to spend some time with Mum.

Still, while hunches and gut instinct were all well and good for a First Level Test, I had to be logical and scientific about this. I needed to conduct a Level Two Test as soon as possible.

My chance came when everyone had cleared out of the receiving bay and returned to their duties. Since I didn't have any duties to return to, I was able to hang back unnoticed.

I went over to one of the shelves that lined the receiving area and took down a small, battered Canopic jar. It had come in badly damaged, and since it wasn't particularly valuable, no one had taken the time to restore it. I had begun using it for collecting wax (old candle stubs, sealing wax, that kind of thing), which I used extensively in my Second Level Test. Wax is very good at absorbing *heka,* or evil magic.

I removed some of the wax bits from the jar and carefully set them in a circle around the base of the statue.

By dinnertime, the entire circle of wax bits was a foul greeny-black color. Drat! I don't think the wax has ever turned dark that quickly before. Now I had to come back and conduct a Third Level Test. Unfortunately, in order to do that, I needed moonlight. Moonlight is the only way to make the inscribed curses visible to the human eye.

Of course, the only way to view something in moonlight is at night.

And I *loathe* the museum at night.

The Moonlight Test

As luck would have it, it turned out to be another one of those nights when Father became so absorbed in his research that he forgot all about going home. It was the fourth night in a row, and for a change, it worked well with my own plans.

Just before midnight, I ventured out of the staff room into the museum. The gaslights had been turned low so that just a tiny blue bead glowed along the dark hallway at regular intervals. The feeble light from my oil lamp barely made a dent in the cavernous darkness, but I didn't let that deter me. I reached up and clutched the three protective amulets that hung around my neck. Father says I let my imagination run away with me, but the truth is, in the darkest hours of the night, if you look very closely (which I try not to) you can see the dangerous dead—the *akhu* and *mut*—rise up out of their urns and sarcophagi like a thick, choking mist. The ancient magic and words of terrible power ooze out of the arcane texts and inscribed objects. They hover in the corners and lurk in the shadows. How could I possibly venture out into that without *some* protection, I'd like to know?

Not wanting to make any noise that might draw the spirits' attention, I padded along in my stockinged feet, which were soon numb with cold.

Of course, Father had moved the wretched statue from the receiving area up to his workroom on the third floor. I hugged the wall as I crept up the polished wooden stairs, careful to avoid the ones that creaked.

No matter how quiet I was, the deep, gaping shadows around me seemed to grow larger and more forbidding. I was painfully aware of the last earthly remains, bones, coffins, and sacred relics of old, long-forgotten religions surrounding me. In the light of my oil lamp, the shadows bobbed and weaved like leering demons.

At last I reached the third floor and entered Statuary Hall. Enormous Egyptian sculptures lined the walls like ever-watchful guardians. The majestic faces of pharaohs stood side by side with mysterious sphinx heads, the smallest of which towered twenty feet high and cast harsh puddles of blackness on the floor.

I hurried past the looming statues until I reached the doorway that led into the Ancient Egypt Exhibit. I paused, bracing myself. Even though I patrolled this exhibit as often as possible, I could never be too sure what might be waiting for me in there. Magic is a tricky business, and the Egyptians were masters of it. Some spells seemed to regenerate themselves after a full moon or on specific unholy days. Others were only visible during certain seasons or when the stars and planets were aligned just so. All in all, ancient Egyptian magic is a horrid jumble of sinister possibilities, and I never take anything for granted when dealing with it.

With one fortifying breath, I made a mad dash through the room, scurrying past the exhibit cases, looking neither to the right nor the left. With one last shiver, I reached the workroom door, yanked it open, and slipped inside.

This room was dark, too, but pale, silvery moonlight shone in through the windows. And in that pale moonlight sat the statue of Bastet, an intricate, malevolent pattern of sacred words and symbols writhing across its surface like a nest of restless vipers.

Sometimes I really hate being right.

As I drew near the statue, I caught the symbol of Anubis, god of the underworld, as well as one for Seth, the god of chaos. There! Another symbol floated by, one I hadn't seen much but I think represented the demonic spirits of the restless dead. Any hopes I'd had of a rather small curse disappeared. I was dealing with an artifact positively steeped in vile, Egyptian black magic.

I needed a closer look, which meant I would have to pick the horrid thing up.

I glanced around the workroom. Wearing gloves wasn't protection enough when the hieroglyphs were swarming like this. The symbols had a way of trying to poke their way through the gloves and into my hands. I wasn't very keen on those words and symbols of evil power running along *my* skin, if you please.

I found an old rag on Father's worktable and wrapped it around my hand like an extra glove. Then I picked up the statue and carried it over to the window to have a better look.

The symbols slowed a bit once the statue was in my hand. I felt them probing at the rag, trying to get past the cloth barrier and worm their way into my flesh. I had to hurry.

The symbol of Apep, the serpent of chaos, floated by, followed by Mantu, the god of war. How odd. I'd never seen him on a cursed object before. There were more symbols: symbols for armies and destruction and—

There was a creak on the floorboards just outside the workroom door. Jolted into action, I scurried across the room, thrust the statue back on its shelf, and frantically searched for a hiding place. There were lots of shadowy corners, but I wanted something more substantial than that.

Spying an old packing crate in the corner, I hopped inside and covered myself as best I could with bits of packing material. I hunkered down, averted my eyes from the door, and waited.

You may wonder why I didn't look up to see the intruder. I can assure you, I wanted to. But I've lived alongside the restless, ancient spirits long enough to know that when you look at things, you focus your whole *ka,* or life force, on them, which causes their power to grow even stronger. If this nighttime visitor was of the supernatural variety, focusing my life force on it was as good as shining an oil lamp in its face.

My oil lamp! I peered through a crack in the side of the crate and saw my discarded lantern off to the side of the shelves. Luckily, the flame had gone out.

The door swung open, creaking slightly on its hinges. The footsteps paused in the doorway, as if the person or thing were surveying the room. Then the floorboards creaked again as someone—or something—stepped inside. I risked a glance through the crack again, just long enough to see a black hooded shape moving across the floor.

I wrenched my gaze away and tried to still the beating of my heart. It sounded like thunder to my ears—surely the intruder would hear it!

The footsteps came to a stop in front of the shelves, mere inches from where I was hiding. Risking another peek, I saw the large black shape studying the middle shelf, where I'd put the statue of Bastet back in its place. As my eyes swept downward again, I noticed two black shoes poking out from under the figure's long cape.

My heart calmed a bit. Supernatural beings don't wear shoes. Whatever it was—whoever it was—it must be human. Which I greatly preferred to the alternative.

Although, anyone skulking around a museum in the dead of night was probably up to no good. Except for me, of course—I had only the noblest of motives.

Slightly more confident now, I risked another glance and saw a long, black arm snake out from underneath the cloak. The movement sent a slight current of air toward me and I caught a whiff of boiled cabbage and pickled onions.

Clive Fagenbush!

Before I could sort out this puzzle, there was another squeak of the floorboards outside the workroom door. With a hiss of indrawn breath, Fagenbush snatched his empty hand back, then stepped around the shelves and flattened himself against the wall so that he was hidden from sight.

He now faced directly toward me. I scrunched down as small as I could in the crate and wished I were invisible.

The new intruder fumbled loudly with the doorknob, not even trying to be quiet. A quick, sure step came into the workroom, accompanied by a tuneless whistle.

I slumped in relief. It was only Father, on one of his midnight ramblings. He turned up the gas and flooded the workroom in soft yellow light.

Wondering if Father could see him, I glanced over at Fagenbush's hiding spot, only to find he'd disappeared.

I craned my neck, trying to see where he had gone, but he was nowhere in sight. Then I glimpsed a flutter of movement near the door as he slipped out of the workroom. Bother! He'd got clean away. But at least he hadn't conked Father over the head or discovered my whereabouts.

As I crouched in the crate, I realized I needed to come up with a plan to get my hands on that statue before someone else did. I considered taking it back to my room, but I couldn't bear the thought of those loathsome curses anywhere near me as I slept. I finally settled on hiding it that night, then returning it first thing in the morning while Father was having breakfast.

It took ages for Father to find whatever it was he was

looking for, but he finally left, turning out the lights and closing the door behind him. I waited a few minutes more to let him get safely out of the way. Once my eyes re-adjusted to the darkness, I climbed out of the crate and went over to the shelf. Using the rag, I lifted the statuette and placed it in the crate where I'd been hiding. I tossed some packing material over it, then grabbed my oil lamp, now uselessly dark, and made my way to the door. I peeked out into the exhibit room.

The museum seemed unusually restless. The creaks and groans had grown louder and more frequent. With my hand clutched firmly around all three amulets, I raced back through the display rooms. I felt disgruntled dead things rustle as I passed, the shadows growing longer as they reached out toward me. I put on an extra burst of speed.

Now do you see why I loathe the museum at night?

Work to Do

"Theodosia Elizabeth Throckmorton!"

"Hm. What?" I sat up and rubbed the sleep from my eyes. Father was standing in the doorway, a ferocious scowl on his face.

"Not the sarcophagus again!" he said.

Oops. I usually try to be up and about before he is for this very reason. But when he spends the entire night in scholarly pursuit and never goes to bed, well, it's rather impossible. "Really, Father. I'm not hurting it a bit and it *is* the best way to keep out the drafts." (It was also the safest place for avoiding all the curses that swirled about the museum at night, but I could just imagine what he'd say if I told him *that*.)

"Yes, but it's a priceless artifact—"

"That is sitting alone in a closet because there's no room for it in the exhibits. Truly Father, I'm very careful. Besides, where else would you like me to sleep when I'm forced to stay here all night?"

He had the good grace to wince slightly at this. "In an armchair, maybe, or curled up on the rug in front of the fireplace in the staff sitting room. Anywhere but in a blasted sarcophagus!"

Yes, but there was no protection in those places. I simply didn't trust the power of amulets alone at night against all the black magic and troublesome spirits. Of course, I couldn't tell him *that*, either.

"But Father, I'm sure Men'naat wouldn't mind."

"Who on earth . . ."

"The young priestess this sarcophagus belonged to," I explained. "She was from the temple of Taweret, an Egyptian goddess and protector of children. Just think how much easier I am to protect in here!"

He sighed in exasperation, then closed the door. I could have pressed my point a bit more, but I didn't want to risk reminding him that I really should be sleeping at school, where all the other girls my age were. I did my best to avoid that topic at all costs.

I crawled over the high stone side of the sarcophagus, which took up half of my room. Well, it was more of a closet, really. But no one else ever used it, so I had it all to myself. There was just enough space for a small writing desk and an even smaller battered old washstand that Flimp, the watchman, had found for me. He'd also pounded a few nails into the wall so I had a place to hang my frocks and pinafores.

As I splashed cold water on my face, I realized I had slept through my best chance for sneaking into Father's workroom unnoticed. I really needed to get my hands on that statuette. And soon. I looked at my watch. Mother was due back in five hours and fifty-seven minutes and she was bound to have loads of new artifacts with her. It was very likely we'd have scads of new, unknown magic swirling around the museum before long. I pulled my gloves firmly into place, then stepped out to face the day.

My next opportunity came when Father left his workroom in search of a cup of tea. I usually brought it to him around this time every morning but I hadn't that day, hoping he would eventually give up and go in search of one himself. It worked.

I peeked inside the workroom. Other than artifacts from every civilization known to man spread out on the worktables in various states of disrepair, it appeared empty. I was halfway to the crate when an obnoxious voice behind me stopped me in my tracks.

"Where is it?"

I turned. Clive Fagenbush stood just to the side of the door—almost as if he'd been waiting for me.

"Where is what?" I asked.

"The statue." His eyes shifted from my face to the roll of papyrus I held in my hand. He strode forward and snatched the papyrus from me.

Just as I opened my mouth to protest, a familiar voice called out, "I say, Fagenbush. What's all this about? Give Theo back her papyrus." Scowling, Nigel Bollingsworth stepped into the room.

Have I mentioned how much I adore Nigel Bollingsworth? In fact, I think I shall marry him when I grow up, although I haven't told him yet. (Father said I mustn't. In fact, when I told Father, what he said was, "What makes you so sure anyone is going to want to marry you, Miss Busybody?")

"I thought she had something that didn't belong to her," Fagenbush muttered.

"Well, you can see that she doesn't. Now go and make the lower exhibits ready for the visit from the Hedgewick School for Wayward Boys, scheduled for this morning. I want everything securely fastened down. You remember the last time they were here."

Fagenbush curled his lip in disgust and shoved the roll of

papyrus back into my hands, then turned on his heel and left.

"Are you all right, Theo?" Nigel asked.

"Yes, Mr. Bollingsworth." I looked up at him and let my eyes fill with gratitude. "Thank you ever so much." I rubbed my wrist so he would know just how horrible Fagenbush had been. In truth, it did ache a little.

He beamed at me. "Very good, then. Carry on." And with that, he, too, left the room.

With no time to waste, I snatched the statue from the crate, hid it in the papyrus roll, and headed down to the reading room on the first floor. I kept a cautious eye out for Fagenbush the whole way, but he appeared to have scuttled back under his rock.

Out of the Frying Pan, Into the, er, Cat

IT'S ALL VERY WELL AND GOOD to know that something's cursed, but you still have to work out what on earth to do about it. Father has taught me that when all the clues fail to lead to a solid conclusion, there is research. Piles and piles of it. Of course, Father didn't realize what I'd spend my time studying, but the fact of the matter was, research was my only defense.

When I was very young and first began to visit the museum, it terrified me, even though I was too young to understand why. Now, of course, I knew it was the evil curses and restless spirits I sensed wandering around the place. But all I knew back then was that if my parents learned of my fear, they wouldn't let me come to the museum. Then I'd never get to see them! So I vowed to keep my fears to myself.

For years my parents thought I had a permanent chill, so badly did I shiver whenever I was near the museum. I still don't know why the curses and spirits didn't harm me. Although we *did* go through an astonishing number of junior curators and clerks. Most of them either had unfortunate accidents or took extremely ill. One or two of them appeared to have lost their minds completely. Fortunately, Mother and Father didn't suffer the fate of those other employees. The only reason I could think that Mother was safe was because without her, the artifacts—and therefore the curses and spirits—would stay buried and obscure and never have a chance to wreak their havoc on mankind. It was almost as if by leaving her alone, they were thanking her for releasing them, although of course she had no idea what she'd done.

Father wasn't as lucky. In fact, that's how he injured his leg. He took a nasty tumble down all three flights of stairs. Afterward, he said it felt as if someone had just reached out and pushed him. I'm quite sure that someone—or something—did. Although I do think they went easy on him too, since he was the one who spent all his time restoring the artifacts to their former glory.

Of course, I didn't understand any of this until I became old enough to read. Then I began researching everything we had in the museum, hoping that knowledge would replace my fear.

It wasn't until I discovered the old, nearly forgotten volumes on ancient Egyptian magic that I began to understand. Once I'd read those I knew exactly what I was dealing with, and it wasn't reassuring. Luckily, the old texts also listed ways to remove or nullify the curses. Slowly I began to learn of different antidotes and remedies. There were a few harrowing mistakes along the way, but mostly I'd been very lucky.

Since I spend so much time in the museum, I've claimed one of the small offices off the main reading room as my own study. (Our reading room is hardly ever used, as most everyone goes to the British Museum to do their research.) Father thinks I am attending to my studies, and I let him believe that. This morning I sat among arcane texts bound in leather and held together with buckles and straps, ancient clay tablets filled with rows and rows of hieroglyphs, and scrolls of parchment and papyrus on which ancient priests and sorcerers made their notations. I finally settled on *Hidden Egypt: Magic, Alchemy, and the Occult*, by T. R. Nectanebus. He seems to have picked up more bits about ancient spells and curses than anyone.

I took a bite of my jam sandwich and began to read. *The cursed statuettes were often made of basalt, a hard black stone associated with the Underworld.*

Now for the difficult part. I had to actually touch the thing with my bare hands. At least there wasn't any moonlight and the curse lay quiet and dormant. Slipping off a glove, I reached out and tapped a fingernail against the statue. It was cold, hard stone, and definitely black. In fact, it looked exactly like the picture in the book. I pulled my glove back on and continued reading.

Once the statue had been inscribed with the necessary hieroglyphs, it was covered with magic spells and philters designed to transfer their power once the proper awakening agent was applied. This was primarily used for healing, but was occasionally used for evil purposes as well. If the statue was intended to curse instead of heal, the philter most likely contained snake oil (cobra or asp), which will give the object an exceptionally glossy texture. If cursed, the book said, *the object will give off the faint scent of sulfur.*

Curses did have a particular smell to them, and it wasn't pleasant. I leaned forward and sniffed. It was hard to tell over the aroma of blackberry jam, but I was fairly certain I *did* detect a whiff of sulfur clinging to the statue's glossy surface.

I resumed my reading, straining to make out the faded, spidery handwriting as dark gray clouds moved in and blocked what little light came in through the window. *To neutralize the curse, make a small replica of the figurine out of wax, four-fingers-width tall. On the bottom of the figure, scratch the indicated hieroglyphs, then make a potion of the following ingredients. Say the indicated spell as you anoint the statuette with the potion. The potion will wake the spell and activate the curse, but the spell you chant will direct it into the small wax figurine, which must then be immediately consigned to flame. It is of critical importance to stay focused on the spell once it has begun.*

Notice how Nectanebus didn't say what the spell *does* once it's activated. These ancient scholars always leave out the important stuff. Frankly, I'm not fond of surprises, as the ones around here tend to be rather wicked. When mucking about with ancient curses and black magic, I prefer to know just how bad things can get if they go wrong. Not that I'm certain I can fix them, but still, there is comfort in knowing.

Just then, Isis, who'd been curled up on the small couch warily eyeing the statuette, leaped to her feet. She arched her back and hissed at the door.

I slammed the book shut and glanced around, trying to find a hiding place for the statue. I snatched it off the desk and ended up shoving it back inside the rolled-up papyrus scroll.

The door burst open and Clive Fagenbush strode into the room. "Where is it, you pest?" he asked me.

You'd think the man was stalking me!

"Where is what?" I asked, taking a bite of jam sandwich, knowing it would disgust him and make him think of me as just a grubby little girl.

"The statuette of Bastet. Where is it?"

"Are you still going on about that? I told you, I haven't the faintest idea what you're talking about. Is Father looking for it?"

"No," Fagenbush said with a snort. "He hasn't even noticed it's missing. But I have. It was an especially interesting artifact and I have . . . plans . . . for it. Now where did you put it?"

"Whatever would I be doing with a statuette?" I asked, trying to look as innocent as I could.

He took two long strides into the room until he was towering above me. His eyebrows drew together, forming a thick black V over his eyes. The cabbagy smell that clung to him, mixed with the sulfur fumes given off by the statue, made my eyes water.

"Give me that statue."

I'd never seen him this furious before, and it took every speck of willpower to stand my ground. I would *not* back away, no matter how hard my knees knocked together. Refusing to let my eyes wander over to the rolled papyrus on the table, I gritted my teeth and stared back. "In case you're hard of hearing, *I do not have it.*"

Fagenbush drew in a deep breath and his long nose quivered. "I know you're lying. I want that statue. I want it back where it belongs by sunset. Do you understand? I have plans for that statue." His eyes raked over me. "And they do not include interference from a nasty, sticky little girl." He smiled, and it was a chilling smile. "But that could change if you don't cooperate," he said meaningfully. Then he stormed across the room, muttering, "The child is a raving lunatic."

When he reached the door, he slammed it shut, certain his threat would be enough to force my cooperation. Fagenbush was revolting, but when he was in a rage he was positively terrifying. Quite frankly, this new side of him scared the stuffing out of me.

I went over to the door and locked it. "Idiot," I whispered, mad at myself for letting him rattle me so. I had an overwhelming urge to snuggle with Isis just then, but there wasn't time. I bent down to give her a quick rub under the chin and promised myself a long cuddle with her after I had dealt with the statue.

I hauled my carpetbag full of curse-removing supplies out from behind the desk and began to rummage around. For any who might be interested in such things, I've made a list of what my kit contains.

Recommended Supplies and Equipment for Ancient Egyptian Curse Removal

Unbleached linen or muslin thread in the following
    colors: red, green, yellow, white, blue, and black

mortar and pestle

loads of wax, preferably white

sharp-edged stick for carving in wax

gold- and silver-colored wire

willow wood twigs

variety of herbs, such as catnip and rue

frankincense and myrrh

red wine

honey

milk

lettuce juice (extracted from lettuce leaves. They are
    often hard to find so I substitute cabbage, then
    water it down a bit. Seems to work fine.)

stones, pebbles, and shells in interesting sizes and shapes

small fish or chicken bones

odd bits of natural bric-a-brac, such as cat teeth, bits of
    lizard skin, a good collection of that sort of thing

small bits of rock and semiprecious stones, like quartz,
    sandstone, lapis lazuli, jasper, malachite, carnelian,
    turquoise, alabaster

Since I am mad about collecting wax bits, there was easily enough to make a small figurine. Once I had formed the replica (which didn't look very much like a cat, but rather more like a slender tree trunk with ears—hopefully it wouldn't matter), I carved the correct hieroglyphs in the bottom of it, then set it down.

I reached back into my bag and pulled out a glass vial, opened it, and sniffed. Claret. I'd had to snitch it from the decanter in Father's library. If he ever noticed it was missing, I would blame it on Fagenbush. Smiling at the thought of this subtle revenge, I groped around until my hand closed around a small muslin pouch.

Since so many magical recipes call for the herb rue, I always try to have a supply of it on hand. (It's good for warding off evil spirits and is useful against the hysterical spasms or afflictions that curses can cause.) It's devilishly hard to find, and takes all my pocket money as well. Removing curses is not a task for the faint-hearted or financially strapped; unfortunately, I am both.

I mixed the two ingredients together in a mortar, grinding the rue down fine with the pestle. When it was ready, I took a deep breath and stripped off my gloves. With the stub of a pencil, I drew a wedjat eye on each of my palms and hoped it would be protection enough. I dipped a clean rag in the potion and began wiping it on the cursed statue. As I chanted the words from the book, I was careful to keep the rag between the statue and my fingertips at all times.

In Egyptian magic, in addition to using the right recipe, the words you use and how you use them are critically important for any curse or spell. You must get the words just so and have the proper tone of voice in order for it to work. Or at least, that's what the books said. I knew I was doing that part right because the statue began to vibrate and the scent of sulfur grew stronger. The hieroglyphs that I had seen last night suddenly rose to the surface in a buzzing frenzy. The good news was, wherever I touched the statue with the potion, the symbols shrank back, as if afraid. Surely that was a good sign.

When I finally ran out of potion, all the symbols had shrunk to half their original size. I stopped dabbing and stepped back, still chanting. Slowly, the hieroglyphs seemed to try and pull away from the surface of the statue, as if the words I uttered were calling to them. With a series of dull pops, they broke free of the statue and rose up into the air above it, where they hovered like a swarm of angry bees. I held my warded hands out in front.

The stench of sulfur was overpowering, and I tried to utter the words of power without breathing in any of the ghastly fumes. Unfortunately, when I came to the phrase "Begone you putrid she-cat," Isis protested by swiping at my ankle with her claws.

Startled, I looked down at her. "Not you," I said. As I

spoke, the buzzing symbols quit hovering and began streaming straight toward my cat. The moment they touched her, she snarled, and every hair on her body stood straight up on end as the hieroglyphs danced along her fur. Isis's eyes grew wild and her ears flattened against her head. An unholy yowl erupted from her throat.

She was no longer my beloved pet, but Evil Incarnate. Was that what Nectanebus had meant when he said it was critically important to focus and avoid distractions? The curse was supposed to rise off the statue and flow into the wax figurine, which I was then to burn. At least, that's what had happened in the past.

But now I had no idea what to do. And I didn't dare take my eyes off Isis long enough to read the book for suggestions.

The bespelled cat reached out and swiped me again, this time with all the furies of hell behind her. Her claws sliced through my woolen stockings and bit painfully into my shin. She arched her back and hissed, then ran to hide under the bookshelf, where she continued to make low, demonic yowls.

I collapsed into a chair and stared at the bookshelf, then turned to look at the sleek statue of Bastet, which now sat as peaceful as you please.

What had I just done? Poor Isis!

Reverse it. That's what I had to do. Reverse it.

But . . . it could be undone, couldn't it? Oh, dear.

And what if that nasty curse had gone into *me*? My stomach twitched uncomfortably. Best not to think about that.

When I was sure I could stand again, I hurried back over to the books spread out on my desk. Surely there must be a way to fix this. Just then, the clock began chiming the hour. Two o'clock! Where had the day gone? It was time to collect Mother.

My joy at Mother's homecoming was somewhat dampened by poor Isis's predicament. I would have to work out what to do about Isis later. I closed the book and snatched the neutralized statuette off the table and rolled it up in an old piece of parchment so I could return it to the shelf upstairs.

Halfway out of the room, I remembered that Father would probably be hungry. I hurried back to the table and tucked the last of the jam sandwiches into my pocket. After one last apologetic glance in Isis's direction, I headed out the door.

I stayed on the lookout for any signs of Fagenbush as I went. Who knows what he would do if he found me with the statue? Probably bash me over the head with it.

I finally reached Father's workroom and made my way through upended dinosaur bones, half-opened crates, cracked urns, and a headless marble sculpture. After I returned the statuette to its shelf, I went in search of Father. I found him at one of his worktables, trying to reconstruct a piece of clay tablet from Mum's dig that had been in the crate with the Bastet statue. The stele was in seven different pieces, and it looked like he was having some difficulty.

I waited patiently for him to notice me. When that didn't happen, I cleared my throat. "Father? It's time to pick Mother up from the station."

"Just as soon as I finish here," he said, sounding as if he hadn't really heard me at all.

I looked out the window, where the clouds had finally joined together and formed a steady gray drizzle. "I don't think Mum's going to want to wait that long."

When he didn't answer, I looked over his shoulder. It appeared he was trying to sort out the hieroglyphs on the pieces of clay tablet. Intrigued, I leaned in closer. I adore hieroglyphs. Some people love to draw and others have a way with music and still others love puzzles, but hieroglyphs are my favorite thing. To me, they make clear and perfect sense, as if they were the way we're *supposed* to communicate. But Father seemed stumped.

"Here you go." I reached around his arm. "What if you put this piece here, then turn it clockwise half a turn?" There. Maybe now he'd begin to see how useful I could be!

"Theodosia, I really don't think you comprehend how complex this is. There is no way a mere child could understand how these pieces—"

"Like so." I slid the last piece into place.

34

"Hmmpf." He leaned forward to study the completed stele. "Now, be a good girl and find me a spot of lunch before we go, would you?"

"I already thought of that." I reached into my pocket and placed the jam sandwich on the table in front of him.

His face brightened. "Oh! Jolly good. Thank you." He took a bite, then grimaced. "Jam? Again?"

My spirits fell. It was something to eat, wasn't it? Besides, it was all I could find in the cupboard. I glanced at the clock again. Poor Mother would be wondering what on earth had happened to us.

But Father was once again absorbed in the stele. *"But let them remember, to be afraid, even after his death,"* he read as the clock chimed two-thirty.

"Come on, Father! Mother is going to be as furious as a drenched cat!"

"Oh," he said, looking out the window. "Is it raining?"

A loud crack of thunder and bolt of lightning shot out of the sky and the rain turned into torrents. "Just a bit," I said.

CURIOUS GOINGS-ON AT
CHARING CROSS STATION

WE STEPPED OUT OF THE MUSEUM into a howling wind that nearly snatched my heavy winter coat right off my back. The sky was leaden with clouds, which pelted us with a furious, stinging rain. Father herded me into the growler, where we shook the worst of the water off then settled back onto the cushions. He rapped on the carriage ceiling with his cane, and we lurched away from the curb out into traffic.

The streets were a mad snarl of carts, carriages, omnibuses, and motorcars, all vying for the right of way. People with large black umbrellas dashed across the street, trying to get out of the downpour. An omnibus swerved to avoid a pedestrian and nearly plowed into us. Our driver swore as the growler lurched wildly and sent me crashing into the side of the carriage. "Watch where yer goin' ye muttonhead!" the driver called out.

As I righted myself, I looked up to find Father scowling at me. "Where *is* your hat?" he asked. "You manage to remember your gloves often enough. Why not your blasted hat?"

Because I don't touch cursed objects with my head, I wanted to say. But of course I didn't. "I hate hats. They feel like they're squishing my head, squeezing and squeezing until my brain feels all mushed up. Like porridge in a too-small bowl."

Father frowned. "Really, Theodosia. You need to get a hold of that imagination of yours. One of these days you're going to catch your death."

Why is it that parents only notice you long enough to scold? If you do something right, say bring them lunch or help them out with a puzzle, they act as if you're invisible. But let one silly mistake slip by, like a forgotten hat, and they read you the riot act.

I looked out the window and forced myself not to squirm with impatience. Mother had been gone for ages, and I couldn't wait to see her. It was my fondest hope that she'd been so homesick, she'd swear she'd never go away again.

Most mothers don't leave their homes for months on end, but then most mums weren't as wonderful as mine. She's dashing and adventurous and oh-so-clever. And an American. She doesn't pay too much attention to stuffy old conventions. Grandmother Throckmorton says I take very much after my mother. I don't think she means that as a compliment.

Hopefully, Mother would want to dash straight home and have one of those warm, happy family evenings that I missed so much. I was getting just a bit tired of sleeping in the sarcophagus—a night or two is an adventure, but four nights in a row is an ordeal. I was running out of clean frocks, I was dying for a proper meal, and there never seemed to be enough blankets at night.

The cab pulled up in front of Charing Cross Station and we stumbled out onto the street. Father managed to catch me just before I landed in a nasty puddle.

We made our way toward the station, jostled this way and that by the crowd. I felt like a billiard ball let loose on the billiard table. Afraid I'd lose Father in the crush, I grabbed the tail of his greatcoat. A path opened up mysteriously in front of him. I couldn't be sure, but I suspect he was using his cane (gently, of course!) to encourage people to make way for us.

After one particularly bad jostle, I felt a cold, small hand next to mine on Father's coat. I watched, shocked, as the hand reached into Father's pocket and pulled out his wallet. Without thinking, I reached out and clamped down on the grimy wrist.

The wallet dropped back into Father's pocket and the owner of the wrist gave a low squeal. "Blimey! Let me go! Let me go! Don't call fer the p'lice, miss. I was just gonna look at it, then put it right back." The squealer had a button nose, and two bright blue eyes peeked out of his soot-covered face.

"You were not," I hissed, not ready to bring a mob of officials down on him quite yet. After all, he looked to be an Unfortunate Soul. (Mother and Father are quite firm in their teachings that we must be kind to those less fortunate than ourselves. Still, I didn't think that meant he should be allowed to pick Father's pocket.)

"Yes I was. Honest." He wiggled frantically, tugging at his arm to get away.

"I won't turn you in, but you stay away from our pockets, do you hear me? Swear it."

"I swears it, I swears it. Now let go already. Them fingernails of yours is right sharp."

They weren't really, but I *had* angled them to their best advantage. It wasn't very nice, but then neither was picking pockets.

"Swear it on your mother's grave," I said solemnly. Through my work at the museum I have learned that swearing on someone's grave is very serious business.

He rolled his eyes and heaved a great, irritated sigh. "All right already. I swear it on me mother's grave."

"Very well then." I let go of his wrist. He gave a quick nod of thanks, then, before I could blink, he melted back into the crowd.

Just then Father glanced over his shoulder at me. "Theodosia, what are you doing back there? Stop gawking and hurry up."

Inside the station we hustled along to the platform where Mum was waiting for us. She was one of the few passengers still there, and she sat perched atop one of her larger trunks. There was another pile of trunks and crates next to her that looked as if it would topple over at the next strong gust of wind.

I was so happy to see her that I wanted to run and throw my arms around her, but it had been so long since I'd seen her, I felt shy. Then she reached out and wrapped her arms around me in a wonderful hug that chased any doubts away. The soft fabric of her traveling suit under my cheek and the familiar scent of lilacs made me horribly aware of just how much I'd missed her. I opened my eyes wide and blinked rapidly to keep from embarrassing myself.

When Mum pulled back, her eyes were a bit damp, too, and she took a minute to adjust her hat. Father had already begun surveying the luggage.

"Good heavens, Henrietta. Just how many new frocks did you acquire in Cairo, anyway?"

Mother laid a gloved hand on his arm. "These aren't my clothes, you ninny. There was some severe competition over there." She glanced meaningfully at me, which meant she didn't want to discuss this in front of me. "I thought it best to keep some of the artifacts close by as opposed to shipping them."

Father beamed at her. "That's my girl."

Mother got a warm look in her eye and I had to look away so I wouldn't have to see them go all mushy.

And it was a very good thing I did.

The platform was mostly empty by this time. If it had been full, I'm sure I never would have noticed the man. Actually, he was trying very hard not to be noticed, which of course made him all the more noticeable. More important, the moment I laid eyes on him it felt as if an icy-footed beetle were scuttling down my back. It was the same sensation I got whenever I discovered a cursed object in the museum. The man lurking in the shadows stared at Mother like a hungry vulture.

No. Not Mother; her trunks.

I looked away before he realized he'd been spotted and sidled up to Mum, tugging on her skirt to get her attention. "Mother, who is that man over there? The one skulking in the shadows," I asked, careful to keep my voice low.

"Skulking in the shadows!" Father said in a rather too loud voice. "Really, where do you come up with these things, Theodosia?"

I glared at him, wishing for a moment that I had let that urchin pinch his wallet. Mother put her hand on my shoulder and gave the fellow a quick glance. The moment she turned in his direction, he looked away and began studying the train schedule posted on the wall in front of him.

"Him? I don't know, dear. He was on the boat when we left Alexandria."

"Another one of your admirers, Henrietta?" Father teased.

"Nonsense!" Mum said, flapping her hand.

Must they carry on so?

The cab driver was not happy when he saw all Mum's trunks and crates. I kept a lookout for the little pickpocket, half convinced he'd try to make off with an entire trunk if given the opportunity. Finally, the driver (with Father's help) managed to get every piece of luggage tied on and tucked in. It was a bit of a squash, but we didn't have far to go.

I sat right next to Mother, pressed up close due to all the

luggage, which I didn't mind. I had six long months to catch up on, after all. I let my mind focus on how wonderful it was to have her home again and actually *go* home for a bit. I was getting tired of dinners out of a tin. I wanted a proper bath and a cream tea, and steak and kidney pie for dinner with a scrumptious pudding afterward.

After six long months away, surely Mother felt the same.

For the moment, I was happy to snuggle up against her and let the two of them talk their boring political talk.

"So, how were things over there, Henrietta?" Father asked.

Mum settled more firmly into the cushions. "Well, the French have calmed down some. The Americans are like puppies bounding all over the place in their enthusiasm, not minding who or what they step on. And the place was absolutely crawling with Germans."

"Any sign of von Braggenschnott?"

"Well, yes, actually. He's risen to a surprising level of influence considering that he's up to his elbows in smuggling antiquities out of the country. But I can't complain; he came to my assistance in convincing the local officials to let me take my discoveries out of the country and bring them home to England."

"I don't know, Henrietta. I don't like having you anywhere near von Braggenschnott or men of his character."

Mother waved her hand in the air. "Nonsense. I'm perfectly capable of taking care of myself."

"Hm, yes, well. The Germans have been busy at home too. Their naval buildup has the entire Ministry uneasy. The Lord Chancellor offered them a treaty again, but Kaiser Wilhelm insists on concessions we refuse to make. Everyone's getting nervous. They're pretty sure he's up to something."

Thoroughly bored with this conversation, I looked out the window. With a sinking heart, I noticed the growler turn away from Chesterfield Place and head down Marlborough Street toward the museum. I gave Father a questioning look. He reached out and patted my arm. "Don't worry, Theodosia. It will only be for a bit. We've got to drop some of these crates off at the museum, and your mother wants to show us a few of her new discoveries."

A bit, my bum, I thought. I settled back against the cushions and resigned myself to spending yet another night in the museum. Which was probably just as well, since I was terribly worried about Isis. I had to find a way to reverse that spell.

Besides, it would only be for one more day. Come tomorrow, we'd have to go home. For one, it was only a few days before Christmas and even my distracted parents emerged from their scholarly pursuits long enough to celebrate Christmas. The second reason was my younger brother,

Henry. He would be coming home from school tomorrow and he *hates* the museum. He is so easily bored, and becomes such a dreadful pest, that by mutual consent my parents avoid having him there for any length of time.

Of course, I should be in school as well. I went for one term and it was so horribly dull and boring. Unfortunately, I had the bad luck to get far better marks than the others, an unpardonable sin in their eyes. (If I'd any idea how unpopular that would make me, I would have flubbed the tests on purpose!) So when I came home for the holidays, I just never went back and, luckily, my parents never remembered to send me. Or, more accurately, I never reminded them. Once, when Father managed to remember on his own, I pointed out that my own studies of history, ancient languages, Greek, and hieroglyphics were far more rigorous than anything any school could come up with. He reluctantly agreed, and so we let the matter drop.

Father had the growler pull round the back to the loading dock. Dolge and Sweeney came out to meet us and hauled the crates and some of the trunks into the downstairs workroom and short-term storage area. Then Father instructed Dolge to hop in the growler and take the rest of Mum's things to our house.

"So," Mother announced after all the fuss of unloading and seeing Dolge off, "who wants to see some new artifacts?"

Father and I crowded around while Mum pulled a key out of her pocketbook and knelt down in front of the first trunk.

"Oh, Alistair! It was all there, exactly as you said it would be. Your research was simply brilliant," Mother said. As she fumbled with the lock, I was relieved to see she still had her gloves on. Father, too, I noticed, as he rubbed his hands together in anticipation.

I studied his face to see if there was any sign of bitterness. There didn't appear to be, but who could have blamed him if there was?

Long ago, when I was only two, Father, after years of painstaking research and study, discovered the likely whereabouts of the tomb of Thutmose III, a powerful pharaoh in Egypt's Middle Dynastic Period. He and Mother made the trip to the Valley of the Kings (leaving me with my British grandmother, who I'm quite sure dressed me up in lacy frills and forced me to sit still for hours on end). Their expedition was a huge success except for the fact that they were betrayed by a colleague, and a man named Victor Loretti claimed the official discovery.

Even worse, the British Museum, which Father was working for at the time, refused to back him and accepted the discovery as Lorretti's.

That's when Father quit that stuffy old museum and came to work for the Museum of Legends and Antiquities.

Anyway, for the last few years Father had been working

on a theory about the location of Amenemhab's tomb. Amenemhab was Thutmose III's Minister of War, and some attributed the pharaoh's great military conquests to Amenemhab's brilliance.

After two years of coming up empty-handed, Mother had finally found the adjoining tomb of Amenemhab.

Father couldn't wait to see what she'd found. Neither could I, for that matter. I stepped closer to her and asked, "Was it scary, Mum, going into ancient sealed tombs like that? Were you the least bit frightened?"

Before she could answer, Bollingsworth wandered in and distracted her. "Hello, Mrs. Throckmorton. Welcome back."

"Thank you, Mr. Bollingsworth. It's good to be back."

Just like Father, Nigel rubbed his hands together. "Did you bring us lots of treasure?"

"Lots," Mum said, then threw open the trunk lid with a dramatic flourish.

A chaotic jumble of foul odors slammed into me like a fist: the coppery tang of blood, the smell of rot and decay, wood smoke, and sulfur. I gasped and my knees nearly buckled at the force of the black magic rolling into the room from the trunk.

Father gave me a sharp look. "What, Theodosia?"

"Th-they're just wonderful. That's all," I replied, trying to look as if all was normal. Could no one else feel this?

"But she hasn't even taken anything out of the trunk yet!"

"Oh, but I know they'll be smashing. Mum always finds the best things."

He narrowed his eyes at me, but was quickly diverted when Mum began unwrapping a large, flat package.

Nigel came over to stand next to me. "I say, Theo. Are you all right? You look a bit peaked. Do you need to go lie down or something?"

I shook my head and took small, shallow breaths as Mother lifted the final wrapping away. After the smell, I was half afraid it would be a severed mummy limb or some horrid thing. But it was a plaque carved with intricate symbols and a drawing of a large man wearing the crowns of Upper and Lower Egypt. He held another man by the hair, his raised arm holding a large knife. My stomach bobbed like a cork as I realized he was about to chop the man's head off. Under his feet were rows and rows of other figures who had met the same fate.

"I say," said Father, "this is rather bloodthirsty stuff."

"Oh, this isn't the half of it," said Mother. "This fellow makes Kaiser Wilhelm look like a nursemaid!"

She reached into her trunk and pulled out another flattish package and unwrapped it, revealing a long, curved knife with the small figure of Anubis on the handle.

Father whistled. "This is marvelous, Henrietta."

"Isn't it?" she beamed. "And there was so much more! All

the walls were covered with detailed histories of every war Thutmose fought, his victories and his strategies. It will take years and years to decipher it all."

I doubted that. I bet if they let me have a go at it, we could have it done in months.

"It contained weapons of every sort imaginable," Mother continued. "Spears and daggers and long swords, quite a lot of them carved with Apep and Mantu."

Father frowned. "I've never seen the serpent of chaos and the god of war used together like that before."

"Me neither," said Mum.

I had a sudden vision of the Mantu hieroglyph I had seen last night. "I have," I muttered. Both Mum and Father looked at me as if they'd forgotten I was there.

"Where would you have seen such a thing, Theodosia?" Father asked, his eyebrows shooting up in surprise. But of course I wasn't about to tell him it had been on the Bastet statue. "Er, can't remember where . . . Sorry," I said.

By the expression on his face, it was clear he thought I was pulling his leg. "Anyway," Mother continued after an awkward moment. "Amenemhab's tomb also contained a small temple dedicated to the god of war, Mantu."

"Really?" Father exclaimed.

We spent the next few minutes happily examining stele after stele, spears, daggers, and all sorts of things. Then

Fagenbush arrived and would have cast a pall over the whole proceeding except Mother got one of her *I am so brilliantly clever* looks. She pulled her handbag out from under her arm and held it in front of her until she had everyone's attention.

"Now, I want you to try and guess what I have in here," she announced, eyes sparkling.

"Oh, Henrietta!" Father said. "We can't possibly guess. Put us out of our misery."

Mum smiled, opened her handbag, and slowly drew out a flat package. She laid it on her still-gloved palm and began unwrapping the paper.

Luckily, everyone's eyes were focused on the artifact so they didn't see me shiver violently, as if I'd just caught a ghastly chill. The truth of it was, whatever was in that package was cursed with something so powerful and vile it made me feel as if my whole body were covered in stinging ants.

When Mother lifted off the last bit of paper, she held a large scarab carved out of precious stone in her hand. It had gold wings curving out of its side and they were inlaid with thousands and thousands of jewels. A large round carnelian, the size of a cherry, sat at the head, and a smaller green stone decorated the bottom of the beetle.

"The Heart of Egypt," she announced. "Straight from Amenemhab's tomb."

THE BOY
WHO FOLLOWED THE MAN
WHO FOLLOWED
THE GIRL

IN ORDER TO RULE, every pharaoh had an enormous heart amulet made for them when they were crowned pharaoh. It is known as the Heart of Egypt, because the health and well-being of the pharaoh and Egypt were one and the same. It was destined to be placed on the pharaoh's body when he died. Thutmose's Heart of Egypt hadn't been in his tomb, and its location had been a major puzzle for years.

"Yes," Mother said, nearly bursting her seams in self-satisfaction. "It was in Amenemhab's tomb the whole time. Not Thutmose's."

As Mum handed the scarab to Father, I glanced at

Fagenbush. His face was positively aglow with pure greed and excitement. Now, most people when they glow look lovely. Not Fagenbush. He looked even more frightening than ever, as if his glow came from the fires of the underworld itself.

Mum took the Heart of Egypt back from Father and wrapped it up once more. She returned it to her handbag and gave it a good solid pat. "We'll stash this inside in a bit, shall we, Alistair?"

"Absolutely."

The adults went back to poring over Mum's haul and frankly, it was hideously boring watching all the adults *ooh* and *aah* over Mum's finds while I was told to not touch and keep my hands off. Besides, all those curses gave me a dull, throbbing headache and made me feel twitchy.

I glanced up at the clock and saw that it was nearly teatime. With luck I could talk my parents into letting me pop over to a shop and pick up some food for a proper dinner.

The only hitch in that plan was that Fagenbush would get to see some of the new pieces before I did. He'd probably try to squirrel them away before I got back. Knowing him, he'd pinch the ones with the worst curses on them.

Then I had a brainstorm. "Oh, Mr. Bollingsworth?" I asked in my most casual voice, the one that always put Father on alert when he was paying attention.

"Yes, Theo?" Nigel looked up from a box of wax shabti figures he'd just opened.

"Has the class from Master Hedgewick's School for Wayward Boys left yet?"

Nigel's face fell as he remembered the group of unruly schoolboys who had descended upon the museum earlier in the afternoon. "Oh, dear. I don't know. I suppose I should go have a look. Make sure they haven't broken anything or absconded with a legendary sword or something."

I came over and stood next to the box of figures he was looking at. "What are these?" I asked. I knew perfectly well they were shabti figures, a common part of any self-respecting Egyptian tomb. The clay and wax figures were buried with the deceased so that they could perform any manual labor the dead person was called upon to do in the afterlife.

But as I drew closer, I saw that these shabtis were different in many ways. They had a rather menacing look to them, for one thing. And each clutched a weapon of some sort in their little clay arms: spears, daggers, swords, each of them had something deadly. Most odd.

With a quick glance at Fagenbush, I asked Bollingsworth, "Are they dolls? Did the mummy children play with them?"

Fagenbush's head snapped up and he narrowed his beady little eyes at me.

"Goodness, no!" Nigel exclaimed, horrified at my ignorance. "They're quite fascinating, actually . . . just a minute. I say, Clive, would you check and make sure those wayward boys aren't up to no good?"

Just as I had hoped! What First Assistant Curator would check on a bunch of bratty schoolchildren when there was a perfectly good Second Assistant Curator to do it for him?

I peered up through my eyelashes as Fagenbush glared sharp, pointy daggers at me. He'd known exactly what I was doing—getting rid of him. I gave him a sweet smile. "Thank you so much, Mr. Fagenbush. I'm ever so curious about these *dolls*."

With a snarl, he threw down the lid he'd just managed to pry off one of the packing crates and stormed off.

"Now, Theo," Nigel began. "These figures are shabtis. They were used for—Theo? I say, Theo?"

But I was busy rifling through the packing material in the crate Fagenbush had just opened.

"Don't you want to hear about the shabtis?" Poor Bollingsworth threw me a puzzled look, but before he could figure out what I'd done, I called out, "Come look at these. I've never seen them before. Have you?"

Immediately the shabti were forgotten (thank heavens!), and Nigel hurried over to see what I'd found.

He reached down and ran his hands through the small black bits. (I *do* wish these curators would learn to wear gloves!) "Curious," he muttered.

"Aren't they?" I let them pour through my hands (which were, of course, properly covered). They were small bits of black stone—basalt and onyx, I think—and they were all very precisely shaped, although what they represented I couldn't tell.

"Grain," Mum announced as she and Father joined us at the crate. "They are all carved to look like grain. Rye, wheat, even rice. I've never seen anything like it before," she said.

"Yes, but why is it black?" I asked. "Isn't grain, well, grain-colored?"

"I don't know why they didn't carve the grain out of sandstone or soapstone or some other, lighter-colored material. Perhaps we'll learn why as we study these finds."

"Speaking of grain," I said, remembering my hunger, now that Fagenbush had been taken care of. "Can I go to the pie shop and fetch us something for dinner? I'm famished. There's been nothing to eat but jam sandwiches for the last two days."

"Oh, darling. Of course you may." Mum elbowed Father. "Alistair, you can't let her eat such rubbish all the time."

"I . . . we've . . . been rather busy here, Henrietta," Father stuttered, looking somewhat sheepish.

To make him feel better, I asked, "Shall I get some nice plump pasties, Father, dear? I know how fond of them you are."

He perked up immediately. "Why, yes. That would be lovely."

I held out my hand for some money. Father scrabbled around in his pockets, put a few shillings in my out-stretched palm, then returned his attention to the ceremonial knife he'd just pulled out of one of Mum's trunks.

I cast a glance up at the darkening sky. If I hurried, I mean, really hurried, I could be back before dark. Probably.

I ran across the workroom and began thumping my way up the stairs.

"Don't forget your coat," Father called out after me. "And your hat!"

The rain let up just enough that I thought I could make it to the pie shop and back before the gray clouds reconvened and began their second assault. It was cold, and the wind was still buffeting people this way and that. But it felt good to be outside, away from foul-smelling evil curses and arti-facts and Clive Fagenbushes.

A few blocks from the museum, the houses and shops grew smaller and the streets more narrow. The clouds were growing dark again and I realized I'd better hurry.

It wasn't until Haddington Street that I heard the foot-steps behind me. I stopped suddenly, pretending I had to rebutton my boot, and the footsteps stopped also. Slowly, I stood up, trying to think what to do. The streets weren't deserted, but there weren't very many people about. I took a few more steps, then paused to look in a nearby shop window. As I stared at bowlers and derbies, I heard the steps start up again, then stop.

I decided the best thing to do was to make a dash for the pie shop. I sped down the street, and heaved a sigh of relief when Pilkington's Pies came into view. I yanked open the door and rushed into the shop, startling poor Mrs. Pilkington. "Goodness, luv. Ye startled me. Why the hurry?"

Mrs. Pilkington was a wonderful person, plump and savory, just like the goods she sold. She always had a delicious aroma of buttery pastry and savory pie filling clinging to her, like a homey eau de toilette.

"Just starving, Mrs. Pilkington. That's all."

She gave me a knowing look. "Aye. Been keeping you cooped up in that drafty old museum too much, 'ave they?"

"Yes, ma'am," I said, with feeling.

"So what'll you have for your supper tonight, luv?"

"Well, Mum's home, so I think we should get extra, just to celebrate."

"Of course you should, dear. And how lovely, yer mum's home."

I made my selections and, at the last moment, had Mrs.

Pilkington keep one of the pies out for me to eat on the way home. I *was* famished. I picked up my purchases, stepped outside, and bit into the flaky meat pasty, nearly choking on it when I found myself smack up against the beastly little pickpocket I'd apprehended earlier at Charing Cross Station. "You!" I spluttered, ignoring the small shower of crumbs that escaped. Served him right for following me.

"Oy, what about me?" he asked, his sharp blue eyes watching my pie with keen interest.

"Why have you been following me? Don't lie, now."

The urchin pulled himself up to his full height, which was a good two inches shorter than me. "I never lie," he said in a huff. "And I wasn't following you, I was following the bloke that was following you."

My knees wobbled a bit. "Which bloke, er, gentleman?"

"The one wot followed ye out of the station today. You know, the swarthy-looking fellow."

I had a good idea who he meant. The fellow that had been staring at Mum's trunks. "But why?" I asked.

"I don't know. Mebbe you 'ave somefink he wants."

"No, no. I mean, why did you follow *him*?" I narrowed my eyes. "Are you looking for a reward?"

He pulled back, indignant. "'Ell no! I just figured I owed ye one, miss. You not turning me in at the station earlier and all. Sticky Will always pays his debts." He eyed my package. "Um, yer supper's gettin' cold."

I looked at the savory pie in my hand. Just minutes before it had tasted lovely. Now I couldn't bring myself to take another bite. Besides, the urchin was studying it so intently, I couldn't help but wonder when he had last eaten. "Here," I said. "Would you like it? Being followed has made me lose my appetite."

The boy's eyes lit up, but he stuffed his hands in his pockets and shuffled his left foot. "Well, I ain't all that hungry. But it'd be a sin to let it go to waste, wouldn't it?"

"Oh, absolutely. Probably a mortal one."

"Well in that case . . ." the urchin said. Then, with much eye-rolling to let me know he was doing me an enormous favor, he snatched the pasty and gobbled it up in two enormous bites.

Which gave me a smashing idea. "I'll give you another pasty if you keep following the bloke after I'm gone and see where he goes," I offered.

Again, he shuffled his feet and tried to look bored, but the effect was ruined when his stomach growled. "'Spose so. Since I got nuffin' better to do." He wiped his nose on his sleeve.

"Right then. Here you go." I handed him another pasty, feeling back in charge now that a bargain had been struck and the situation dealt with.

He stuffed the meat pie into his jacket. "When I finds out, should I come by yer museum?"

"Oh. Er, no." I wasn't sure Flimp, the watchman, would let him in. Besides, however would I explain him? "But I'll be at Charing Cross Station again tomorrow. Around the same time. Could we meet then?"

"See ye then," he agreed.

I watched him slip off into the shadows between the buildings. Frankly, it felt good to have someone on my side for a bit. Even if it was only a pickpocket. At least *someone* was covering my back.

I squared my shoulders and started walking down the street. I tried very hard not to think about being followed, but it was difficult. Doorways loomed like gaping maws, and the windows seemed to watch me as I passed. The streets were deserted, except for the old lamplighter who'd begun to light the lamps, which glowed feebly against the thick puddles of fog that descended upon the streets. The sludgy fog also did odd things to the sounds of the street, making the steady click of boot heels behind me all the more noticeable. I couldn't be sure, but it sounded as if they were drawing closer.

Just as I was preparing to run the rest of the way back to the museum, I heard the rattle of a carriage. I glanced over my shoulder. I knew that brougham!

I weighed my options: being followed through the streets of London by a menacing stranger or catching a lift with

Grandmother Throckmorton. It shouldn't have been such a difficult choice, but then, you don't know my grandmother.

I took a step toward the carriage, waving at the driver. It took him a moment or two to recognize me but then he pulled over. When the carriage had stopped, I rapped on the door. Inside, a curtain was yanked aside to reveal the arrogant beaked nose of my grandmother.

She frowned at me, scrunching her mouth up tight as if she'd put too many lemons in her tea.

I glanced over my shoulder. The footsteps had grown silent. Had my pursuer given up? Or was he waiting in a doorway somewhere just outside my line of vision? Would he follow Grandmother's brougham? Would Sticky Will follow *him*?

The driver jumped down from his seat. "Hello, miss," he said as he opened the door for me.

Grandmother poked her head out. "Well, hurry up then. You're letting all the cold air in. You can explain yourself once you're inside."

I clambered in and perched myself on the edge of the seat opposite Grandmother Throckmorton. It was never a good idea to get too comfortable around her.

She thumped her cane on the floor of the carriage. "I demand to know what you are doing out here unchaperoned."

I squirmed on the seat, suddenly aware of how grubby I

must look. "Father sent me round to pick up something for dinner."

"Unattended?" She was well and truly shocked, as I knew she would be. "And just where is your governess?"

She had left months ago. Bored out of her mind, she'd claimed. She had been hoping for tea parties and dancing lessons, not clattering around in an old museum.

But if Grandmother Throckmorton knew that, she'd find me a new governess by luncheon tomorrow. "She, um, went to visit a sick relative," I said.

Grandmother peered down her nose at me and sniffed. "Hmm. Is that mother of yours home yet from her gadding about?"

I gritted my teeth. "Yes. Mother just returned from Egypt this afternoon." Grandmother Throckmorton always says the most awful things about Mother. She thinks Mum is far too modern and unconventional. "She found some absolutely wonderful artifacts," I said in her defense.

"Hmph. Rummaging around in dusty old tombs. Can't imagine there's very much that's wonderful in there."

I clenched my fists but didn't rise to the bait. After all, Grandmother Throckmorton had just rescued me from my pursuer, even if she didn't realize it.

"When is that scamp of a brother of yours due home?" she asked.

"Tomorrow."

The carriage rolled to a stop and the footman opened the door. Staring straight ahead at no one in particular, he announced, "We've reached the museum, ma'am."

I leaped to my feet. "Thank you ever so much for the ride, ma'am."

"I should think so," she said. As I scrambled down out of the carriage she called out, "I'm going to speak to your father about that governess of yours."

Bother.

THE COZY FAMILY DINNER
THAT WASN'T

I MADE IT BACK TO THE MUSEUM just as darkness swallowed up the streets of London. Shivering, I climbed the front steps and slipped inside just before Flimp locked the door for the night. I thought briefly about trying to coax Mother and Father out of the workroom, then realized the fastest way to get their attention was to entice them with the smell of food.

As I headed down the dim hallway that led to the staff rooms, a dark squalling blur shot out of the shadows. My heart leaped into my throat as the blur attached itself to my shoulder with a vicious yowl.

I was halfway to apoplexy before I realized it was not a true demon, only Isis. I still couldn't believe I'd botched things so badly.

Her little heart was pounding as fast as mine was and her claws were firmly enmeshed in my coat. Her ears lay flat against her head and her eyes swirled madly in their sockets. "Isis, shh. It's all right. Here, let's get you a bite of sausage, shall we?" I wrestled a bit of meat out of one of the pies and held it out to her. She paused and her eyes cleared, just for a second, and I caught a glimpse of my old cat. Then the wild look was back and she hissed at me before launching herself back into the shadows, where she streaked away.

I had to fix my cat. Soon. *If* I could catch her, that is. And *if* I could find a way to de-curse her. Was that even possible? Finding out would be my first order of business after dinner.

I reached the staff breakfast room that we used as a family room and got busy unwrapping the food, hoping the delicious aroma would reach my parents.

Two minutes later, Father poked his head in the door. "Back already, Theodosia?"

Already? It felt like I'd been gone ages, what with being followed and all, but I just said, "Yes, Father."

"Excellent." He came into the room and put the kettle on. "Mum's on her way up."

"Was she really in a lot of danger on this trip?" The question popped out. I hadn't even realized I'd been thinking it until it landed on the table like a flopping fish.

Father turned to face me. "Really, Theodosia. If I had thought your mother was in true danger, I would have gone with her myself."

Charming! Then I would have been missing two parents!

"Your mother knows her way around Egypt. And she could twist a German or two around that little finger of hers if she'd a mind to. However"—his face grew stern—"you shouldn't listen in on conversations that don't concern you. We'll have to be more careful next time."

Honestly. What was I? A cab cushion? How could I *not* have heard their conversation? That's why I rarely ask my parents anything—when they realize I've heard them they resolve to clam up whenever I'm about. I don't know how they expect me to learn anything . . .

Just then Mum walked in. "Ooh, darling! It smells wonderful in here." She came over and kissed me on the cheek. I pressed up against her face as long as I could before she pulled away. I did have six months to catch up on, you know.

"Thank you so much for getting us a decent supper tonight." She began to rummage around the sideboard until she found enough plates and cutlery to set the table.

Then we all three sat down to dinner. It wasn't steak and kidney pie, and it wasn't home, but it *was* family, and mostly it *was* lovely.

Father bit into a plump, savory pasty and closed his eyes in appreciation.

"So, Mum," I asked, leaning forward. "What was it *really* like? Did you have to sleep in a tent this time? Did you see any live scarab beetles?"

Father opened his eyes. "I forgot to ask you earlier: has the Egyptian independence movement gotten any worse?" he asked.

"Well, The Consul General definitely has his hands full with the growing Egyptian nationalist movement," Mum said around a bite of meat pie. "They're still demanding that the British evacuate the country."

I sighed and began munching on my pasty while the conversation wandered back to Egyptian politics.

Then I flinched as Father's fist crashed down on the table. "That wouldn't be an issue if that confounded Lord Cromer hadn't been so bloody-minded and autocratic! It could bring our work in the Valley of the Kings to a standstill."

"True," Mum agreed, not even batting an eyelash at Father's outburst. She had nerves of steel, my mum.

Anxious to turn the conversation to happier things, I asked, "Did you get to ride a camel this time?"

Mum leaned across the table toward Father. "You had heard that Kamil went and formed a National Party, hadn't you? Lots of anti-British sentiment there."

"Yes. Is there any substance to the rumor that they're being funded in part by the Germans?" Father asked.

"No one knows. But, in response, Lutfi as-Sayyid has formed a People's Party. He'll be a bit more cooperative but is probably still aiming toward eventual home rule."

I heaved another sigh of boredom. How my parents could make something as exciting as Egypt sound boring, I'll never know.

"I'm sorry, dear." Mum reached over and patted my arm. "How tedious this must all be for you. Tell me, what have you been doing with yourself since I was gone?"

Delighted that the conversation had turned to something interesting—*me*—I happily began telling Mother everything I'd been doing while she was away.

After dinner I kept talking, trying to keep us all at the table so I could savor being together again. As we sat there, Mother suddenly put her hand to her cheek. "Oh, darling! How could I have forgotten? I brought you something."

I perked up at that. Sometimes Mother found the most lovely presents.

She got up from the table and rummaged around in her traveling satchel and pulled out a long, rolled-up parchment. "This is a rubbing of the tablets we found in the section of the pyramid we opened. They are Amenemhab's secret writings on the art of war." She squinted at the first line of hieroglyphics. *"How to Cast Your Enemies into Chaos,"* she read aloud, rather pleased with herself.

"Oh, Mum! That's wonderful. Thank you." I reached out for the parchment and unrolled the thick paper, my eyes dancing over the rows and rows of hieroglyphs that paraded across the page.

I threw my arms around her. "I'll just curl up in the chair by the fire and read now, so you and Father can talk."

"Well, darling, your father and I need to talk business."

"Don't worry. I'll be as quiet as a mouse, I promise."

"Actually, Theodosia," Father said, "your mother and I need to talk in private. Why don't you go off to that closet of yours? You can read your new rubbing in there."

My shoulders drooped. "Yes, Father. If you insist."

"I do. Go on now."

I shuffled toward the door, then turned to look at them over my shoulder. "You won't forget to come and get me when it's time to go home, will you?"

"Of course not, dear," Mum said. "We won't be long."

As I stepped out of the sitting room into the cold, dim hallway, I tried to remind myself that this was an excellent chance to try and get to the bottom of the Isis situation.

I hurried through the corridors, then went downstairs to the reading room library. But when I reached out and turned the handle, it was locked. Bother! Which idiotic curator took it in his head to lock the library up at night?

Probably that rat, Fagenbush.

Discouraged, I went back upstairs to my room. I lit the oil lamp and climbed into the sarcophagus, making myself comfortable by pulling a blanket up under my chin. I unrolled the scroll and began to read:

Hail, O Seth, Master of Chaos, hail Mantu, Destroyer of our enemies, hail Anat, whose terrible beauty strikes fear into the heart of our enemies, hear our pleas.

Through Thutmose, our land's most powerful ruler, the land's power has grown great, our enemies bow down before us, beseech us for mercy, which flows from Thutmose . . .

I was soon lost in Amenemhab's theories of how to bring death and destruction to one's enemies. Famine, plague, flood, locusts, pestilence—he had them all covered with curses and amulets and secret rituals designed to bring his enemies to their knees.

After hours of reading, my eyelids began to grow heavy. I missed Isis terribly. She normally curled up at my feet, and it just wasn't the same without her. I missed the warmth of her small furry body. The comfort of her contented purring. I tried my best not to think of her ricocheting around the museum in a cursed frenzy. However, if she was feeling demonic, at least she wasn't feeling lonely. Or scared.

As I drifted off to sleep, I had to remind myself that sleeping in a sarcophagus wasn't creepy. Not really. Not if you don't think about it . . .

Besides, even if it was scary, it certainly was safer with three tons of solid stone covered with protective symbols between you and whatever spirits lurked in the museum at night.

Fagenbush Gets an Unexpected Bath

I AWOKE THE NEXT MORNING with a fuzziness behind my eyes that let me know I hadn't slept well. And no wonder! My dreams had been filled with images of marching Egyptian armies and other horrors of war. That Amenemhab fellow certainly was descriptive; his writings made for rather questionable bedtime reading.

Worse yet, I was still in the sarcophagus, which meant Mother and Father never went home last night. Or they had forgotten to come and get me. That thought had me sitting bolt upright, heart pounding. They wouldn't really forget me, would they?

I scrambled out of bed, then poured cold water from the pitcher into the basin and splashed it on my face, washing the sleep out of my eyes and, hopefully, any clinging memories of my strange dreams. That was another thing that had kept me awake last night. The museum had been positively lively with creaks and groans, as if all the artifacts had decided to throw a party. I couldn't help wondering if it had something to do with the new collection. Finding out would be my first order of business for the day. (After making sure my parents hadn't forgotten me!)

Oh, dear. Make that my second order of business. My first and most important task was to locate Isis and try to set her right.

I brushed the wrinkles out of my frock as best I could, frustrated at having to wear the same one two days in a row. Honestly, it made me feel only one step up from a street urchin. I slipped my cleanest pinafore off its nail and shrugged into it. Lastly, I buttoned up my gloves, then headed round to the sitting room, hoping for a sign of my parents, or at the very least, a bit of leftover pasties. But no such luck. No parents and no leftovers. I used the last bit of jam to make a quick sandwich. As I ate, the sound of Father's voice drifted down the stairs from his workroom. The tightness in my chest disappeared. They *hadn't* left me behind.

On my way to the reading room, I decided to stop and pay Edgar Stilton, the Third Assistant Curator, a visit.

In spite of being named after a cheese, Stilton is a very handy chap to have about. He is a simple man, but intelligent and honest and, for some reason, he's like a lightning rod for the unrest in the museum. Whenever I have any doubts, I have only to pay Edgar a visit to get a reading on the museum's current temperament. Since Stilton is the most junior curator, he tends to arrive at work earlier than the others as he has three higher-ups he needs to impress. (Although, he really shouldn't worry about Father; he simply doesn't notice that sort of thing.)

When I reached the second floor, Stilton's door was open. His office wasn't much bigger than my closet, which was most likely another reason I felt a sort of kinship with him. His desk was stacked high with papers and scrolls and bills of lading. Even with the gaslight turned up high, the room was dim and dark feeling. I popped my head in. "Good morning."

He startled badly, nearly knocking his teacup to the floor. Not a good sign.

"Oh, Miss Throckmorton, hullo." He righted his cup and pulled out a handkerchief to wipe the spilled tea off his hand.

"Theo," I said as I came fully into the office and sat down

across from him. "Have you heard about Mother's new findings?" I asked, not because I was particularly interested, but because I needed to watch him for a few minutes in order to get an accurate reading.

"Yes, Bollingsworth told me a little about it on his way out last night. Smashing find." His left shoulder twitched ever so slightly.

"Yes, isn't it? And she brought me a rubbing of some of the tablets they'd found. It makes for interesting reading."

"I should say," Stilton said, a tic beginning just under his right eye.

Just then, the bell sounded from the receiving dock, and Stilton jerked as if he'd been burnt. He cleared his throat. "Delivery's here."

"Lovely," I said. That meant another of Mother's trunks had arrived. Hopefully everyone would be distracted by the new artifacts and I could spend the morning researching a cure for Isis. "I think I'll go help them unpack."

I bid poor Stilton goodbye and left him jerking and twitching like an insect at the end of a pin as I hurried toward the reading room. When I reached it, whom should I see but Clive Fagenbush unlocking the door. His expression darkened when he saw me. "What are you doing here?" he asked.

I smiled sweetly at him and resolved to locate a key of my own. "I had planned to work on my studies."

"I don't think so," he sneered. "Your father told me to tell you that he wants your help in Receiving."

Bother. How many times I had longed for Father to ask for my help, and the one time he did, I had something vitally important to do. Wasn't that the way of it? Very well. I would just have to slip away at the earliest opportunity.

When I reached the receiving area, my parents were up to their elbows in shabtis. Hundreds and hundreds of them. And every beastly one was carrying a curse.

It took ages to unpack them. Mum and Dad were thrilled because having an entire army of shabtis would make an impressive exhibit. I thought it was tedious, especially since the curses made my eyes water and my stomach queasy. I kept glancing at the clock, wishing Henry's train would hurry up and get here.

Which just shows you how bored I was. No doubt by tomorrow I'd be wishing Henry's train would take him *back* to school.

Finally the shabtis were unpacked and Mother and Father became so absorbed in cataloging them that I managed to slip away.

It was time to un-demonize my poor beloved cat.

I'd thought about it quite a lot as I unpacked the shabtis.

The first thing I would try was belling the cat, only not with a bell, but an amulet. I hoped that if Isis was wearing some protection, the curse's effect would diminish.

But first I had to make the wretched thing.

I went back up to the reading room and pulled out the copy of Erasmus Bramwell's *Funerary Magic, Mummies, and Curses.* I carried it into my small study and pored over it from front to back. For the first time ever, research failed me. Bramwell hadn't a single idea. He wrote quite a lot on how to mummify a cat (something quite a lot of ancient Egyptians used to do) and how to properly mourn a cat (one must shave off one's eyebrows) but nothing on how to exorcise a cat. Which meant I was on my own. No ancient books or scholars from centuries gone by to guide me through this one. I'd have to make something up and hope it worked.

I needed to find a way to use Isis's own regenerative powers (cats do have nine lives, you know) to throw off the curse and grow back her original personality. I had to purify her *and* offer her protection against the powers of evil that coursed through her small furry body. Plus, I had to try to remind her of what her true nature was. A tall order.

I searched through my carpetbag (which I had forgotten to put away the day before. Very careless of me!) and was able to find all the ingredients I needed. I have recorded them below, for posterity, as Father always says.

THEODOSIA THROCKMORTON'S RECIPE
FOR UNDEMONIZING YOUR CAT

1 small square of white linen

1 stick of willow wood, burned at the tip

1 small baby tooth from when cat in question was a kitten (Luckily, I had one of those!)

1 small fishbone (to stimulate her senses and remind her of her true nature)

1 thimbleful of dried Nepeta cararia, commonly known as catnip (to stimulate her senses even more)

1 drop of blood (the spellmaker's, not the cat's)

1 vessel of pure water

1 hippopotamus tusk carved with magic symbols and used in magic ceremonies during the Middle Egyptian Dynasty period (borrowed from the Museum of Legends and Antiquities Egyptian Magic collection #736)

26 threads—12 white (for purity), 8 green (for the power of growth), 6 red (for rebirth—Isis needed to be rebirthed in a hurry!)

The first thing I did was strip off my gloves. They would be much too clumsy for the fine work required in making the amulet. Next I drew a wedjat eye in the middle of the linen square with the burned end of the willow stick. This would give poor Isis the healing power of Horus and the protection of the fearsome goddess Eye of Ra.

Then I placed the tooth, fishbone, and catnip in the middle of the linen square. I poked my finger with a small needle, then let one drop of blood fall on the small pile. Next, I carefully folded the linen over and over again until it was nothing but a lumpy square. I plaited the twenty-six threads together so that they formed a small collar. After that, I had to poke holes in both ends of the linen pouch with my needle, then thread the collar through the pouch so I could attach it to Isis's neck. The wand and water would be used later, during the ceremony.

But before I could begin the ceremony, I had to find the poor bedeviled cat.

How does one catch a demonic cat, anyway? Let alone hang on to it long enough to remove a curse? Cats are so contrary, even when they aren't possessed by black magic. No sooner do you decide you need to find one than they go into hiding. Of course, if I wanted the cat out of the way, she'd be under my feet, winding herself between my ankles and tripping me.

I spent ages wandering around the cold, cavernous museum looking for Isis. I checked all her favorite places; behind the furnace, in the loading dock where the mice and rats live, in the family room under the wardrobe, and under the display cases in the bird gallery (she likes to pretend she is stalking them). But she was nowhere to be found.

When the museum's various clocks sounded, I counted the chimes; twelve. It was lunchtime! Which meant Isis might be lurking about hoping for dropped bits of sandwich or whatnot. Dolge and Sweeney weren't the neatest of eaters. Neither was Flimp.

I spent the better part of the next hour skulking around like a cat myself. While there was no sign of Isis, I did manage to collect a nice pile of crumbs. In the foyer, under the balcony that Isis seemed to enjoy launching herself off of, I arranged a blob of liverwurst, a tiny crumble of cheddar, and part of a boiled egg white.

Just as I was setting a very promising Isis trap, I felt a *whoosh* as a small furry shape whizzed past me, then vivid pain as razor sharp claws swiped my hands away from the scraps.

I was so startled that it wasn't until Isis had nearly swallowed the last bit of egg that I remembered to grab her.

Howling like a banshee, she twisted violently, trying to wrench herself from my grasp. It was like trying to hang on to a small whirlwind! I clutched her close and prayed the reading room was still empty. It would be just my luck to have some crusty old scholar show up while I was trying to smuggle my cat in.

With relief, I found the room empty and hurried into my study. I held on to Isis with one hand while I groped for my supplies with the other.

Unfortunately, this left her arms and legs free to slash and swipe. I winced as her claws made contact with my torso, then nearly dropped her when her paw sliced through my left sleeve.

I wrestled her down to the floor and held her in my lap with one hand while I tried to wrap the collar around her neck with the other. Luckily my heavy layers of clothing protected me from any further damage. Finally, I got the collar wrapped around her scrawny little neck. Then I had to release my hold on her so I could tie the horrid thing, which left her free to try to run away or claw my arm off.

She gave both a rousing good try.

As I tied on the collar, I mumbled the charm as quickly as I could. "May the healing power of Horus fill you. May the strength of the Eye of Ra shine down upon you. May you revert back to your charming little self." At those last words, Isis wrenched free of my grasp. As she streaked toward the door, I lurched to my feet and grabbed the vessel full of water. "May this water purify your soul!" I cried out, tossing it at her as she disappeared through the door.

I heard a bellow of surprise, then who should stick their ugly head in the door but Clive Fagenbush! His eyebrows were drawn together, like one huge mustache across his forehead, and there was a big wet blotch right in the middle of his chest. You can just imagine how happy he was about *that*.

As he took a single, slow step into the room, a drop of water dangled from his long pointed nose. "What do you think you are doing, you miserable child?" he asked.

His fury was like a wall, pushing up against me. I took a step back. "I was giving Isis a bath," I said.

He took another step closer. "A cat? A bath? In winter? Tell me, do you always invoke purification rites when you give your cat a bath?"

Bother. Heard that, had he? I stopped backing up, folded my arms across my chest, and gave him a haughty glare. "Of course. Don't you? How do you expect to get really clean, then?"

His frown deepened.

Just then I heard Father's voice from down the hall. "Theodosia! Get out here! We're going to be late picking up Henry!"

Oh, dear. He sounded angry. "Sorry. Got to go." I took a step forward to make my escape, then realized I would be leaving him here alone with my things.

He glowered at me. "I'm warning you . . ."

"Now!" Dad's voice barked out, and Fagenbush and I both jumped. Father stood in the door behind us. When he saw the Second Assistant Curator standing in my study, he did a double take. "I say, what are you doing in here, Fagenbush?"

Yes, I thought. What *are* you doing in here? I tilted my head to the side, waiting for his answer.

"I, uh, thought Theodosia might have had, er, something that I was looking for."

"Nonsense. Theodosia doesn't have anything in here." He frowned at me, suddenly wary. "Do you?"

I gave a little laugh. "Whatever would I have in here?"

Father nodded. "Quite. Now, move along, Fagenbush. Theodosia needs to come with me."

Fagenbush nodded, then beat a hasty retreat. Just as I was feeling rather smug, Father turned back to me. "What on earth has happened to you? Look at you! You're a mess."

I rubbed my elbow, then pushed my hair back out of my eyes so I could look down and see how much damage had been done. The bottom of my right sleeve was in tatters, and my wrist had a number of scrapes on it. "Isis and I had a bit of a disagreement."

"That confounded cat will be our undoing," Father declared, then strode out of the room. "Now come along. You're making us late."

As I followed, I could only hope that the amulet would work its magic on Isis. Hopefully by the time we returned from the holidays, she would be cured.

HENRY'S HOMECOMING

CHARING CROSS STATION was even more of a madhouse than the day before, if that were possible. Families dressed in traveling clothes and lugging valises were shepherding excited children into the station, while porters wheeling carts of towering luggage did their best to avoid them. Trains pulled up to the platforms and belched out groups of schoolchildren home for the holidays like puffs of gray smoke. As I searched the most recent batch for signs of Henry, I felt a slight tug on the back of my coat. I whirled around and found myself face to face with the urchin, Sticky Will.

"'Ello there."

He looked a little grimier than he had yesterday, and his collar had sprung loose. "Hullo!" I said. "I was hoping I'd find you—"

"Seems to me as I'm the one wot did the finding."

I waved my hand. "Never mind. What did you find out?"

"Blimey, miss!" the urchin said, staring at my arm. "Was you in a fight?"

"No, I wasn't in a fight," I said. "My cat and I had a misunderstanding, that's all."

The pickpocket eyed me up and down. "Must be some cat. 'As 'e got lion blood in 'im?"

"At the moment she seems to," I muttered. "Now, what did you find out?"

"The bloke made 'is way to some digs on Carleton Terrace Gardens."

"Carleton Terrace! Isn't that right next to the German Embassy?" Did that mean this skulky fellow was a German? And why would a German be following Mum? Or care so much about her trunks?

The urchin shrugged. "I just follows 'em, miss. I don't tell 'em where to go." His eyes darted over my shoulder, then back at me. "We're even now, right miss?"

"Yes, I suppose—"

"Got to go," he said, turning to dart back into the crowd.

"Wait a minute," I said. "How can I find you?"

The urchin grinned, revealing a missing tooth. "I'm usually here most days." He glanced over my shoulder one more time, then was gone, disappearing into the crowd. I was surprised at how alone I felt all of a sudden. A person could get used to having an ally.

Just then I heard an all too familiar voice behind me. "Does Father know about this?"

Slowly, I turned around. "Henry. You're home." I tried to keep the disappointment out of my voice. Well, I tried a little. Why couldn't *he* be helpful like Sticky Will?

"Are you so desperate for friends that you're picking up strays?"

My face grew hot and I clenched my fists to keep from socking him. "I have plenty of friends," I spluttered.

"Really? Who? A scrawny cat? Flimp? A boring curator you make cow eyes at?"

"I do not make cow eyes at him!"

"Street urchins?"

"Oh, shut up. I do too have friends." I did. Really. Sticky Will was my ally, wasn't he? Or was he just a pickpocket hoping for another pasty? Oh, who needs friends anyway? "Where are Mother and Father?"

"Getting my luggage. They told me to run on ahead and see if I could find you."

Behind him, I saw my parents making their way through the crowd, along with a porter juggling Henry's luggage. "How many days' break do you get this winter?" I asked.

"Three weeks," Henry said. "And if you're snotty to me, I'll make sure they put *you* on a train to school when they send me back."

The cad.

After we picked Henry up from the train station we went directly home to our house on Chesterfield Street. It was wonderful to be home! Thick curtains and even thicker carpets kept all the drafts away and there was a fire burning in every room in the house. Cook, relieved to have something to do, made a fabulous dinner of steak and kidney pie, and even Henry wasn't too much of a bore.

Then, after dinner who should show up but Uncle Andrew, Mum's brother and my favorite uncle in all the world. Of course, the townhouse was much too cramped for all of us so Mum and Dad made a last-minute decision to go to the country. We all packed like madmen, bundled up, and piled into a carriage that carried us off to our home in Surrey. I have to say, I think it was the best Christmas ever! Except for the rain.

The only awkward bit was when Mother and Father

opened their presents from me. They tried to be polite, but I saw the puzzled looks they exchanged when they thought I wasn't looking. I'd made them each an amulet. Of protection. To be worn when we're at the museum. Honestly. You'd think they'd have sorted this stuff out by now.

Uncle Andrew showed me how to throw knives that afternoon. We didn't tell Mum. She got angry enough last year when he showed me how to shoot clay pigeons with a shotgun. I landed flat on my backside in the muddy slush with a bruise the size of a pudding on my right shoulder. But I blew that clay pigeon to smithereens. I don't know why Mum got so upset. According to Uncle Andrew she's a crack shot herself. But she says I'm too young. What I'd like to know is how old does a person have to be before they get to do all the fun stuff?

The Same but Different

USUALLY WHEN I RETURN TO THE MUSEUM after a long absence, it feels like I'm being welcomed by an old friend. All the creaks and groans seem cheerful. As if the wraiths and spirits are relieved to have me back, as if they *liked* having someone around who was aware of their existence.

But not today.

Today, the minute I stepped foot into the building, it felt different. Colder. More still. As if everything were holding its breath. I gazed around the vast main hall, peering up into the small balconies and archways that lined the stone walls, but saw nothing out of the ordinary.

It was unsettling, to say the least.

When I set my valise down on the tiled floor, the soft *click* echoed down the chamber and disappeared into utter silence. Father started to walk around me, but I put out my hand to stop him. "Do you notice anything?"

He scowled at me, then concentrated a moment. "No," he said, rather crisply. "Nothing. The only thing I notice is that you're about to go off on one of your tangents. I'm warning you, Theodosia."

Father turned toward the stairs and tripped over my valise. "What in heaven's name is that?"

"Just a few things I brought with me. Supplies, that sort of thing." Clean clothes, to be exact. Just in case we got stuck at the museum for days on end again.

"Hmph," he growled, then strode out of the foyer toward the stairs that led up to his workroom.

I heaved a sigh, then looked away from Father to find Henry grinning at me. "You made a good impression on him, there, Theo."

I glared at him. "Yes, almost as good an impression as you made when you tried to light the gaslight at home with your finger and nearly burned your hand off."

Henry kicked halfheartedly at my bag. "It was supposed to be an experiment. On static electricity."

Henry looked so dejected I was almost sorry I'd brought it up. But really, I didn't need Henry to remind me how iffy my position was. It wouldn't take much for Father to decide I was suffering from nerves or some equal nonsense and pack me off to some cold gray school to cure me of them.

I left Henry in the foyer studying his bandaged finger and went up to the second floor to stash my case in my closet. Then I went up to the third floor and the Ancient Egypt Exhibit, curious to see if I could work out what was making the museum feel so wrong. Besides, if I pretended I wasn't really looking for Isis, maybe I'd have a chance of finding her.

When I was halfway up the stairs, a voice behind me made me jump.

"So what *is* wrong?" It was Henry.

"As if I'd tell you, you little beast. You'd be off to Father in a minute flat, tattling and trying to get me locked up in another of those hideously boring schools."

"They're not so hideous. They've got sports, you know. Besides, maybe I won't tattle. Not if you make it worth my while," he said.

I stopped and whirled around to face him. "And why would I want to do that?"

"If you tell me what's wrong, I'll even try to help you work out what's going on."

"I don't need your help to work out anything."

Henry's face fell and I immediately felt awful. Then I had

a brilliant idea. What if the reason Henry hated the museum was because he could sense all the black magic? He was my brother, after all. Shouldn't we share the same traits, just like we share the same eye color (hazel, if you're wondering)? "Actually, there is something you can help me with," I told him. "But keep your voice down and your hands in your pockets."

He muttered something about bossing not being part of the deal and shuffled along after me.

As we walked among the Egyptian statuary on our way to the exhibit room, I could detect nothing out of the ordinary. I paused at the door leading into the exhibit and closed my eyes. Again, I sensed nothing.

"What are we looking for?" Henry asked. "And how are you going to find it with your eyes closed?"

"Henry," I asked, opening my eyes and watching him closely. "Do any of these exhibits ever give you the willies or make you uneasy?"

"Uneasy how?"

"Like make your skin crawl—"

"No. Never. How about you?"

"No. Never."

"Then why do you ask?" He thought for a moment. "Is that what's wrong with you? Are you frightened of these stuffy old exhibits?"

"No! But you hate being in the museum, so I thought perhaps it made you uneasy."

"I'm no coward!"

Drat. I'd so hoped he felt some of the same sensations I did, but just didn't know how to say so. Bringing Henry along was already proving to be a bad idea. "Look, I'm just trying to detect what is off with the museum. Something feels wrong somehow. As if someone were here while we were away, or one of the exhibits had been tampered with, something of that nature."

"You're off your nut," he said. "Forget about school, Father needs to send you directly to Bedlam."

I whirled around and scowled at him. "Take that back! Right now! Take it back, I say!"

Stunned, he just stared at me.

I clenched my fists and took a step toward him. "I'm warning you, Henry. I'm deadly serious. Take that back now or I'll—"

"All right already! I take it back. Don't get your knickers in a twist."

I glared at him. "You're not helping." I turned away from him and stepped fully into the Egyptian Funerary Magic room. It was morning, so the presence of the long-dead spirits was subdued. Maybe that was it. Were they too subdued?

I gave one last look around the room. Everything here

seemed perfectly normal. Well, as normal as the Egyptian exhibits ever got.

We left the room and headed toward the armory. Occasionally a bespelled sword found its way into the museum. Maybe I'd missed one and the sensation was coming from there.

Henry and I walked among the tall glass display cases that held spears, swords, and battle axes from every historical battle ever fought. Or so it seemed. It didn't take long before Henry became completely absorbed in all the weaponry in the room and I was able to conduct my examination without any interruptions. As I walked among the full-size suits of armor posted around the room like so many silent guards, I felt nothing. No sign of what was wrong with the museum and no sign of Isis either.

Fighting off a feeling of discouragement, I chewed my bottom lip and tried to think what to do next.

But of course! Our next stop would be Edgar Stilton's office. If something were truly off, he would be feeling it as well. It was early and he was likely the only assistant curator who had made it in so far.

When I tapped on his door, Stilton called, "Come in," his voice cracking horribly on the "in" part, which caused him to turn bright red.

"Good morning, Stilton," I said.

"Hullo, Theo. And Henry! Welcome home from school."

He let loose with a whopping big sneeze, then fumbled for his handkerchief.

"Thanks," said Henry, stepping back a pace or two.

"Have you got a cold, Stilton?" I asked.

He dabbed his honker with his handkerchief. "No," he said. "It only just started this morning when I got here. Must be the dust or something."

Aha! I knew it. Something unusual *was* afoot!

We said our goodbyes and then, reluctantly, I headed for the short-term storage area downstairs, where we had unloaded Mum's discovery last week. Wanting to avoid the nasty swarm of curses the artifacts were carrying, I'd put it off as long as possible.

"What's down here?" Henry asked, nearly treading on my heels.

"Mum's latest discoveries. You'll like this one, Henry. It's got loads of weapons."

His face brightened at this news and he stopped dragging his feet.

There was no one in short-term storage when we arrived, so I parked Henry in front of a box of evil-looking shabtis and set to work.

The sense of malevolence coming from the cursed artifacts was exactly the same as before Christmas, so I ignored them and began examining the contents of the other crates to see if anything was missing. The steles were there, and the revolting ceremonial dagger. I rifled through another crate and found a pile of scarabs that had a distinctly malicious feel to them, but it wasn't strong enough to account for the whole museum being off.

Four new crates sat nearby, but they hadn't even been opened yet. When I looked up from the boxes, I saw Henry had taken a dozen shabtis out of their crate and had set them up along the floor as if they were tin soldiers.

"Henry," I hissed. "They're not toys! They're four-thousand-year-old artifacts. Now put them back." I glanced down at the clay figures. With my heart beating faster, I slowly picked one up.

"Hey! You just ruined my troop formation!" Henry protested.

Ignoring him, I studied the figure in my hand. It had changed. The features were sharper, clearer. The expressions more harsh.

But no. That was impossible, surely. I closed my eyes and tried to concentrate. Was the uneasy sensation I had coming from these shabtis?

I waited a second and felt . . . nothing. No. Whatever strange things were going on with these clay soldiers, it wasn't what I had sensed when I came in this morning. Although, that now meant there were two things I had to investigate.

"Okay, Henry," I said as I put the shabti back in the crate. "Put those away. Our next stop is the catacombs."

"Oh, give off," Henry said uneasily. "They aren't really catacombs."

"If you say so," I said, heading for the door.

"They're not," he insisted, hurrying to catch up to me. "It's just a bunch of old stuff down in the basement. Stuff Dad's not using."

Henry was right. They aren't really catacombs, but long-term storage for things we're not currently using in the exhibits. But they are very creepy. All sorts of dead things, mummies and coffins and ancient skeletons of who-knows-what lurking twenty feet underground. Sounds like catacombs to me.

I opened the door, shuddering as a thick blast of icy cold stale air hit me. It smelled dank and musty and . . . "Okay. Nothing's been disturbed down there." I turned around and bumped smack into Henry, who was trying to peer over my shoulder down into the depths of the stairway.

"How can you tell?" he wanted to know.

"I just can, that's all." I could tell by the feel of the air, dank and heavy, with no fresh eddies or swirls cutting through its depths for months. The whole place had the feel of a sleeping beast that hadn't been disturbed in ages.

I didn't want to be the first one to do so. And certainly

not without more protection than I had on me at the moment.

"Tea," I announced, putting as much cheer into my voice as possible.

"There's no tea down there," Henry said, still peering into the dark passageway.

"Of course there's not." I shut the door, narrowly missing his nose. "But it's time to take Mother and Father their tea," I said firmly.

Henry shrugged and followed along, saying he hoped I'd make him some as well.

And they say he has no imagination!

As I started the midmorning tea, I wondered if all the unsettledness in the museum could be Isis. Setting out the mugs, I shook my head. That's not what it felt like. It felt more sinister than that. Although, Isis was quite sinister enough, come to think of it.

After I buttered up my parents by taking them their tea, I started in on Mum, insisting she inventory all the things she'd brought back. Maybe something in one of the unopened crates was causing this sensation. Finally, in complete exasperation, she caved. "But only because it must be done anyway, Theodosia. Not because of this melodrama you're inventing."

Doesn't she realize I have enough work to do around here without making things up?

We'd been down in short-term storage for almost an hour when Henry came thumping loudly down the stairs.

"What was that again, Mum? I couldn't hear you because *somebody* was making too much racket."

"This crate has six steles, each with war scenes on it," she repeated.

I made a note in the ledger in front of me. "Next?"

"Mum," Henry interrupted. "Dad says you're to come at once. That blasted old fool Snowthorpe's here."

"Henry!"

Henry shrugged. "Sorry. Those were his exact words."

With a sigh of exasperation, Mother got to her feet and brushed off her skirts. "What does he want, I wonder?"

Lord Snowthorpe is some muckety-muck high up at the British Museum whom Father used to work for. None of us like him much, especially Father. He's a greasy fellow, and whenever he pays us a visit, Father falls into one of his moods for at least two days.

I thought briefly of staying and continuing on with the inventory without Mother, but sometimes interesting things happen when Snowthorpe's about. I decided to follow her. I turned to Henry. "You coming?"

"Nah. I think I'll stay down here."

I saw the keen way he stared at the exposed weapons

we'd just inventoried. "Come on," I urged. "You can't be down here alone."

"Says who?"

"Me. Now come along. We'll spy on Snowthorpe, if it makes you feel any better."

His face brightened at this and he followed me up the stairs, sounding like a herd of hippopotami the whole way. How does he think to spy if he can't keep quiet?

When we reached the top of the stairs, I put my hand back to shush him. Lord Snowthorpe was leaning against one of the marble columns in the foyer, tapping his cane impatiently against the floor. Mother and Father were nowhere to be seen. Must be bracing themselves.

Snowthorpe's a tall man with a hooked nose and a very red face, as if he'd stayed out in the sun too long. He's got a tremendously round belly that he can barely manage to stuff into his coat and a superior air about him that would choke a pharaoh.

Just as I wondered if Mother and Father were making him wait on purpose, I heard a faint hiss from above. I looked up to find Isis poised in a crouch at the top of the balcony under which Snowthorpe stood.

Before I could do anything, she screeched, sounding more like a panther at the zoo than a cat, and flew at Lord Snowthorpe.

As her sharp claws dug into his shoulders, he gave a mighty bellow and tried to reach around and snatch her off his back.

While I ran forward to rescue Isis, Henry sniggered.

At Snowthorpe's shout, Mother and Father came running, and soon it was true pandemonium as we all tried to pry Isis from Snowthorpe's back without ripping his morning coat or hurting Isis. Although the way Father was going on, I suspect I was the only one worried about Isis.

Finally, Father got the cat untangled from the coat and shoved her at me. "Take this accursed cat, Theodosia, and get her out of here. Now!"

Isis struggled in my arms, whirling like a dervish, trying to escape. With one excellently placed swipe of her claws, she leaped from my arms and ricocheted back into the bowels of the museum.

Everyone was going on as if Snowthorpe had nearly been murdered and scowling at me like it was all my fault!

After everyone fussed over Snowthorpe a bit, he finally got down to business, looking significantly less jolly than when he'd first come in.

"I say, Throckmorton. The reason I've come down here is because I'd heard you'd found Thutmose III's Heart of Egypt. Been waiting all my life to see one of those, and I thought you might appreciate the chance to show it off."

The minute he said "Heart of Egypt" I knew. *That's* what was missing. Of course!

Mother was dying to show off her newest find and toddled off to fetch it.

I followed her, leaving Henry to spy solo. The two men would only sip tea and murmur stupid things about the weather. Surely, even Henry could manage that.

When I caught up to Mother she glanced over at me. "You're going to have to do something about that cat of yours, darling. She's gone feral on you."

"Not feral, Mum. Demonic, more like," I said under my breath.

As I followed Mum, it occurred to me that I had no idea where they'd hidden the Heart of Egypt. At last she reached the upstairs workroom and went to the far back wall and moved a section of books from the second shelf. There was an old tapestry hanging on the wall behind it (Late Medieval period). What an odd spot for a tapestry!

Mother pushed it aside and revealed a small safe.

Honestly! No one tells me anything.

I stood on tiptoe and tried to look over her shoulder as she spun through the combination, but she was too quick for me. She swung open the safe door and revealed a much larger chamber inside, containing all sorts of bulky wrapped objects. What else were they keeping in there that I didn't know about?

She reached in and found the velvet wrapping that had covered the Heart of Egypt and pulled it out of the safe. Carefully, she unwrapped it. When she lifted the last of the velvet away, we found ourselves staring at a dull black object.

It was not the Heart of Egypt.

Gone Missing

"It's gone!" Mother gasped, then whirled around to face me.

The thing in her hand was shaped like a real heart and made of blackest black. On the front of it, a coiled serpent—Apep—was painted in gold leaf.

"Whatever shall I tell Snowthorpe?" Mum cried. "Oh, whatever shall I tell your *father?*" she asked with true distress in her voice. She shoved the black heart at me, then turned back to the wall to lock up the safe. As my hand closed around the artifact, I braced myself, expecting to feel curses rolling off it in waves.

But there was nothing.

I studied the cold black stone, then leaned closer to sniff it. No trace of sulfur. I rubbed one of my fingers along the surface, but there was no oily residue. I set the stone heart on one of the shelves, near the back, where hopefully no one else would see it before I had a chance to conduct a few more tests.

Mum finished locking up the safe, then headed for the door. "We can't tell Snowthorpe it's missing. I'm not going to give him the satisfaction of thinking us amateurs."

"Mum?" I asked as I followed her out of the room.

"What is it, Theodosia?" she asked impatiently.

"Did you *tell* Snowthorpe about the Heart of Egypt? I mean, how did he know about it? You've only been back a few days."

Still puzzling out what to tell everyone, Mum waved her hand in the air. "I didn't announce the find, if that's what you mean. But I did have to declare it to get it out of the country."

"Yes, but did you declare it to Snowthorpe?"

"Of course not, Theo. I imagine someone he knew got wind of it."

Perhaps, but who would that someone be? And how would they have learned about it so quickly? Mother had it carefully hidden on her person during the whole trip. She hadn't even wired Father to let him know she was bringing it home.

Something about this wasn't quite right.

As we reached the anteroom, I could hear Snowthorpe's voice coming from within and could almost feel Father sending out mental SOS signals.

"What are you going to tell them?" I whispered.

"Don't worry. I have it under control," Mum said.

That didn't comfort me as much as she thought it would.

Mother straightened her spine, smoothed her skirts, and plastered a cheerful smile on her face (which looked more like a grimace) and marched through the door. I followed in her wake, not wanting to miss this one.

"There you are, ladies," Snowthorpe nearly bellowed. "I'd thought perhaps you'd got lost." He chuckled at his own feeble cleverness.

"Not at all, Snowthorpe," Mum replied, rather harshly.

He clapped his big hands together. "Well, let's see it, then."

"Yes, well." Mother cleared her throat. "I'm afraid you've chosen a particularly bad time, Snowthorpe. It's being cleaned at the moment."

The man frowned. "Cleaned? Well, I don't mind seeing it in progress, as it were."

Mum glanced desperately at Father. He knew at once

something was wrong, even if he hadn't caught on to exactly what yet.

I jumped into the fray. "It's a very delicate process. Er, due to the condition of the piece." I used my most knowledgeable voice, the one Father calls my Miss Bossy voice.

Mother leaped onto my reasoning like a cat pouncing after a mouse. "Yes! That's it. The cleaning process on a piece like this is very complex, as you can imagine." Mum went over and took Snowthorpe's arm and began gently steering him toward the door. "Once it's ready, you'll be the first we show it to."

Her voice faded away as she led him down the hall.

"Theodosia?" Father's sharp voice cracked through the room. "What's going on?"

"The Heart of Egypt's gone missing, that's what's going on."

As soon as Mum came back, she and Father disappeared into Father's office and closed the door. I could hear them talking in clipped, urgent tones. In minutes, they would no doubt begin tearing the museum apart, looking for it.

I didn't think they'd find it.

It was just too odd a coincidence that Snowthorpe should show up on the very morning we learned the Heart of Egypt was missing. I mean, how did he even know it was here?

Snowthorpe was our only clue as to who else might have

known about the artifact—someone had told him it was here. And before we could figure out who had taken it, we had to discover who else had known about it. If I got the Heart of Egypt back for my parents, surely *that* would impress them. Then they'd see what a huge help I could be, if only they'd let me.

I grabbed my things and slipped out the front door after Snowthorpe. I ignored the dark gray clouds that were lazily spitting down rain and hurried after him. Spotting the fluttering of his coattails as he turned the corner, I quickened my pace.

After several blocks, we reached the British Museum. I hurried up the stairs and followed Snowthorpe into the marble foyer filled with elaborate buttresses, gothic arches, and an enormous diplodocus skeleton. (I half hated the museum for how much grander it was than ours.) As I forced my gaze away from the display, I caught sight of Snowthorpe turning down a hall on the left.

Of course, even the hallway was grand here. It had lush carpet and deep, rich paneling, and mahogany doors with shiny brass nameplates. As Snowthorpe paused to talk to a man in the hallway, I quickly spun away and pretended to study one of the nameplates. I didn't want Snowthorpe to see me. Besides, a young girl viewing the museum's collection was explainable, but a young girl hanging about the offices was not.

The two men finished speaking and went their separate ways, the unknown man raising his eyebrows when he spotted me in the doorway. I flashed him a quick smile, pointed toward Snowthorpe, muttered some nonsense, then hurried along.

Snowthorpe turned into one of the offices and I stopped two doors away, straining to listen. It wasn't too difficult. Not with the way Snowthorpe tended to shout whenever he spoke.

"Well, Tetley," Snowthorpe barked. "You were dead wrong. The Throckmortons don't have the Heart of Egypt."

Aha! So it was this Tetley fellow who'd known about the artifact and blabbed to Snowthorpe.

There was a murmured reply that I couldn't quite hear. I glanced around, relieved to find the hallway empty, and inched closer.

"No. No. I think they're bluffing. Made up some story about it being cleaned. Next time check your sources better!"

"Yes, sir. Very sorry about that, sir," I heard Tetley say.

Snowthorpe cleared his throat. "Very well, then. Carry on."

Panic raced through me as I realized the conversation was over and Snowthorpe would be stepping out of the office—and directly into *me*—any second. I looked around at the long hallway. There was no place to hide, except for the door in front of which I'd been standing. I pressed my ear up to the wood and heard nothing, no murmur of voices or rustle of paper.

I had no choice. Ever so quietly I turned the knob and opened the door a crack. It was a storage closet of sorts. I stepped inside and pulled the door closed, careful that it not make too loud a *click*.

I backed up and bumped into a bolt of rolled-up carpet. Discarded chairs and unused lamps were tucked in corners. Dusty old scholarly journals were stacked on the floor in towers nearly as tall as I was. Ignoring the clutter, I focused my attention on the hallway on the other side of the door and listened. Merely a second later, I heard, or felt, rather, Snowthorpe's heavy tread as he retreated down the hall.

That was close. How on earth would I have explained my presence to that know-it-all? And who was this Tetley fellow anyway? How had *he* heard about the Heart of Egypt?

It seemed I had discovered nothing but more questions!

I heard the soft *click* of a nearby door being closed. Once again I heard footsteps in the hall. "The old codger wasn't supposed to go looking for it," someone muttered as they passed the closet door.

I waited a second or two, then quietly opened the door a crack. I looked to the right and saw that Tetley's door was now closed. When I looked to the left, I saw a young man with a hat and cane walking briskly, as if he were heading out. Odds were that was Tetley.

Interesting. As soon as he heard Snowthorpe report back on the absence of the Heart of Egypt, he had to leave the museum suddenly? Really, it was just too suspicious. Once again, I needed to follow.

Following the Leader

It was much easier following Tetley. He'd never met me before and had no idea who I was, so it didn't really matter if he spotted me.

I strolled along behind him as he made his way down Great Russell Street, then turned left on Bloomsbury. We walked along that street for a couple of blocks until we came to Oxford Street, which presented a bit of a problem. First of all, it's very busy road, and getting across it without being plowed into by a hansom, growler, or omnibus, or worse yet one of the new motorbuses, required quick thinking and even quicker feet. Second, Oxford Street was my boundary, the street past which I was not allowed to go without my parents. Ever.

I would like to say my conscience caused me to at least pause before I stepped into the street and dashed across, but that would be lying. I valiantly forged ahead, visions of Mother's and Father's faces alight with joy as I presented them with the lost Heart of Egypt filling my head.

Once we crossed Oxford Street, Tetley led me through a maze of dark streets and winding alleys that housed pubs, pie and chip shops, lodging houses, and pawnbrokers. The houses grew shabbier, the air thicker and danker with the black smoke and fog that hang above London like a nasty ghost. Forgotten laundry hung from the windows, now sodden with rain. Small bodies crouched in doorways and looked out at me with large, bleak eyes. Few of them had coats. Most huddled in old shawls that were little more than rags. I wished I had some pocket money on me so I could have shared it with them.

Quite frankly, I was beginning to feel a little nervous. I'm sure this is why I've been told *not* to cross Oxford Street. I glanced ahead at Tetley and drew a little closer.

He paused for a moment to consult his watch, then looked up and down the street. I bent over to fiddle with the button on my shoe. That's when I heard the sound of footsteps behind me come to a sudden stop. A small greasy fear clutched my stomach.

I forced myself to stand up and casually glanced over my shoulder. I saw no one, well, no one who looked as if they were following me. But then, they wouldn't look as if they were following me, because they would be trying to hide it, now wouldn't they?

But wait. There was a set of rather nice clothes back there, being worn by a boy just a tad smaller than me. He had a cowlick like a single devil's horn. "Henry!" A jolt of relief shot through me.

Henry smiled at me—smiled, mind you! As if this were all a lark!—then pulled his hands out of his pockets and trotted toward me.

Tetley began walking again. My fear of losing him was greater than my desire to bean Henry for scaring me half to death, so I turned to follow.

"Wait! Theo!" Henry called after me in a harsh whisper.

I whirled around. "Henry! You ninny! Don't you know anything about spying? You cannot make noise like that when you're following a person!"

Henry caught up to me with a wide grin on his face. "But I followed you pretty good, didn't I?"

"Come on. We're going to lose him." He *had* done a good job of following me, but I wasn't about to tell him and have it swell his already inflated head. However, I must confess to being glad of a traveling companion on these streets.

"Why are you following him?" Henry asked.

I stepped into the street, careful to keep my eye on Tetley. "Well, if you don't know, then why are you following me?"

He shrugged. "It was better than hanging around a moldy old museum."

"Our museum isn't moldy," I corrected.

We paused at a junction that connected seven streets, each leading off like the spoke of a wheel. With a shock, I realized we were standing in the Seven Dials, one of the most notorious neighborhoods in all of London. I would be in a whole tubful of hot water if my parents ever found out. Hopefully, they'd be so thrilled at getting the Heart of Egypt back they'd forget all about it.

Tetley stopped to look around, as if he were expecting someone to meet him. Henry whispered, "So, what *is* going on, Theo?"

I wondered if I could trust him. He *had* risked an awful lot to follow me. And it wouldn't hurt to have someone else know what was going on . . . in case things went wrong. "First you need to promise you won't tell anyone."

"I promise!"

I quickly filled him in. When I'd finished, Henry whistled. "That *is* suspicious."

"Exactly. I'm certain he must know something about its disappearance."

"I'm sure you're right," Henry said.

My chest swelled with pride. Perhaps my instincts had been right to trust him.

Tetley took off again, and away we went. He turned down a side street where the houses went from shabby to downright grim. The dank, rat-infested streets were lined with listless, exhausted men and women. Dirty, hollow eyed children huddled at their feet. Their pinched faces and dull eyes were haunting. Henry moved closer to me and I took a deep breath to steady myself. My lungs filled with grimy London air that reeked of the Thames, which we seemed to be winding our way toward.

"How long are we going to follow him?" Henry asked, uncertain.

"I'm not sure." I was wondering the same thing, trying to decide how much farther I wanted to go in this part of town. But I didn't want Henry to know I was uneasy. I was the oldest and it was my duty to present a bold front. Still, it did seem as if we were getting nowhere—at least, nowhere we'd want to be.

And I didn't want to get our throats slit in the process.

"It looks as if he's heading to the river. We'll follow him there and if nothing's happened by then, we'll high-tail it back." Only I'd choose an alternative route.

Just then Tetley turned down a particularly filthy street

that reeked of sewer. I nearly reached up to pinch my nose shut, but realized that might offend someone. This was not the sort of neighborhood you went around offending people in.

"Breathe out of your mouth," I advised Henry.

"Don't worry. I am," he answered, his voice thick.

I glanced nervously into the shadows that lurked near the houses, nearly fainting in fright when one of them detached itself and began walking in our direction. "Run!" I whispered urgently.

A COSH TO THE HEAD

I DIDN'T NEED TO TELL HIM TWICE. We took off at the same time, not caring how close we got to Tetley. Hopefully, he had a wicked little blade hidden in his walking cane like Father did and could protect us all.

I'm afraid our running was rather pitiful, and the heavy footsteps drew closer.

I grabbed Henry's arm. A church. We'd dash into one of the churches. I looked around desperately. For blocks and blocks there'd been a church on every corner. Now, when I needed one, all I could find were breweries and inns. Botheration!

We'd nearly caught up to Tetley now. Surely that was the lesser of two evils? Even if he did have something to do with the stolen artifact, that wouldn't make him the sort of fellow who'd refuse to help children, would it? Or would he just cut our throats and toss our bodies into the Thames?

I decided to go with the villain I knew instead of the villain I didn't. Just as I opened my mouth to call out to Tetley, I felt a cold, clawlike hand clamp down on my elbow.

I nearly screamed. Would have if I hadn't immediately recognized the assailant's voice. "Wot you doin' down 'ere, miss?"

"Sticky Will!" Relief, as warm and welcome as treacle syrup, coursed through me. "What are you doing here?"

Henry leaned over to put his hands on his knees while he caught his breath.

Will removed his hand from my elbow and shrugged. "This is part of me territory."

"Territory? You mean pickpockets have territories?" Fascinating.

"'Course they do. Otherwise we'd all be fighting over every pidgeon that crossed our path."

"But no one's tried to pick our pockets," I pointed out.

Will looked scornful. "'Course not. I been following you since you turned into Broad Street. Signaled the other blokes to lay off."

"Oh." So we hadn't been in any real danger, thanks to Will. "Well, thank you. Very much." Once again, Will had been covering my back. And I hadn't even had to ask! I glanced ahead to Tetley, who was turning the next corner.

"Well, don't thank me too much, miss. There's one bloke back there who ain't getting the signal."

"You mean someone else is following us? Besides you?"

"Aye. Attached himself at Queen Street."

"Is he the same one who followed me from the train station?"

"Nah. That was me first thought, too. But it weren't."

"Well, who is he then?" I asked, turning to see if I could spot him.

"Don't look! 'E'll know yer on to 'im. Who knows what 'e'll do then?"

I clutched Will's arm. "We mustn't let the man up in front of us get out of sight. I think he's stolen something valuable from the museum. I have to find out what he's doing with it."

"Blimey, miss. This is just like one of them penny dreadfuls." He sounded very cheerful about it. "Let's go." He shoved his hands in his pockets and sauntered, acting for all the world as if he were merely out for a morning stroll.

I tried to seem as casual, but it is terribly difficult to saunter when you know you're being followed by someone.

What little sense of adventure there had been in the beginning was gone now and it felt like grim dogging of duty. Then it occurred to me—we were a team! Just like a group of archaeologists on a dig or exploration. A small warmth lodged itself in my chest and my steps felt somehow lighter. We walked for about two more blocks before Tetley suddenly picked up his pace and made a quick, unexpected dash into a small alley just off Parker Street.

Behind us, we heard the footsteps of the person on our trail break into a run. I whipped my head around. Was he going to make his move on us now that Tetley was out of sight?

I saw Will glance around, looking for a hiding place. The dreary building nearby, with its even drearier inhabitants, didn't look as if it'd offer us much protection.

In no time the footsteps were upon us. I took a deep breath, put on my fiercest scowl, and braced myself.

But the man barreled past us. He wasn't following us at all. He was following Tetley!

And if that was the case, the pursuer most likely knew about the wretched Heart of Egypt. Bother. Why not just announce it in the *Times* for goodness' sake?

In silent agreement, the three of us inched our way into the alley. All sorts of filth mixed with the rainwater and ran over the cobbles. The brick walls were black with grime and crumbling with damp. The alley looked more like a cross between a sewer and a rubbish bin than anything else.

It was also a dead end. Tetley's path was blocked by a brick wall.

His pursuer drew closer and pulled a long black club out of his coat.

Tetley turned just in time to see the stick come down upon his head.

"He coshed the blighter!" Will said, sounding suspiciously cheerful about the whole thing.

Tetley crumpled like a falling soufflé, folding his body into a puddle on the ground. My hand flew to my mouth as I vowed not to scream. Was he dead? Or just unconscious? I couldn't tell. But it was obvious this fellow was playing for keeps!

The attacker (tall and very dashing, really, in a villainous sort of way) quickly knelt down and began searching Tetley's pockets. He found something in the upper coat pocket, which he took out and put in his own. He felt for Tetley's pulse, then stood up, adjusted his coat, straightened his hat, and turned back toward the street.

We jerked back out of sight. My mind was racing. Poor Tetley! Had I just witnessed a murder? Should I abandon the Heart of Egypt and go for help? I was at a loss for what to do. Luckily, Will took command.

"You two wait by the chip shop on the corner. I'll go this way and wait fer 'im down by the brewery. That way, whichever way 'e goes, we'll have 'im covered."

My indecision lifted when I heard a groan from the alleyway. Hopefully, if Tetley was well enough to groan, he was well enough to wait for help until Henry and I had retrieved the Heart of Egypt.

But before Will could get into position, the attacker quickly emerged from the alley and headed down Drury Lane toward the river. We all followed.

This time we hadn't even managed a whole block before we heard the sound of footsteps behind us. Honestly! Doesn't anyone in London have anything better to do than follow other people around?

Will caught my eye and jerked his head slightly up the street. I gave a tiny nod to let him know I'd heard the footsteps, too. He held up three fingers. Three pursuers.

And this time, of course, we couldn't count on the fellow we were following for any sort of help at all.

At Russell Street the man in front of us seemed to realize he was being followed (although I doubt he realized he was being followed by half of London!). He switched directions and moved away from the river, walking at such a furious clip that we had to trot like horses to keep up with him.

Of course, the pursuers were no idiots and quickly

increased their pace until the whole lot of us were galloping down the street.

And nobody seemed to give a fig. On my side of Oxford Street, people would have at least stared, or shouted out a "Hey there!" But not on this side of Oxford Street. Here they shuffled quickly out of the way and stood back to watch the show.

The man ahead of us now seemed rather desperate to lose his pack of followers. He twisted and turned, taking side streets and back alleys, but we all doggedly stuck to his trail. We finally emerged along the back side of Covent Garden. The man tore around to the east side of the gardens, expertly dodging the straggling carts left over from the morning's market.

We emerged at the west end of the gardens into the courtyard of St. Paul's Church. Of course—he was going to seek sanctuary inside the church! Brilliant!

His other pursuers soon realized this as well. They oozed toward the stranger in front of us, moving with a lethal grace that reminded me of Isis when she was hunting mice. They fanned out, cutting off the victim before he could reach the church door. The three of us ducked behind one of the large columns to watch, hoping to stay out of sight.

The man who'd attacked Tetley drew out his truncheon and crouched in a fighting stance. Outnumbered, he struck first, taking the attackers by surprise. The surprise lasted only a moment before they swarmed him, fists flying.

Cornered now, he fought like a madman, swinging his bludgeon like a sword, using his elbows and kicking, but in the end, there were just too many of them. Two of the men finally grabbed his arms, and one of the others strode up to him, placed his arm around the man's neck as if he were hugging him, then jabbed him in the gut. As the assailant pulled away, the stranger collapsed to the ground. There was a vicious-looking knife in the other man's hand, covered in blood.

"Blimey," Will whispered.

"Blimey, indeed," said Henry, his eyes big and round.

I elbowed him in the ribs. These men were truly evil. We would be lucky to get out of this with our lives, never mind the Heart of Egypt.

"Shhst," Will hissed. "They're searching him like he did the other bloke."

Quickly and efficiently, they emptied the fallen man's pockets of everything they found, including whatever it was he had taken off Tetley (and I was betting it was the Heart of Egypt by their excited voices). One of the men—the one who'd stabbed him—pocketed this find and shouted triumphantly.

"That's German!" said Will.

He was right. I turned to look at him. "How do you know that?"

"Ain't I good enough to know German when I 'ears it?" he asked, sniffing.

"Oh, don't be ridiculous. Of course you are! I just meant where have you heard it before?"

"At one of them political rallies, that's where."

Ignoring Will's fit of pique, I turned my attention back to the men, who had stepped away from the body and were having a quick, hurried conversation in low voices. Then, one man at a time, they left the churchyard, each going in a different direction.

I was torn. We needed to check on the injured fellow. But I also needed to keep my eye on the Heart of Egypt. And at some point we had to get back to Tetley.

I turned to Will. "Can you follow the one who nabbed the package out of that man's coat?"

Will nodded.

"Don't do anything! Just follow him and find out where he goes. And for goodness' sake, be careful."

Will gave a quick nod. "Right-o. If I can get close enough, I might be able to pinch it right out of his pocket."

I grabbed his arm and gave it a little shake. His eyes widened in surprise. "Do not tangle with these men. They just stabbed a man in cold blood in the middle of a church square. I hate to think what they could do to you."

"Why, thank ye, miss. That's right kind o' you to care. But this is my territory. I'll be fine."

He got to his feet, still crouching low, and slipped away. Henry jumped up and tried to follow. I grabbed the back of his coat and yanked him back down. "What do you think you're doing?"

"I'm going to follow the German. With Will."

"You'll do nothing of the sort. Will's a professional and can take care of himself. You'll just get into trouble. Besides, we need to see if we can help this fellow."

Henry muttered something about a bunch of tommyrot.

"Look," I whispered. "This is much more dangerous than merely following someone! He's a known attacker and basher of heads! He could still be alive and dangerous."

Henry perked up at that and followed me as I eased out of our hiding place.

We made our way over to the fallen man. My heart was thumping so hard in my chest, I feared it was going to leap out and run and hide in the church.

I've never been anywhere near a dead person before. Not even a dead thing. Well, except for the mummies and such, but they've been dead for such a long time they don't really count.

It was eerily quiet. No sounds of traffic or noise from the surrounding streets, as if the very stillness of death itself lay over the spot.

"It's jolly creepy, isn't it?" Henry whispered.

"Don't be such a little beast," I whispered back. I don't know why we were whispering, but it seemed the right thing to do in the presence of Death.

I saw the man's legs first, sticking out from behind the side of the building. I put my hand out to slow Henry down so he wouldn't tromp right over them. Slowly, I inched around, following the long black legs up to the man's body. He was so still, and his face was deathly white, as if all the blood had drained from it.

And so much blood! His entire waistcoat was dark red and there was a small puddle gathering off to his left. I strained to see if he was still breathing, but his chest didn't seem to be rising and falling. Not a good sign.

Gingerly, I knelt down as close to the body as I dared. I leaned forward, staring at the whiskers of his mustache. Were they moving at all?

I turned to Henry. "He's not breath—"

Hard, strong fingers clamped down on my elbow. I nearly shrieked, but ground my teeth together so no sound would escape. I scrabbled as far away from the man as I could, which wasn't very far, since he had attached himself to my arm like a limpet.

Henry was just putting his arms around me to help pull me away when the man croaked out a single word. "Help."

It was very feeble, but it was a word. And if he could speak, he wasn't dead. Which meant we had to help him. I let out a breath and forced myself to scoot closer in case he said anything else.

"Henry, I think we passed a police station on Bow Street. Do you think you can go back there and fetch some help?"

"Aren't you afraid they'll think we did him in?"

"That's rather wishful thinking. We're children. Children don't go around stabbing strangers."

The man's hand tugged on my sleeve, pulling me closer. "No p'lice," he managed to get out.

"But you're bleeding buckets all over the ground! We've got to get you some help."

"Som set hoo," he said.

Botheration! Now *he* was speaking a foreign language. Didn't anyone speak the Queen's English anymore? "I'm sorry. I don't understand."

The man licked his lips and tried again. "Somerset House. Help there."

"Somerset House?" Henry said.

"Yes. It's down a few blocks near the river," I explained.

"I know where it is!" Henry said. "But what kind of help will be there? I think it's very suspicious he doesn't want the police. How do we know he isn't leading us into a trap?"

"Why would he do that if we're trying to help him?

Besides, if he gets patched up, he might be able to tell us how he found out about the you-know-what and why he coshed Tetley on the head to get it."

"You're daft if you think he's going to tell you that. He's got 'secret' written all over him."

I turned back to the man as he tugged on my sleeve again.

"Thir' floor. Antique S'ciety." The man stopped talking and I thought perhaps he had fainted, or worse. Then he spoke again, only this time I had to practically put my ear on his mouth to hear.

"Wigmere. Only Wigmere." He clutched my sleeve and fought desperately to get the words out. "Tell him"—he drew one last shuddering breath—"forces of chaos . . ." Then his words dribbled to a stop.

Somerset House

THE MAN WAS SO PALE AND STILL, I was afraid he wouldn't survive long enough for us to bring help. If only we had some medicine or bandages. Something that could help him hang on.

But of course—my amulets!

I reached up and lifted my small heart amulet out from under my collar and pulled it over my head.

"What are you doing?" Henry asked.

"Trying to save him," I said, carefully laying the amulet directly over his heart.

"By giving him a silly-looking necklace?"

"Oh, do shut up. Make sure this stays right where it is. Don't let him accidentally knock it off."

"But what is it?" Henry insisted.

"How can you spend half your life in a museum and not know what that is?" I asked, thoroughly exasperated. "It's an amulet. It will protect his life force until I return with help."

I frowned down at the injured man. He needed more than just spiritual help. I quickly stepped out of one of my petticoats. (How lucky I'd put two on that morning for extra warmth!)

"Here," I said, thrusting the petticoat at Henry.

He recoiled. "What am I supposed to do with that?"

"Make bandages, you ninny!"

Reluctantly, he reached out and clasped the petticoat gingerly between two fingers.

I gave him a disgusted look, then headed out of the churchyard. But as irritating as he was, I did not envy Henry having to keep watch over a nearly dead man.

I ran back through the narrow streets until I finally emerged on the Strand. There, directly across from me, stood Somerset House. It was large and imposing—nearly the size of a palace—with a thousand windows facing the street. Not wanting to call attention to myself, I slowed to a walk in order to cross the enormous courtyard. At the entrance, the doorman raised an eyebrow at me (I'm quite sure I looked horribly grubby) and asked my business.

I straightened my spine and tilted my chin, giving him my best imitation of Grandmother Throckmorton's haughty stare. "I'm here to see Wigmere with the Antique Society on the third floor."

"You mean the Antiquaries Society?"

"Er, yes. That." The man blinked once, then pointed me in the direction of the stairs. Perhaps having an over-grand relative comes in handy sometimes.

I went up the stairs, drawing a number of curious glances from the men who had business there at Somerset House (there didn't seem to be any women about). When I reached the third floor, I saw a large brass sign announcing the Antiquaries Society. Almost there.

A young, rather prim-looking gentleman with wire spectacles stepped out of his office. "May I help you?" he asked in that tone of voice that lets you know he has no intention of helping, he's just trying to shame you into stopping whatever it is that you're doing.

Once again I assumed my best Grandmother Throckmorton stare, the one where she looks down her nose. (Things end up going a bit fuzzy and double sometimes, but it is a very effective look.) "I am here to see Wigmere, if you please." Which, of course, did not mean please at all, but rather, if you get out of my blasted way.

The young man's mouth pinched. "Have you an appointment with *Lord* Wigmere?" he asked, knowing full well I didn't.

Oops. Hadn't realized the fellow was a lord. "No. I'm afraid something rather sudden has come up. I've an important message for him."

"Best give it to me and I'll pass it along."

I shook my head. "I was told to give it only to Lord Wigmere."

The man was decidedly put off that I should know something he didn't. "Well, I'm afraid that's impossible."

How was I going to get past this interfering watchdog? "How about if I write him a note, you take it to him, and then he can decide if he wants to see me or not."

The fellow sighed. "You know, we are very busy here. We don't have time for children's games."

"Excuse me, sir"—I let the slightest bit of contempt into my voice on the "sir"—"but I have no more time to waste on games than you do. This is a matter of gravest importance. Life and death, actually. Will you get me a piece of paper or should I try another office?"

That stopped him cold. His mouth tightened and he withdrew into his office and returned with a piece of paper, which he handed to me.

I looked up at him in annoyance. "What shall I write on it with? Blood?"

He looked appalled at that suggestion and went back to his office, returning with the most abused stub of a pencil I had ever seen. Ignoring the intended slight, I placed the paper against the wall and wrote my note.

Dear Lord Wigmere,
    Man dying. Must see you at once.
Sincerely,
    Theodosia Elizabeth Throckmorton.

I carefully folded the paper twice, then began to hand over the note. The man's eyes were fastened on it like a bloodhound on point, his eyes gleaming.

"Excuse me," I said. "But may I have an envelope, please?"

He looked as if he'd like to box my ears. Instead, he marched back into his office, then came out to shove an envelope at me.

I carefully placed the note in the envelope, praying that all these horrid delays wouldn't end up costing the injured man his life. I sealed it quite thoroughly so as to keep the man from peeking, then handed him the note. He took it (grabbed it, actually) and stormed off down the hall, walking so stiffly that I had to wonder if he had a steel rod attached to his spine.

Not wanting to go through this again, I kept a careful eye out as to which office door he knocked on. He entered, then quickly returned, his mouth all puckered up as if he'd been forced to take Gladwell's Health and Liver Tonic.

"He will see you, miss." He put a rather sarcastic emphasis on the "miss," which I decided to ignore because, after all, I was in. When we finally arrived at Wigmere's door, the annoying little man gave a single knock before opening it. "Miss Throckmorton to see you, sir." I stepped inside the room and he closed the door behind me.

Lord Wigmere sat at his desk, his head bent over something he was writing. "I'll be with you in a moment," he said without looking up.

Cool as a cucumber, he was. If someone had written me a note announcing that a person was dying, I would have paid attention to them straight away.

He was also old, older than Father, with a shock of white hair and a luxurious white mustache. He had an intriguing gold and lapis ring on the third finger of his right hand. It was beveled, and had small hieroglyphs carved in it. It reminded me of one of Ramses II's rings I'd seen in the British Museum.

"Now, Miss Throckmorton," he said, making me jump. "What's all this about a man dying?"

I looked up to meet his gaze and found myself staring

into eyes that were as blue as the ocean and nearly twice as deep. His face was deeply wrinkled and he looked as if he carried the weight of the whole world on his shoulders.

"One of your men sent me, sir. I don't know his name as he was stabbed in the ribs and found it difficult to speak. But he did say to tell you something about forces and chaos."

Wigmere snapped to attention.

"Where did this happen?" he barked.

"In St. Paul's churchyard. My brother Henry is staying with him until you send someone."

Wigmere shoved to his feet and grabbed the cane that was leaning against his desk. He made his way to the door, flung it open, and called out, "Boythorpe!"

I heard steps hurrying down the hall and the annoying guard dog of a man appeared in front of Wigmere. (Although, I could almost forgive him his horrid personality, what with having a name like Boythorpe and all.) "Get me Thornleigh, right away. And Dodson and Bramfield too." He started to turn back into the room and his eyes fell on me. "And bring Miss Throckmorton some refreshment, Boythorpe. She looks like she needs it."

Wigmere thumped his way back over to the desk and sat down. "Now, Miss Throckmorton. If you would be so good as to start at the beginning."

"Please call me Theodosia. Everyone does."

He nodded his head.

What should I tell him? I had no idea who's side he was on. Or even how many sides there were, come to think of it. How trustworthy could he be if one of his fellows had attacked a man and stolen a precious artifact?

"Ah," Wigmere said, leaning back in his chair. "You're no doubt wondering if you can trust me."

"Well, something like that. Your friend did bash someone over the head and take something that didn't belong to him."

Wigmere stilled. "The Heart of Egypt? Did Stokes get it?"

"The Heart of Egypt! What do you know about it? And yes, Stokes got it, but the men who attacked him stole it."

"I can assure you that my man Stokes was only trying to keep it from falling into the wrong hands. Now why don't you tell me what *you* know about it?"

I was loath to give away the museum's secrets or worse yet, have Wigmere think I was starkers. But I looked into his great, heavy eyes, stern with justice and strength, and found myself spilling the whole story.

When I had finished telling him of Snowthorpe's visit to our museum that morning and the discovery that the Heart of Egypt was missing, there was a knock on the door. Without waiting, three gentlemen stepped in. Wigmere made the introductions. "Dodson, Thornleigh, Bramfield, this is Theodosia Throckmorton and she has come to tell us that Stokes is down, badly injured, perhaps dead, in the churchyard at St. Paul's. Her brother Henry is with him. You are to go and fetch them both at once and bring them back here. Dodson, you and Bramfield take Stokes down to Level Six when you return. I'll have a doctor waiting. Thornleigh, escort Master Throckmorton to my office when you get back."

All three men took their instructions with no questions and left immediately.

"You may continue, Miss Theodosia." Wigmere said it in a very kind voice, but there was iron in there as well. You knew if you didn't do something the first time he asked, he would make you do it anyhow.

I explained how Henry, Sticky Will, and I had followed Tetley because he was the last possible connection to the Heart of Egypt. I told him how Stokes had then come on the scene. Wigmere's eyebrows raised higher and higher the longer I talked, until they finally disappeared into his hair. "You say Stokes killed this fellow Tetley?"

"Well, he did bash him rather hard, sir," I explained.

"I doubt the blow was lethal, Miss Theodosia. Our operatives have been trained to disable and disarm rather than kill."

"Oh." This made me feel rather better about helping Stokes, I must say.

"Well, all three of you have been very brave and very clever," Wigmere said at last.

I cannot tell you how good this felt to hear. Every other grownup I know calls me a silly little girl or accuses me of having too much imagination, but not Wigmere. And *he* seemed the sort of fellow who ought to know.

"Has anything of this sort happened before?" he asked.

"What? People stealing artifacts from our museum?"

Wigmere leaned forward. "There *have* been strange goings-on, haven't there?"

Did he mean the curses? How would he know about them? Unless there were other strange goings-on that I didn't know about . . .

Luckily, I was saved from answering by another knock on the door. Then a tea tray was brought in.

The fellow set it down on a small table and left the room.

Wigmere waved at the tray. "Please help yourself to refreshment."

"May I pour for you, sir?"

"No, thank you. I will just write a quick note while you have yours, if you don't mind."

I didn't mind a bit and poured myself a cup of tea, adding plenty of milk and sugar. There were some delicious-looking cucumber sandwiches and Banbury cakes on the tray, which made me aware of how violently hungry I was.

I munched my sandwiches as quietly as possible and sipped tea to the sound of Lord Wigmere's pen scratching across the paper on his desk. His office was grand. Just the sort of office I intend to have when I am grown up and no longer have to settle for an old closet. It was lush, with thick curtains and an elegant carpet, comfortable chairs, and wonderful artifacts on display.

Finally, Lord Wigmere got up, grabbed his cane again, and limped to the door. He stuck his head out and called for Boythorpe, who appeared so quickly I couldn't help but wonder if he'd been trying to listen in.

"See that Dr. Fallowfield gets this immediately."

"Yes, sir."

Lord Wigmere closed the door and returned to his desk. I was just considering whether or not he'd notice if I had a fourth sandwich when he said, "Now. You were going to tell me about the strange goings-on at that museum of yours."

Bother. I had so hoped he would be sidetracked from this question. "What sorts of goings-on do you mean, sir?"

He gave me a reproachful look. "I expected something rather more truthful from you, my girl."

My cheeks burned at his admonishment, but once again I was saved from answering by a knock on the door. A look of severe annoyance passed over Wigmere's face. "Come in."

It was Thornleigh, and beside him a very wide-eyed Henry.

"Henry!" I said, jumping up from my seat and nearly toppling the tea tray. "Are you all right?"

"'Course I am. Not a milksop," he muttered, his cheeks turning pink.

I turned to Thornleigh. "How is the, uh, your associate? Is he . . ." I couldn't bring myself to say the word "dead." There was too much finality to it.

Thornleigh glanced at Wigmere, looking for permission to speak. Wigmere nodded. "Stokes is alive, but barely." Thornleigh lifted his hand, my amulet dangling from one of his fingers. "We found this on him, sir. Placed directly over his heart."

Wigmere lifted an eyebrow at me. "Yours?"

"Yes."

"Where did you get it?" he asked.

"I made it, sir."

"And how do you come to know so very much about protective amulets, I wonder?"

Thornleigh cleared his throat. "This lad"—he gestured to Henry—"used his head and applied a pressure bandage to Stokes's ribs to slow down the blood loss."

Henry shrugged, red-faced at the unexpected attention. "Learned it at school," he said.

"Was there any sign of another boy?" Wigmere asked. "The one who followed the attackers?"

"No, sir. But we'll have Dodson head right back to the church and wait for him once we get Stokes settled on Level Six."

"Excellent."

"Excuse me, sir," I said.

"Yes?"

"How will you recognize him?"

"I beg your pardon?"

"I mean, sir, you've never seen Will before. How will you know it's him? I should probably go with Mr. Dodson so I can identify him." And so I could avoid any further interrogation by the sharp-eyed Lord Wigmere.

"Hm, yes. I see your point." He speared Henry with a keen look. "What do you say, young man. Are you up to the task? Can you return with Dodson and point out this Will to him?"

"Be happy to, sir. Let me just grab a sandwich or two and I'll be on my way."

Lord Wigmere turned back to me with a meaningful look. "You and I still have things we must discuss," he said.

Bother.

THE BROTHERHOOD OF THE CHOSEN KEEPERS

"MY DEAR GIRL. THIS IS NOT A GAME. Very serious things are afoot here in Britain and it appears you are involved. Your mother's and father's reputations are well known. Many of the items your mother brings into the country have rather . . . remarkable properties. I need to know how many other artifacts with these same properties reside in your museum."

My earlier caution forgotten, I jumped out of my chair and took a step toward the desk. "You know about the spells?"

He came to full attention at the word "spells," and for one horrible moment I thought I'd made a hideous blunder.

"Yes," he said slowly. "I know about the spells. Why don't you tell me what *you* know about them?"

"Well, you're the first person I've met who actually knows they exist. Besides me, I mean. Mother and Father never sense them, but I can usually tell the first time I lay eyes on an artifact. It feels like icy-footed beetles are crawling down my back. Is that how you know they're there, too?"

Lord Wigmere's mustache twitched slightly. "Ah, no. We have other ways of telling if the objects are bespelled."

"Wax? That's my Second Level Test."

Wigmere sat back and folded his arms. "Tell me about this Second Level Test."

"Well, when I've determined the artifact might be cursed I place a small circle of wax bits—"

"Where do you get this wax?"

"I save up the ends of candles and such. Anyway, I place a little circle of wax bits around the object. I check it a few hours later and if the wax is a dirty gray or black, I know I was right and the object is cursed."

"Have you ever been wrong? Has the wax ever stayed white?"

"Never."

"Fascinating," he said under his breath. Then he asked, "Do you conduct any other tests?"

"Well, yes. If it passes the wax test I then do a Level Three Test. The Moonlight Test."

Wigmere raised his eyebrows, and I rushed my words because when you say them out loud they sound foolish. "I have to check the artifacts at night. When moonlight shines on them, I can . . . I can see the curses swimming around on the object."

Wigmere's eyes burned with interest. "Really? What do they look like?"

"Well, they're hieroglyphs. But they move and swim, like a swarm of bees looking for someone to sting, and they give off a buzzing feeling." I paused. "Haven't you ever seen them? In the moonlight like that?"

"No." Wigmere shook his head and looked a bit sad about it. "So the hieroglyphs tell you the nature of the curse?"

"No. They actually *are* the curse. As written on the object by whoever cursed it in the first place."

Wigmere leaned back in his chair, studying me as if I were a particularly interesting artifact he'd just stumbled upon. "Remarkable. And when did you first discover you had this unusual talent?"

"Unusual, sir? But isn't that how you do it?"

"No. I'm afraid not. Our ways are much more mundane and laborious. Indeed, it would save us all a great deal of time and trouble if we had your gift."

For some reason I couldn't explain, this made me a bit queasy. "Well, I've had it since I was very young." Then I explained to him how I'd discovered research and used that to arm myself. "That's how I learned about the different tests and found the different recipes for removing the curses."

"Recipes?"

"Well, yes. Aren't they rather like recipes? You follow the steps using the right ingredients, only instead of a cake or a leg of mutton you end up with an uncursed object."

"Well, it's not quite that simple for most people." Abruptly, Wigmere turned his chair around to a large cupboard built into the wall behind his desk. He pulled a key from his trousers and unlocked one of the doors, then took out a long, black stone box. He turned back around and placed it in front of me. His eyes fixed on me the whole time, he carefully lifted the lid.

Inside there was an ornately carved, long thin statue of the most hideous gaping serpent I had ever seen. It had jagged scales and enormous fangs, and the eyes were two small bits of red carnelian. It felt old, older almost than time itself. I raised my eyes from the artifact and saw Wigmere watching me intensely.

"Well, it's as ugly as sin," I said when I realized he was waiting for me to speak. "And one of the most vile representations of the Serpent of Chaos I've ever seen. But there's no curse on it, if that's what you're wondering."

Wigmere fingered his chin and looked thoughtfully from the serpent back to me. He turned back to the cupboard and pulled another box from the shelves. This one was of light gray soapstone, and carved with many hieroglyphs and symbols, some I'd never seen before.

He placed the box on the desk in front of me and removed the top. As soon as the lid was off, the skin on my back lifted from my spine and felt like it was trying to run out of the room.

I stared down at the small, carved hippopotamus that looked as harmless as a child's toy. It wasn't. I could sense ill luck and abominable curses writhing on its surface. I shuddered, then reached for the lid and plunked it back on the box. "Seth. In one of his more innocent forms." Not that anything about the god of chaos and destruction could be called truly innocent. "Heavily cursed. Feels like death-and-destruction stuff, but I'm not sure."

A slightly triumphant look crossed Wigmere's face. "But I thought you said you could see the curse on the object itself?"

I sighed. "But only in the moonlight." How disappointing. I suppose it is too much to ask that an adult, especially one as grand as Wigmere, pay attention to everything someone my age has to say.

His mustache twitched, a response I was beginning to recognize. "You *were* listening! This was just a test! To see if I was telling the truth!"

Wigmere looked a bit sheepish. "Well, you can hardly blame me. Your talents are truly remarkable. Never seen anything like them."

Pride warred with dismay. While I fancied being unique, I wasn't sure how I felt about being the only one with this particular skill. That was too uncomfortably close to being off one's nut. "Well, how do *you* tell, then?"

"By studying the origins and history of the piece. Sometimes we get hunches, but never a shiver down my back that nearly shakes me out of my chair. It's a lot of guesswork, actually."

I didn't know what to say.

Lord Wigmere continued. "It must be some inborn trait, some intuition or talent you possess. Like being able to ride a horse well or being good at playing the piano."

"But then, wouldn't my parents be able to see the curses? Or Henry?"

"Henry doesn't see them, then?"

"No."

Wigmere shrugged. "Well, I'm just hazarding guesses here. This is something I've never run into before. Although I do know that some people's natures are simply more open to magic than others'." He paused for a moment, his eyes focused just past my head.

"What?" I asked.

"I was just remembering something. From when I was a boy."

I scooted forward to the edge of my seat. "What?"

"It was my first trip to the British Museum. I remember being fascinated by the Egyptology room. As an adult, I've always thought that's when my career decision was made, but now I'm remembering it wasn't so much the artifacts, although those were very interesting."

He paused again. I wanted to get up and shake him. "Yes?" I prompted.

"But now I remember having a distinct case of the willies the whole time. I remember wondering why the place was so blasted cold. My parents finally bundled me out of there, I was shivering so badly."

"And now you're wondering if you weren't reacting to the exhibits the same way I do to cursed objects?"

"Exactly. As if it were an ability one has as a child, but loses as an adult."

Well that was rubbish. I had no intention of losing this ability when I turned into a grownup. "But wait," I said. "What about all the people who wrote the books on Egyptian magic in the first place? They weren't children."

Wigmere reached up and began stroking his mustache. "No. That's true enough. But those books were also written centuries after the fact. Those authors most likely never ex-

perienced any of the magic firsthand. They were just copy-
ing from the ancient Egyptian texts."

"Well, what about the ancient Egyptians, then? They
weren't all children."

"No, but they lived in much closer contact with their
gods than we do. However," Wigmere said, turning away
from the past. "None of this conjecture will help us today.
It is very possible, Miss Theodosia, that we will need to tap
in to your talent from time to time."

"I would be honored to help in any way I can, Lord
Wigmere. But who is *we*?"

"We, my dear girl, are the Brotherhood of the Chosen
Keepers. A group of men, a society if you will—"

Just then a quiet knock at the door brought Wigmere in-
stantly to his feet. Honestly. The comings and goings here
were far worse than at Charing Cross Station! "Excuse me,"
he said, then limped over to the door, opened it, and spoke
in hushed tones.

"Are you up to taking a short walk down to Level Six?"
he asked. "Stokes has regained consciousness and is asking
for me. I thought perhaps you'd like to see him yourself so
he can thank you."

I jumped to my feet. Of course I was dying to see Level
Six, but all I said was "If you'd like."

LEVEL SIX

WE WALKED DOWN THE HALL until we came to a small narrow door marked PRIVATE, NO ENTRY. Wigmere ignored the sign and stepped inside, with me close on his heels.

It was a small room, no bigger than a large closet really, with heavy curtains covering the east wall. Wigmere went over to the curtains and pulled them aside.

There was a door behind the curtains! A flat shiny metal door with no handles, only a seam running down the middle.

Wigmere pushed a button on the wall and they opened. I gasped. It was a lift. Right here in Somerset House. Amazing!

I followed him into the small compartment. He nodded at the fellow manning the control panel on the wall. "Level Six, please." The man pushed a button, then the whole world dropped out from under my feet and my stomach nearly came out my nose.

I reached out and placed a hand against the wall to steady myself.

"All right?" Wigmere asked.

I nodded.

"Takes a bit of getting used to."

I'll say.

With a grind of gears and a lurch we reached Level Six. I followed Wigmere off the lift, none too sorry to have solid floor beneath my feet.

The excitement of the lift was quickly forgotten as I stared at the hustle and bustle all around me. Dozens and dozens of desks were set up in tidy rows. But that was the only neat thing about the place. Everything else was a jumbled mess. Men sat at desks stacked with old parchment, papyrus scrolls, and clay tablets. Telegraph machines tapped out messages in quick staccato bursts. Men scurried back and forth, carrying files and books. It was like a library gone mad.

A thoroughly modern library, I might add. There wasn't a single gas lamp in sight. It was all electric lights!

"Welcome to Level Six, the heart of our operations," Wigmere said, with no small amount of pride in his voice.

I estimated there were somewhere between twenty and thirty men (it was hard to tell because they all kept moving around). There were worktables and workstations and artifacts spilling about like so much forgotten rubbish. Everything was a tangled, disorderly mess, and it was absolutely lovely to behold! Well, except for the faint smell of curses that clung to the corners of the room.

Wigmere limped along at a rather furious clip. I had a hard time keeping up because I was so busy trying to take everything in.

We passed several large basins of quartzite and a huge sarcophagus made out of alabaster. Very curious. I'd never seen anything that big made out of alabaster before. A few feet away from that was a tub, a regular clawfooted bathtub like we had at home. Only this tub was full of thick reddish mud.

"Mud?" I asked.

"Yes. Nile River mud. We find it can sometimes absorb the curses and nullify them. What do *you* do when a curse escapes an artifact and works its way into a person?" he asked.

A vision of poor Isis flashed in my mind. "Oh, that's never happened," I said, eyeing the mud thoughtfully. It wasn't strictly a lie. Isis *isn't* a person.

We resumed walking and passed a wall of offices with large glass windows. In one of them, two men leaned forward, examining something on a table. An artifact of some sort. One of the men reached out and lifted it up.

I could see the air swirl around the artifact and the man's arm, like heat waves rising up from the pavement in the dog days of summer. Suddenly, the man screamed and clutched his hand. His partner leaped up from the table and ran over to a switch on the wall and flipped it.

Immediately a buzzer sounded and the entire room erupted into frenzied activity. "Stay here," Wigmere barked, then limped as fast as he could toward the commotion.

Needless to say, I followed.

A crew of operatives burst into the small office and dragged the man out into the main room, toward the large mud-filled tub.

As I drew closer, I could see the skin on the injured man's hand hiss and bubble and blister all the way up to his wrist. There was the foul stink of sulfur in the air.

They shoved his arm into the tub, covering it completely in the Nile River mud.

A few seconds later they removed his arm from the tub and rinsed it off. We all watched the man's arm closely. Slowly, like a serpent waking, the bubbling resumed and began working up toward his elbow. The poor fellow was close to panicking. The medic treating him looked to Wigmere for direction. "Now what, sir?"

"What kind of curse was it, Danver?" Wigmere asked the injured man.

"I d-don't know, sir. We hadn't gotten that far yet." Poor Danver couldn't take his eyes off his arm as the blisters and boils covered his elbow and continued upward.

Wigmere exploded. "You mean to tell me you touched a cursed object without knowing the nature or power of the curse?"

"Excuse me," I said, worming my way forward. "Perhaps this might slow it down." I reached up and lifted another of my amulets off my neck. Without touching Danver's skin directly, I wrapped the leather cord with the amulet around his upper arm, like a tourniquet.

The bubbling boil of the curse lapped up against the tourniquet, then pulled back, like a wave at the seashore. Again it surged forward, and again the amulet repelled it. In the background I heard voices murmuring, "I say, jolly good," and, "Clever, that."

"This won't hold all day." My mind was scrambling, sorting through all the curse antidotes I knew. "Wax! We need wax. Do you have any?"

"Wax?" Wigmere said.

"Yes. Now, hurry. *Please!*"

"How much?" one of the medics called out even as he began moving away.

"Enough to cover his whole arm up to his shoulder," I called back.

People finally got the message and propelled themselves to action. I gave Danver my most confident look. "Don't worry. This amulet should hold the curse off long enough for us to remove it." I *so* hoped I was right about that.

I turned to Wigmere. "We'll need to melt the wax. Do you have an electric coil or a chafing dish or something?"

He studied me closely, then nodded and barked out an order.

Before long there were men scurrying everywhere, finding the wax, breaking it into bits so that it would melt quickly, setting it up to melt. As they made the preparations, I checked Danver's arm to see how it was doing.

A small sliver of the curse, like a fine thread, had just found its way under the tourniquet and was working its way to his shoulder. "We really need to hurry up with that wax!" I called out.

"Ready in two minutes," the medic called back.

Danver's eyes were practically rolling back in his head. "Don't panic, please don't panic," I said. "Everything will be all right." I think. I hope. I'd only done this twice, and only on artifacts, never on humans. But according to Hassam Fahkir in his ancient scroll on remedies for Egyptian magic, it should work.

Finally they brought a basin full of melted wax. "Take off his shirt," I told the medic.

There was a general gasp at the thought of a man removing his shirt in front of a girl.

"Oh, stuff and nonsense! Do you want to remove this wretched curse or not?"

With a glance at Wigmere, the medic removed Danver's shirt.

"The wax will be hot, but, um, it shouldn't be any worse than the curse," I warned.

Danver nodded. "Just get on with it," he replied between clenched teeth.

"Right."

I pulled the shallow dish closer. "Shove your arm in that, as far as it will go."

Danver took a deep breath and did as I instructed. (I do so love a grownup who can follow instructions!)

He sucked in a breath, then the whole room fell silent as his arm sat bathed in the wax.

Keeping my hands clear of the curse-infected arm, I pushed on his shoulder to help get as much of his arm down in the wax as I could. Glancing around, I spotted a letter opener on the desk. I picked this up and used it to spread the wax so that it completely covered the skin.

After a few minutes had passed, I said, "Right. You can take your arm out now."

Slowly, Danver lifted his arm from the dish. His entire limb was encased in soft warm wax, all the way up to his shoulder. "Perfect," I said.

"Now what?" asked one of the medics.

"Now we wait," I said.

Within minutes, the wax began to turn murky as it drew the curse from Danver's skin. It quickly went from a dirty gray to a greeny-black color, and the smell of sulfur rose up into the air. As it hardened, it began to crackle, a soft sound that worked its way up Danver's arm as the fouled wax crackled and peeled itself away from his skin, falling in a vile mess.

I caught the wax bits with the dish, then shoved it at the medic. "This needs to be thrown on a fire immediately."

"But it will foul the hearth," one man said.

Wigmere shut him up with one look.

I bent forward to examine the arm. The curse was gone. No lumps or bumps or boils or blisters, or—"I say, it took all your hair with it." I stepped back and wiped my brow.

Wigmere skewered me with a look.

"You mean to tell me you've never done this before?" he said.

I gulped. "Well, yes. But not on a man with a hairy arm." I rushed to explain. "In his writings from the Middle Dynastic Period, Hassam Fahkir said it would work. And it did, didn't it?" I braced myself for his anger.

Wigmere's sharp eyes studied me. "Rather quick thinking, that," was all he said. Then he turned back to his injured operative. When he was satisfied the man was out of danger, he motioned for me to follow him to the infirmary.

I was shocked by how pale Stokes was. He looked well and truly dead. I was afraid there'd been a blunder and someone had mistaken his death rattle as a call for Wigmere. (Really, if you mumble the name Wigmere, it sounds quite like a death rattle.)

The man who'd been tending him stepped back from the bed. Wigmere pulled up a chair and eased himself into it. "Stokes? Wigmere here. They say you wanted to see me?"

Nothing happened, and I began to worry that I'd been right. But then there was a sort of gasping sound, like I imagine a fish makes when he swallows the hook.

"Steady now," Wigmere said.

Stokes's eyes fluttered open. "Chaos," he said. "It was Chaos."

He was right about that. The whole morning had been a madhouse, if you asked me.

"Blast," Wigmere said softly. "Do you know who?"

Stokes nodded again, then fell silent. Once he'd gathered enough strength he said, "Von Braggenschnott."

"Von Braggenschnott!" exclaimed Wigmere.

I knew that name! Where oh where had I heard it before? Stokes nodded and tried to continue.

"What was that?" Wigmere leaned even closer.

"Forces . . . of chaos . . . are rising . . . once more," Stokes managed to get out.

"Blast!" said Wigmere. He pushed to his feet and barked out orders regarding Stokes's care, then headed back through Level Six toward the lift. I hurried to keep up. For someone who needed a cane, he could gallop along surprisingly well when he'd a mind to.

"What does that mean, *The forces of chaos are rising once more*?" I asked when he finally paused to wait for the lift.

He glanced down at me as if weighing whether or not he should tell me. "It means bad things are going to happen for a while, until we can sort this mess out." He stopped and ran his hand over his face. He suddenly looked ten years older and infinitely more weighted down by the cares of the world. "This Heart of Egypt situation has the power to topple our entire nation if not handled properly."

The full implications of what he was saying struck me. "What exactly do you mean, *topple*?" I have found it always best to be absolutely clear on death-and-destruction stuff.

Wigmere began pacing in front of the lift door. "The curse on the Heart of Egypt is designed to weaken a nation, to make it easy to conquer. It was very cleverly designed by Thutmose III's minister of war—"

"Amenemhab."

He looked at me in surprise.

"Yes. Exactly. Anyway, it is extremely powerful. It was a way to guarantee the power and glory of Thutmose III's kingdom, even after his death. Whoever lifted the Heart of Egypt from the tomb would bring down upon their head famine, plague, pestilence. Destruction."

For once, I was speechless. I could barely fathom the enormity of it all. A little thread of worry began unraveling in my stomach. "It will topple the Germans now that Von Braggenschnott has it. Right?"

"No," Wigmere said, running his hands through his thick white hair. "It was removed by a British subject—"

I squirmed as I realized the British subject in question was Mother.

"—who brought it to British soil. It is Britain that is in danger. We must retrieve the Heart of Egypt and return it to Thutmose's tomb. That is the only way to stop the bloody curse. Then we need to make sure it stays there!" He pushed the lift ringer with considerable force.

We rode back up the lift in silence. I was in such turmoil

over the news I didn't even notice my stomach when it dropped down to my ankles.

"And another thing," Wigmere finally said, staring straight in front of him.

"Yes?"

"You've got to keep quiet about all you've seen here today. We're a very secret operation. Very few people know about us. You mustn't tell a soul."

"No one? But surely Henry, since he's been here."

"Not a soul," Wigmere said firmly. "Not your brother, not your parents."

"But surely I can tell Mother and Father what's happened to the Heart of Egy—"

"No! It is of utmost importance that you tell no one."

"Very well," I said solemnly, my heart sinking at all these new secrets I had to keep. "My lips are sealed."

No matter what it might cost me.

A Sardine Trap

THORNLEIGH AND HENRY WERE WAITING FOR US in Wigmere's office. According to their report, Will never returned to the churchyard. Worried, I reminded myself that Sticky Will was very good at taking care of himself. He'd had lots of practice, and if he could survive the Seven Dials, he could survive anything.

Wigmere sent me and Henry back to the museum in one of the Brotherhood's coaches. Henry peppered Thornleigh with questions the whole way, but the man kept mum. He had the driver let us off at the corner so that no one at the museum would see the coach. "Bye, then," he said, as we stepped onto the sidewalk. "Excellent job, saving Stokes and Danver."

"Who's Danver?" Henry asked as the coach drove away.

"Never mind," I said. We climbed up the stairs to the museum's front entrance, and just in time. Flimp was getting ready to lock up. He rocked back on his heels as he waited for us to clamber through the door. "Someone's been looking for you two all afternoon, they 'ave," he chided us.

Henry and I stood in the anteroom for a moment, trying to get our stories straight. We were still whispering, trying to think of a story that wouldn't get us in too much trouble, when who should come thundering in but Fagenbush.

He strode over to where we stood and peered down his long beak directly into my eyes, as if he were trying to read my mind. "Where have you been?" he demanded.

"We went to visit the British Museum. To get out of the way. Everyone seemed extra busy today." When fibbing, it's always best to stick as close to the truth as possible.

Fagenbush's eyes narrowed until they were slits of malevolence. "I don't belie—"

"Theo! Henry! There you are!" Mum came hurrying into the foyer. "That was lovely of you to lay low today. Your poor Father's got enough on his mind."

Why, she'd never even realized we were gone! But now I

was committed to the partial fib I'd told Fagenbush, who continued to hover. So I told her the British Museum story.

"Really, Theodosia. You know how your father feels about that place. Let's not tell him, shall we? It will spoil his mood." She paused, then added, "Even more."

A stab of regret sliced through me. I so longed to tell her what had happened to the Heart of Egypt. To tell her how close Henry and I had come to getting it back. But I couldn't. In truth, none of that mattered anymore. It didn't matter how clever I or Henry had been, not when the well-being of all Britain was at stake.

Since Mother and Father were still distracted over the Heart of Egypt, they had dinner brought round. We all ate together in the sitting room, which should have been nice but wasn't. Father's foul mood infected us all, and I had plenty of worries of my own after talking to Wigmere. We all sat in a rather melancholy silence, our bleak thoughts circling around the dinner table like vultures.

After we'd finished dinner, Henry curled himself up in the chair in front of the fire with his new book, *The Treasure Seekers*. Mother and Father retired to discuss their problems in private. Feeling guilty about all my secrets, I retired to my closet, one of my best thinking spots.

Safely in my sarcophagus, I vowed to pore over Amen-emhab's *Book of War* first thing in the morning, after a good night's sleep. Maybe there was a clue to solving the toppling problem in there. It was worth a try.

But of course, I couldn't sleep. After the day I'd had, I should have been out in minutes. Every fiber of my being was exhausted, but my mind wouldn't switch off. When I wasn't worrying about the Heart of Egypt toppling Britain, I was marveling over a whole society of people who studied for years in order to do what I did without even trying. Who would have guessed such a thing? The idea made me uneasy, as if I were some kind of freak.

The problems before me were huge, and it seemed as if there was nothing I could do about any of it. Finally admitting that sleep was miles away, I crawled out of the sarcophagus and tiptoed to the door, which I had left open a crack. I checked my Isis lure (a tin of sardines stationed just inside the door) to see if she had snuck a nibble when I wasn't looking.

She hadn't.

I grabbed a blanket from the sarcophagus and wrapped it around my shoulders. Sitting down on the floor near the door, I leaned up against the wall. I would just sit here and will Isis to come, that's what.

I sorely missed her tonight. I needed the feel of that

small, warm furry body next to me to chase away, well, everything. Then I had an idea.

One of the cornerstones of Egyptian magic is the art of creative utterance. Which is basically a fancy way of saying, it's all in how you say a thing. And the words you use. True names can be a very powerful tool. So, what if I tried to see if I could make it work for me? Wigmere said I had a unique talent and it wasn't all about following recipes; maybe I could use that to my advantage!

I reached over and traced the hieroglyphs for "Isis" on the floor near the sardine tin, then whispered, "Isis, come." Nothing happened. Then another thought occurred to me. "Come, Isis," I called again, only this time I used the ancient Egyptian I'd learned from my study of hieroglyphs.

I did this quite a few times, stopping every now and then to check for signs of her. Nothing. As I sat there, my thoughts drifted to Wigmere and his Brotherhood. I wondered if they had all stayed up tonight in order to try out the Moonlight Test for themselves.

I wondered if it would work for them.

Then, of course, thinking about Wigmere got me thinking about Stokes. I was glad he was going to be all right. If I closed my eyes, I could see the cold flat stare of the German fellow as he shoved that knife into Stokes's ribs.

Germans. Knife. Stabbing. Stop it, you horrid brain!

Why does one's mind always think of the truly awful things in the middle of the night when there's no one to talk to and nothing to distract oneself with?

I heard a creak on the floorboards outside my door. Oh, please let it be Isis.

I stood up as quietly as I could and tiptoed to the door, peering out into the gaping black of the hallway. There was nothing there.

Uneasy, I sat back down against the open door. I had to come up with a plan. After everything that Wigmere had told me, it was more important than ever to find the Heart of Egypt. And more difficult. Just how was I supposed to retrieve the wretched thing?

I shifted my position, thinking I'd return to bed, when once again I heard a slight creak on the floorboards outside in the hallway.

Which made me wish doubly hard I hadn't just been thinking about bloodthirsty Germans and stabbings and such.

Nonsense. Determined to be brave, I leaned forward and peered back into the dark hallway. "Isis?" I whispered.

My heart kicked into a gallop when I saw a tall, slender woman standing in the hallway. "Mother?" I breathed, but even as I said the word, my brain registered that this was most definitely *not* Mother. The woman wore a linen sheath with a wide gold collar. There appeared to be a solar disk held between two horns on top of her head.

I blinked to clear my eyes, and when I opened them again, she was gone. I slumped back against the door as relief surged through me. Perhaps Father was right. I really did need to get a grip on my imagination.

Just then, two iridescent golden-green orbs appeared in the hallway. Isis! I pulled back behind the door, my hand ready to close it once she decided to come in.

It took forever, but she finally nosed her way to the sardines, crouching like a panther and stopping every few inches to check for . . . something. I don't know, whatever demonic cats check for.

When she finally reached the sardines, Isis tossed all caution to the wind and tore into the things as if they were dangerous cat-hunting rats. She'd take one in her mouth and shake her head back and forth (flinging sardine juice everywhere) as if killing the sardine all over again. Only then would she settle down and eat it.

While she was thoroughly absorbed in her meal, I reached forward and very slowly closed the door. As soon as she heard the click, she paused and looked up at me, a low caterwaul starting deep in her throat.

"Isis," I said, carefully enunciating her name. She stopped snarling and went back to eating her fish. I spent the next few minutes talking to her, saying calming things and using her name every three or four words. It seemed to work. She calmed down quite a bit and even ate the last sardine without having to kill it all over again.

Then I had to decide how to coax her over to the bed. If I'd been thinking properly, I'd have saved the last sardine and put it at my feet once I lay down in the sarcophagus.

Why is it that all the really great ideas always come too late? I went and settled myself in the sarcophagus, calling Isis's name and that of Horus, the god whose protection I'd put in her amulet, the whole time.

Her eyes grew more focused and less frenzied looking. After many stops and starts, she made her way to the sarcophagus and gracefully hopped up onto the edge, balancing delicately as she tried to decide what to do. Finally, she hopped down to my feet and began knitting at the blanket with her claws. Soon a loud rumbling purr started up. With a sigh of relief, I allowed myself to fall back against my pillow. It looked like that amulet might be doing the trick after all.

I could only hope a great idea on how to solve the whole toppling of Britain would come as easily.

Chaos Rising

I woke up to the sound of sawing. Well, it sounded like sawing. When I managed to pry my eyes open and look around, I saw Isis raking her claws on the door, trying to get out. She'd left big raw gashes in the wood. Father was going to kill me.

I leaped out of bed. She took one look at me, arched her back, and hissed ferociously. Clearly whatever magic I'd woven last night was gone this morning. Heart sinking, I opened the door and watched her dash out of sight.

My eyes were gritty with sleep, so I washed my face, then changed into a clean frock.

Starving, I hurried to the sitting room to start breakfast, hoping Mum had thought to bring some supplies from home. When I reached the sitting room, I stopped to sniff. "Is something burning?" I asked Henry.

"No. Mum's making us breakfast," he said, fidgeting and banging his heels on the bottom rung of his chair.

"But Mum doesn't cook," I reminded him.

"Well, today I decided to," Mum announced as she carried a plate of charred toast and an eggcup over to Henry. "I've neglected you horribly for months. I want to make it up to you."

I stared at Henry's blackened toast. By poisoning us?

"I'll start one for you." She went back to the sideboard and slipped a thick piece of bread onto the toasting fork. "How many eggs would you like?"

I watched Henry pick up one of his blackened toast strips and *boink* it against his egg. He frowned. It was supposed to dip, not *boink*.

"Only one," I said, my eyes still glued to Henry's plate.

"Coming right up, dear."

Henry *boinked* his toast once more, then gave up. He picked up the egg and took a bite.

"Mum?" I asked.

"Yes, dear?"

"How do you decide which artifacts to bring back with

you when you're on a dig? You mentioned that you had to leave lots of things behind, so how do you choose?"

"Oh, I don't know. Sometimes it's because we don't have anything else like it in the museum, or it might be one of a kind. Mostly I just rely on instinct."

Ah! Perhaps Mother was mistaking a tingle of warning for an instinct. Surely this ability of mine came from *somewhere*. "Instinct?"

"Hm-hm. I let my instincts guide me as to which will make the most striking exhibit." She carried a plate and eggcup to the table and set them in front of me. "Why do you ask?"

"Just curious." I stared at my egg for a moment, then lifted my spoon and sliced off the top. Just as I feared. Hard as chalk. "Do you ever get the willies when you're down in the tombs? Just you and all those ancient relics?" I asked.

"What a ridiculous question! Of course not."

"Who actually knew about the Heart of Egypt, Mum? Knew that you'd found it?" I took a small bite from an unburned corner of toast and began to chew.

"Well, there was the work crew, Nabir, Hakim, Stanton, and Willsbury. And the director of the Antiquity Institute. I had to tell him so I could get permission to take it out of the country."

I choked down the bite of toast and took a sip of tea. "That's quite a lot of people." I had hoped there were only one or two. Then it would be easy to trace the leak directly back to who was responsible for stealing the artifact.

I looked over at Henry, who'd stopped banging his feet and was listening intently.

"Oh! And von Braggenschnott knew. He was the one who helped convince the director to let me take it out of the country."

There it was! I knew I'd heard that name before. "Who is this von Braggenschnott fellow, anyway?" I asked as casually as I could. "I heard you and Father talking about him."

"He's the head of the German National Archaeological Association."

"What are the Germans doing in Egypt?"

"Oh, they've always been in Egypt. Just like us, the French, Americans, Italians, they all have archaeological teams over there."

"But didn't you say there were more Germans than usual this time?"

Mother frowned. "Yes. That's true. They've been increasing their presence there over the last four years. Ever since von Braggenschnott took over."

I studied my egg. Surely there was a way to avoid eating it without hurting Mother's feelings.

"He's a rather disreputable fellow, I'm afraid. Which is unfortunate as it casts a taint over all of Germany's excavations."

While Mother wasn't looking, I fished my handkerchief out of my pocket, snatched the egg out of its cup, and shoved it into the crumpled linen. "What makes him so disreputable?"

"He deals in black-market antiquities and smuggles artifacts out of the country for private collections. Among other things. Why all the questions?"

"No reason. Just trying to get a feel for how things work over there."

She cast me a puzzled glance, then shook her head. "I'm going to be down in Receiving cataloging the new things if you need me."

"Thanks for breakfast," I said, slipping the wrapped egg into the pocket of my skirt. "It was very thoughtful of you."

"My pleasure, dear. We'll have to do this more often."

Henry rolled his eyes at me and I gave him a sharp kick under the table. When Mother had gone, I reached over and took the newspaper from Father's place. He hadn't even touched it yet so I tried not to wrinkle it too badly. I wanted to see if there was any mention of the adventures over in St. Paul's churchyard the day before.

As I scanned the paper, a headline caught my eye. "Crop Blight Appears in Northern Counties. Record Shortfall Expected."

Lord Wigmere's words rang in my ears: *plague, pestilence, famine.* At the word "famine," my mind turned to the bleak, hungry faces I'd seen yesterday. I had a good idea what famine looked like.

I turned back to the paper and began reading about the record flooding and freezing temperatures in the north. Henry came round the table and began reading over my shoulder.

"What's a pustule?" he asked.

"It's disgusting, is what it is," I told him.

"No. I mean, what *is* it?"

"Where did you see it?" I asked.

He pointed to a small item on the bottom-left corner. I leaned over and read the headline: "Virulent Illness Strikes Dozens in Hampsford."

"Bother. Now all we need are locusts."

"What's a locust?"

"It's a big, beetley grasshoppery type thing. Eats crops," I explained, my mind churning furiously.

"Do you mean like that?" Henry asked, pointing to a big beetley grasshoppery thing clinging to the outside of the windowpane in the pouring rain.

"Oh, lovely."

"What?"

"Nothing." I wondered how hard it would be to get in touch with Lord Wigmere. Mum had just launched the end of civilization.

Going on an Ally Hunt

NOW I *HAD* TO DO SOMETHING. There was simply no choice. Not with the Heart of Egypt's curse beginning to do its damage here in Britain. I glanced back down at the paper, intending to read the article again, hoping I might be wrong. Instead my eyes landed on a photograph on the right-hand corner of the front page. "It's him!" I said, startling poor Henry so badly that he dropped his last piece of toast—butter-side down, of course.

"It's one of those Germans we were following yesterday. The one who stabbed Stokes."

Henry's eyes grew wide. "Crikey!" He leaned forward and shoved me out of the way so he could see the picture better.

The article was dreadfully boring, full of politics and treaty negotiations between Britain and Germany. The main thrust of it was that Britain could hold off entering into a substandard treaty with the Germans as long as we remained strong domestically. For now, the German delegation was giving up and returning home. The writer of the article made it quite clear that Britain would be able to negotiate in her own best interests only as long as her economy remained strong. Further talks were scheduled for the spring.

Of course! If Britain was in a weakened state, brought on by plague, pestilence, and famine, we would lose our bargaining power. A weakened Britain couldn't possibly negotiate in her own best interests because she'd be dependent on other countries. Wigmere was right. How wickedly brilliant! Germany was using the power of ancient Egyptian magic to topple its adversaries. Just like Thutmose III and Amenemhab had.

I hurried through the rest of the article. It didn't mention von Braggenschnott by name, but it did say the delegation would be leaving their residence in Carleton Terrace Gardens and returning to Germany tomorrow on the *Kaiser Wilhelm der Grosse*. That cinched it—Will had said he'd followed the man tailing me back to Carleton Terrace. They had to be connected!

The easiest solution would have been to leave it all to Wigmere and his Brotherhood, but he hadn't looked too hopeful yesterday. Plus, it was Mother who'd brought the vile thing home—it seemed as if someone in our family ought to take responsibility for it. I quailed at the enormity of the task, then forced myself to look on the bright side: surely saving Britain would impress Mother and Father. I mean, they'd notice *that*, wouldn't they?

After hours of thinking, I finally came up with a possible plan. Unfortunately, there was simply no way I could do this on my own. I would need help. I loathe asking people for help. First of all, they rarely say yes. And second, even when they do, they can rarely be trusted to do as they're told. Wigmere had been adamant about not telling my parents, which left Henry and Will.

Henry was the only other person who knew of Wigmere's organization, even though he didn't realize the half of it. But perhaps I could gain Henry and Will's cooperation without telling them anything they didn't already know. Then I wouldn't be breaking my promise to Wigmere. Will, in fact, would be a key player in this plan of mine. If he was agreeable, that is. His part was rather dangerous, which worried me, but then so did plague, pestilence, and famine.

The weakest link would be Henry, but I wasn't going to think about that just yet.

I looked out the window, hoping against hope it had stopped raining.

No such luck. Which meant I would have to make my way to Charing Cross Station in the freezing rain. It was the only place where I knew to find Will, and time was of the essence. I had to reach him today so we could put our plan into action for tomorrow.

The tricky part was getting out of the museum without attracting Henry's attention. I didn't want to risk him following me again. Last time I saw him, he had muttered something about being sick of all this Egypt rubbish and headed off toward the armor exhibits.

I grabbed my thickest coat and an umbrella and stepped out into the downpour. The wind had picked up and was blowing the sheets of rain sideways. Small streams of water ran down the gutters, and the traffic in the street was a hopeless tangle. Of course, now that I knew about the curse, the rain seemed much more sinister, as if the very drops themselves were laying a thin film of chaos over the land.

With one last, longing glance at an omnibus, I began trudging my way to Charing Cross. I so wished I had enough money for an omnibus today *and* a cab tomorrow. But I didn't. And tomorrow was when we would need a ride most.

Once I reached Charing Cross Station, I realized that getting here was the easy part. Now I had to find Sticky Will.

There was an absolute wall of bodies everywhere. The smell of wet wool and smoke filled the damp air. I stepped back from the crowd and tried to guess where I would be right now if I were a pickpocket.

Well, that was obvious. Right in the middle of the potential pickings, of course. You wanted lots of people jostling about so your movements would be well hidden. And you'd want to be near the richest-looking pockets.

I took a few more steps back and found a bench to stand on. As I peered over the mob of people, I spotted a man with a very well cut suit holding an ivory-handled cane, a gold watch chain dangling from his waistcoat.

He looked like a good target to me. Not that I was planning on picking his pocket. I just wanted to find the person who might be thinking of it.

I pushed and squirmed my way through the crowd toward the man.

Just as I reached him, I saw a small, grimy hand reach out and slip itself into the man's pocket. Honestly! How could no one notice such a thing?

"Caught you," I said under my breath.

Sticky Will startled so badly that he dropped the man's wallet back into his pocket.

"Blimey, miss! You scared the snot outta me!"

"Sorry about that," I said. "I need to talk to you. *Now.*" As I dragged him to the edge of the crowd, he mumbled something about me costing him a pretty penny.

I found a spot out of the rain under an awning where we wouldn't be crushed to death before I'd explained what I needed.

"Wot's up?" Sticky Will asked.

"First, tell me what happened to you yesterday. Were you able to follow that fellow?"

"Aye, miss. He went ter Carleton 'Ouse Terrace, too. I tried to get close enough to get yer thingamajig, but he was guarded up too tight like."

"Did he see you?"

"No. I'm sure of it. Is that wot you came all this way to find out?"

Now that it was actually time to lay out my plan, I was suddenly tongue-tied. What if he thought I was off my nut like everyone else? I mean, Will didn't know what was going on, and I had to get his cooperation without betraying Wigmere's trust. I would have to appeal to his sense of adventure and national pride; hopefully, he would never find out that I hadn't told him the full truth. "No. It has to do with that artifact we were chasing yesterday."

Will nodded. "Go on."

"It is vitally important that we get it back. Those German fellows who nabbed it are up to no good. The artifact has, er, special properties that make it more dangerous than most."

His eyes widened and he leaned forward. "Wot properties?" he asked. "Is it cursed?"

I started. "Cursed? What do you know about curses?"

Will leaned back and sniffed. "Ain't I good enough to know about curses?"

Oh, no. Not that again. "Of course you are, you twit. It's just that so few people believe in them, I hadn't expected you to."

"Oy. All you have to do is read one of them penny dreadfuls to know curses is alive and well."

I started to remind him that penny dreadfuls were make-believe, then realized it didn't matter *why* he believed what I said. "Well, you're right. It *is* cursed. A horrible, vile curse."

"Blimey," he said, his eyes now as round as saucers.

"Exactly. And in order to make sure that nothing bad happens, we have to get the artifact back from the Germans. That's where you come in."

"Me?" he squeaked.

"You." I nodded. "Only someone with your skill and experience can do what needs to be done."

"Wot needs to be done, then?"

"Well, here's my plan. I saw in this morning's paper that the Germans are leaving tomorrow on a ship. You, Henry, and I will follow them down to the docks. We'll have Henry create a diversion, and while everyone's attention is distracted, you'll sneak in and pinch the artifact right out of one of the Germans' pockets." I leaned back. "What do you think? Can you do it?"

"It'd be the pinch of a lifetime! They could even write one o' them books about me!"

"Exactly! And you're the only one I know who can do it. You're small, you're quick, and, thanks to me, you know who has it. But you won't get to keep it. It will have to be returned to . . . be taken care of properly."

His face fell a bit at that but, really, what could a pickpocketing urchin do with something like the Heart of Egypt?

"It's not like you could use it to pay for sausages or a new coat," I explained as gently as I could.

He puffed himself up, bristly as a hedgehog. "Wot's wrong with this coat, I'd like to know?"

"Nothing! Absolutely nothing. I just meant, the artifact is so unique and recognizable, it's not like you could sell it or anything without getting caught."

"You mean fence it?"

"Yes. That's the word."

"Wol, me friend could fence anything, but I get what you mean."

"Then you'll do it?" I asked.

His eyes sparkled. "Yes, miss. I will."

Wonderful. That was one problem solved. Now I just had to work out the two dozen other obstacles that stood in our way and we'd be all set.

A Mud Bath

I HADN'T BEEN BACK from my trip to Charing Cross Station for more than ten minutes before a loud bloodcurdling yowl came from somewhere up on the third floor.

"Theodosia Elizabeth Throckmorton!" Father yelled. "Come and get your blasted cat! Now!"

"Uh-oh." I hurried up the stairs.

When I reached the workroom, I found Isis attached to Father's back like a demonic cocklebur. Father kept turning round and round trying to bop her with his cane so she would let go.

He mostly ended up beaning himself instead. Which served him right for even thinking to take a cane to my cat.

"Theodosia? Come get this cat or I will cheerfully hand her over to Henry for his mummifying experiments."

No he wouldn't, he was only teasing. Wasn't he? "I've got her. Just hold still a minute, would you?"

Father stopped spinning around like a top and I grabbed Isis. I tried to pull her off his back, but she clung as if her claws were embedded in his skin.

Finally, after many attempts and frustrated curses by Father, I freed my poor cat. She squirmed and fought in my arms. "Sorry about that," I said over her caterwauling.

Father just glared at me.

I could no longer put it off. Isis was getting a mud bath.

Unfortunately, I didn't have any mud from the Nile River. Mud from the small square across the street would have to do. It was made from rainwater, so perhaps the purity of that would be similar enough. One could always hope.

I snuck back into the museum carrying a small bucket of the wet, juicy mud and headed toward my closet, where I'd left Isis. I could hear her low-pitched growling. I put the bucket down close to the door so it would act as a barricade when I opened it. Bending over with my left hand at the ready, I opened the door with my right.

As soon as there was enough space for her whiskers to

clear the door, Isis leaped over the bucket into the hall-way—straight into my waiting hand.

I'd positioned myself just right and was able to grab a handful of her fur, right behind her neck. I quickly used my other hand and gathered her into my arms, holding her close. It was a challenge trying to reassure her and avoid her needlelike claws while using my foot to scoot the bucket of mud through the doorway.

Of course, it would have been much more convenient to use the museum's main lavatory, but I couldn't risk one of the museum's visitors wandering in at the wrong moment. How would I explain giving a cat a mud bath? Even *I* couldn't talk my way out of that one!

I shall spare you the details of the bath. Suffice it to say, I don't recommend it. Not unless there is no choice. What Isis didn't realize was that if the mud bath didn't work, it would be a waxing for her—just like that fellow at Level Six. But a hairless cat was too hideous to bear thinking about.

I opened my door a crack to see if the coast was clear, but Isis had no such qualms and burst through the door, careening down the hall. The good news was, she didn't slash at me with her claws or give one of those terrifying yowls of hers. The bad news was—

"Theodosia?" Mum called out. "Was that your cat? Whatever is wrong with that creature?"

—the coast hadn't been clear. "Just feeling frisky, I think."

"Well, that's very frisky indeed. Is that mud on your frock, dear?"

I stared down at myself in dismay. It looked like someone had tried to imitate a primitive cave painting on the front of my gown.

Mother waved her hand. "Well, never mind. We're going home now. Just put your coat on over it so your father doesn't see."

I ran to get my coat, buttoning it up tight to hide my sins. I even squashed a beastly hat on my head, just to keep Father happy.

That night, when I was sure my parents had retired to the library, I snuck out of my room down the hall to Henry's bedroom. I hadn't mentioned anything to him yet about my plans for tomorrow. With Henry, it's best not to say anything until one has all one's ducks in a row.

I scratched lightly on his door. "Henry," I whispered. "Can I come in?"

His door swung open and he stood in his pajamas, rubbing his eyes. "What do you want?"

"Henry, did you mean it the other day when you said you wanted to help me?"

He looked suspicious. "Maybe."

This looked to be harder than I thought. I twisted my hands together. "Here's the thing. I have a plan to get the Heart of Egypt back, but I need your help."

A gleam of interest shone in his eye.

"Would you let me in so I can tell you about it?"

"Oh, all right. But what do you need my help for? You're always telling me to mind my own business." Henry is always sullen and cranky when he's sleepy. I followed him back to his bed, where he crawled under the covers. I perched myself on the foot of the mattress.

"Henry, this is important. And it's bigger than just you and me. It's for Wigmere and Stokes and all of them." I reminded myself that I wasn't telling Henry anything he didn't already know. Well, not much anyway. And certainly none of the details.

He perked up at that. He'd been going on for two days now about his heroes at Somerset House.

"I know where the Heart of Egypt is, and I have a plan to get it back. You, me, and Sticky Will all have to work together, but if we do, we have a shot. What do you say?"

"I say you're off your nut! What can three kids do against a whole mob of cutthroats?"

"Yes, but Henry, that's just it. Because we're kids, no one will be on the lookout for us and we'll have a chance. Don't you see? But here's the really hard part. We can't tell Mum or Dad. Wigmere says the Heart of Egypt needs to go back to the Valley of the Kings. We can't keep it here at the museum." I cringed and hoped I wasn't telling too much of Wigmere's secret, but Henry already knew about the missing Heart of Egypt and he needed *some* explanation.

Henry tilted his head thoughtfully, and I could tell he was listening to me.

"So," I said. "Here's the plan. We'll go to Carleton House Terrace first thing tomorrow morning so we can be in position to follow von Braggenschnott and his gang when they leave for the docks. After yesterday, we know what they look like, and thanks to this morning's paper, we know when they're returning to Germany: tomorrow on the *Kaiser Wilhelm der Grosse* at one o'clock."

I had his full attention now. "Why don't we just meet them at the dock? Wouldn't that give us less chance of being spotted?"

"We need to be sure they're taking the Heart of Egypt with them and don't hand it off somewhere along the way. We'll wait outside Carleton House Terrace until they leave. I have enough money so we can follow them down to the docks in a hansom cab. While they're waiting to embark, Sticky Will can sneak in and pick von Braggenschnott's pocket. Don't you see? It's brilliant!" But only if it works, I thought (though I didn't say that out loud). If it didn't work, it could be disastrous and we'd end up being in all sorts of hot water.

"If you don't mind poor Will being skewered like a bug. What's to keep this Bragging Snot fellow from sticking him, like he did Stokes?"

Drat. Found that hole, did he? "First, we'll be in a crowd; it's unlikely he'd pull a knife when he knows he'd get caught."

Henry frowned. "You don't think he'll say that Will was trying to pick his pocket and he was just protecting his property?"

I frowned at Henry's unexpected logic. "Will says he's much too good to get caught. Let's hope he's right. Besides, that's where you come in. You'll need to create a diversion so that the Germans' attention will be focused on something else."

The scowl disappeared. "Like what?"

"Oh, I don't know. Like that explosion you made up at Christmas. Or those whirligigs you launched last summer that had everyone scrambling for cover. Something like that."

His face brightened. "That was a bang-up trick, wasn't it?"

"Pure genius. And now you can do it again and become a hero!"

"And what will you be doing all this time?"

"Oh, Henry! I'll be orchestrating and scheduling and making sure everything is going as planned."

He got a smug look on his face and pulled the covers up under his chin. "In other words, you'll be bossing."

To the Docks

I SLEPT WRETCHEDLY. My brain was buzzing like an electric wire as I reviewed all the plans and backup plans we'd need. When I finally fell asleep, I dreamed of a thousand shabtis rising up and banging on their crates, trying to get out.

The next thing I knew, Betsy, our housemaid, was knocking on my door.

I got out of bed and looked out the window. Still gray, but the downpour had subsided into a soft rain. That, at least, was good news.

Downstairs, Mother and Father dawdled over breakfast

and the paper, taking their sweet time. "Really, Theodosia!" Father said. "Must you fidget so? You act as if you're sitting on an anthill!"

Henry sniggered and I gave him my best quelling look. Today was *serious*.

"I'm sorry, Father. I'm just anxious to get to the museum and . . . er . . . check on Isis."

"Don't even mention that cat. She's still in disgrace for attacking me."

"I'm sure she'll never do it again, Father. I gave her a cure . . . a tonic, to calm her down."

He took his eyes off his newspaper and peered at me over the top. "What tonic?" he asked.

I shrugged. "Oh, you know. A mixture of sardine juice, cream, some paté, ground-up catnip, and a raw egg."

Father got a funny look on his face. He put the paper down and shoved his half-eaten breakfast away. "Go and get your coat." He sighed heavily as he got up and left the room.

As I stood up to follow, I glanced over at his discarded newspaper. My heart sank as I read the headlines. "Hundreds Hospitalized with Virulent Influenza."

We really had to hurry.

I had told Sticky Will that we would meet him at the Duke of York Column at 10:30 a.m. Since the ship didn't leave until 1:00 p.m., I simply couldn't imagine the Germans departing for the docks any earlier than that. However, our slow start had put me on edge. As soon as we arrived at the museum, Henry and I made ourselves scarce. Ten minutes later, we snuck out the east side entrance and hightailed it to Pall Mall.

By the time we reached the Duke of York Column, we were both hot and sweaty, in spite of the gray, wet weather.

As we approached our meeting place, Will popped out from behind the column. "Wot took you so long?"

"Parent nonsense," I wheezed, still trying to catch my breath from our mad dash across town.

"Seems to me that 'aving parents might be more trouble than it's worth," Sticky Will said with a superior air.

I knew it! He *was* an orphan!

"Well, come on then," he continued. "'Ow do we find these blokes?"

"Well, the embassy is in number nine. So we hang about near there and wait for them to leave."

Henry gaped at me. "That's it? That's your plan? Crikey. I could have thought of that."

I sniffed. "But you didn't. Now come on."

We headed for number nine Carleton House Terrace. It was an elegant building, with loads and loads of windows,

like hundreds of unblinking eyes watching us. Or maybe that's just what it feels like when you know you're skulking.

We spread out and positioned ourselves so we could see all the doors, then settled down to wait.

You would think loitering would be the easiest thing in the world, but after about thirty minutes of it, one begins to feel highly conspicuous. After an hour of it, one becomes bored witless. Consequently, when a nearby clock chimed noon, I had a bad case of the fidgets. I mean, just how close were they going to cut this!

I made my way over to where Will was waiting. After a quick conference, we decided to peek in the bottom-floor windows and see if anything was happening inside.

Of course, no sooner had we left our hiding places than one of the doors burst open. A group of men exited the building, speaking German fast and loud. A motorcar was brought round and they all piled into the thing, then it putted off down the street.

Caught off-guard, we ended up scrambling. "We need to find a cab! Quick!" I looked up the street and down, hoping a hansom would appear. But of course no cabs were in sight. Then an ear-piercing whistle split the sky, nearly deafening me.

I turned to find Sticky Will with two fingers stuck in his mouth. He took a deep breath, intending to whistle again. "No! Stop! What do you think you're doing?" I asked.

He looked at me as if I were bonkers. "Callin' a cab. What else?"

"Yes, but also calling the attention of every German within miles. Not to mention causing severe damage to our eardrums."

Will shifted from his left foot to his right. "Look, do you want a cab or not?"

I nodded, then clapped my hands over my ears as another one of those whistles sliced the air. But, wonder of wonders, here came a hansom!

"Told you, miss. You got to whistle if'n you want a cab."

"You were right. Henry! We're leaving now."

Henry stood up from where he'd been using the long stick he was carrying to float leaf boats down the gutter. He reached us just as the carriage pulled to a stop.

The driver peered out of the hansom with a scowl on his face. "Who here was whistlin' for a cab?"

"He was," I said, nodding my head in Will's direction.

"I oughtter get down out of here and box your ears. Don't you know better than to be wasting my time!"

"But we truly need a cab."

The cabbie looked suspicious. "'Ave you got the blunt?"

"Yes, yes. Of course." I dug the money out of my pocket and waved it at him.

He grunted. "Very well. Get in with you, then."

We all clambered up into the cab. Before we'd got our-

selves seated, the driver cracked his whip and the horse lurched forward, sending us all tumbling to our seats.

"Where to, miss?" he called down.

"Queen Victoria Docks, please."

"Very well." The hansom was much slower than the fancy motorcar the Germans were in. I was frantic, sure von Braggenschnott and his men would board the ship before we arrived.

The driver steered his horse down to the docks, a teeming rabbit warren of shipping offices, warehouses, and quays that went on for miles. Towering over all the piers and barges were rigged beams and pulleys. It was like a small city—a loud, jostley city that smelled of fish and salt and the Thames' unique stench.

As soon as we pulled to a stop, Henry and Will leaped out of the cab. I shoved the money at the cabby. He took forever with the change. I think he was hoping I'd tell him to keep it.

Finally I got away and hurried after Henry and Will toward the ship. My heart seemed to be lodged in my throat and my stomach was twirling as badly as one of Henry's whirligigs. The *Kaiser Wilhelm der Grosse* was enormous; the ship towered above the docks as if someone had picked up three city blocks of very tall buildings and plopped them down next to the river.

We quickly spotted the Germans' motorcar. They had

parked it right up on the wooden dock next to the ship it-self. Will, Henry, and I skidded to a stop when we realized they had only just got out of their car. We weren't too late. That was one problem solved. We trickled into the milling crowd and began working our way to the boarding area where the Germans were headed. Will had that sauntering thing down pat. Even Henry seemed to be doing a pretty good job of acting casual. But me, well, I felt as if anyone could take one look at my face and know I was up to some-thing. My guilty conscience, Father would say. Thinking of him finding out about this made my knees go weak.

By the time we reached the boarding area, my nerves were stretched so tight I was afraid they might snap. I tried to focus on the lay of the land and picked out my position right away. I gave Will the signal and he strolled to the mid-dle of the crowd. He could do this. I just knew he could. *He had to.*

Firmly pushing aside any doubts, I turned to Henry. After a quick conference we decided the best place for him to work his distractions would be up behind a large barri-cade of cargo containers. He took off in that direction, and I headed up a small ramp that led to a balcony outside the second story of a shipping office. From there, I would be able to see everyone else and give the signals.

When I reached my position, I glanced down, dismayed

to see that the Germans were quite close to the loading ramp.

Almost as if he sensed something, Will glanced up in my direction. I jerked my head toward the Germans and he switched course and moved in that direction.

It was stunning how well he managed to blend in with the crowd. He moved through the throngs of people as if he were a cork bobbing on the ocean, letting the crowd's momentum carry him forward.

I looked at Henry. Even from this distance I could see the tense excitement running through him. To him, this was all a ripping game. I left it that way. If one stopped to think of what we were risking, of what might happen if the Germans were on to us . . . I gulped. I forced myself to concentrate on what was happening down below and not let my imagination run wild.

Finally, the crowd's movements carried Will within reach of the German delegation. Without looking at me, he reached up and adjusted his hat, his sign that he was in place and ready. Steady now, I told myself, my heart thumping in my chest as loudly as a big brass drum.

I caught Henry's eye and flipped my hair over my shoulder, which was the signal. Henry nodded, then lifted the long flexible stick he'd been carrying all morning. He loaded the small leather pocket on the tip with birdshot, pulled it

back, and then bent down out of sight. He took careful aim, then released the tip of the stick, sending the small lead bits raining down into the crowd.

Immediately people began slapping at their faces and necks as if they were being stung by insects. A low murmur rose up as people broke off their conversations and began looking around.

Will used the opportunity to get right behind von Braggenschnott. All the Germans had ignored the stinging shot and were looking into the sky, eyes alert, trying to find the source of the attack. No shrugging it off for them.

As they stared up toward the stack of containers where Henry lay hidden, Will lifted the coattails of von Braggenschnott's morning coat.

I held my breath.

Will's fingers slipped into the German's back pocket—and came out empty.

I nearly fainted as a thought occurred to me: What if he wasn't carrying the Heart of Egypt on him? What if he'd hidden it somewhere in his luggage? What then?

It was a horrible revelation. *Was* this the right thing to do? *Were* we putting Will in too much danger?

I gave myself a mental shake. It was too late for second thoughts now. We'd just have to brazen it out.

Will pulled back from von Braggenschnott and waited for

the next distraction. I turned to Henry, who sat leaning against a container, well hidden from the crowd. He was watching me and awaiting further signals.

Very carefully, I bent down and gave him the next signal—I adjusted my left shoe.

When I stood up again, he nodded. Time for the thunderbolts.

Within seconds, small whirligigging objects came zooming over the crowd. I knew they were just paper twists weighted with pebbles, but they certainly surprised the people below. Startled and confused, people cried out and ducked for cover.

Will stepped toward von Braggenschnott. But alas! Instead of moving away from the disturbance like everybody else, the man turned toward the commotion and slammed smack into Will, who clutched at the German's coat to try to keep his balance. The vile man shouted something, then backhanded Will across the face.

Will staggered backward and von Braggenschnott and his men drew guns—real live guns—and began shooting at the silly thunderbolts!

Mass confusion and pandemonium erupted as everyone hit the ground to avoid having their head shot off.

Henry leaped to his feet to go to Will's aid. Frantically, I motioned him back to his hiding place. If they discovered

that Henry was behind all this, who knew what they'd do to him? Shoot him, that's what.

Von Braggenschnott motioned at two of his men to head in the direction of the thunderbolts.

I motioned to Henry like mad, trying to get his attention. Finally, he looked over at me and got the idea. He scuttled away, weaving a crooked path between the cargo containers, and disappeared out of sight.

This wasn't going at all how we'd planned. Who would have guessed that von Braggenschnott and his men would be so horrid about a little thing like cracking thunderbolts?

I looked back and saw Will struggle to his feet, blood pouring from his nose. He wiped his hand across his face and spotted the blood. His expression grew furious and he drew back his leg as if he were going to kick von Braggenschnott. But if Will did that then von Braggenschnott would take him apart limb by limb. Apparently Will stumbled onto the same idea, for he backed off a bit, then sauntered away. Sauntered, mind you—I would have torn out of there like all the furies of hell were behind me!

Henry reached me first. "Did he get it?"

"I don't know. I couldn't see."

"Did you see that Bragging Snot beast take a swing at him?"

"Yes, I did. His nose is bleeding buckets, too."

"Vermin."

We heard a shuffling sound off to the right. Will appeared, blood streaked across his face, and a black eye already beginning to form, but he was grinning from ear to ear. "Blimey! Did you see that Bogeyfellow take a swipe at me?" He sounded highly indignant, but proud, too.

"I certainly did. The rotter." I discovered I couldn't bring myself to ask if he'd got the Heart of Egypt. If he failed, I wasn't sure I wanted to know quite yet. The fact that Will was smiling was promising, but he *was* a boy. He could just as easily be smiling at the adventure of it all.

Henry, however, had no such reservations. "So, did you get it?"

Will smiled so wide, I was afraid his face was going to split in half like an overripe squash.

He patted his front trouser pocket. "That I did!"

I went weak with relief. I closed my eyes and slumped against the wall behind me. "Oh, well done, Will! Very well done!"

His cheeks grew red and he shuffled his feet on the ground. "Oh, 'twer nothin' miss. Really."

"Nonsense! That foul man struck you! You could have—"

"Give off," he mumbled, clearly not wanting to talk about this.

Henry piped up. "That *was* bloody brilliant!"

Will's head jerked up and he and Henry exchanged devilish grins.

"May I have it now?" I asked, trying to change the subject.

"'Course." He reached into his pocket, pulled out a velvet pouch, and placed it in my hand.

I shuddered as the force of the curse hit me.

"You all right, miss?" Will asked, concern in his voice.

"Yes, I'm fine. Let's go home, shall we?" As we made our way home, a swell of pride surged through me.

We'd done it.

A Triumph Sours

THE REST OF THE DAY, Henry and I basked in the glow of our smashing success. It was a heady feeling. Whenever Henry caught my eye, he would break into a grin. I should have scolded him for being too obvious, except I was too busy grinning back.

There was one sticky moment when I told him he couldn't come with me to return the Heart of Egypt to Wigmere. But when I explained it was his job to keep Mother and Father from discovering I was gone, he was a little more cooperative.

And of course I felt ever so guilty having the Heart of

Egypt right under my parents' nose and not being able to tell them. How furious they'd be if they knew! They'd most likely ship me off to some horribly grim school for the next five years. (I tried to tell myself I was only saving them the pain of losing it twice, but it wasn't helping much.)

I set off bright and early the next day and headed to Somerset House and the Society of Antiquaries. It was pouring rain and the wind was howling as if every disembodied spirit on earth had decided to join in. It was eerie, but I was confident. I patted the pocket of the old waterproof I was wearing. I had the means of saving our entire nation safely tucked in my pocket.

Because of the nasty weather, there were very few people about. It was a long walk, but satisfaction at having retrieved the Heart of Egypt gave me a rather lot of cheerful energy.

At Somerset House, I marched with confidence up the stairs to the third floor. The doorman must have sensed my resolve because he only threw me a quick glance and didn't try to stop me. Perhaps he recognized me.

After my last visit, I intended to avoid Boythorpe at all costs. I kept my steps light and walked straight past his door, hoping he wouldn't pop his annoying little head out to see what was going on.

Once safely past his office, I went to Wigmere's, sixth

door down on the left. I looked to make sure no one else was in the hallway. The place seemed quite deserted.

I knocked. There was no answer. I knocked again. Still nothing. Well, stuff and nonsense. How was I to return the beastly artifact if Wigmere didn't have the decency to be here?

I stood there for a moment, thoroughly stumped. But then I remembered: the lift! I headed down the hallway and found the last door on the right, the skinny little one that looked like a closet. I stepped in, then shut the door behind me.

The attendant was surprised to see me. "What are you doing here, miss? All by yourself?"

"I need to see Lord Wigmere and he isn't in his office. Is he on Level Six?"

The man hesitated, studying me with suspicion.

"It's all right! I'm allowed down there. You saw me yourself not three days ago. Besides, it's urgent that I see Wigmere."

"Very well, but if there's hell to pay, you'll do the paying."

I nodded. "Fair enough."

I was a little more prepared this time when my stomach tried to shoot out of the top of my head, but not much.

When the lift stopped, the attendant opened the door. Before he could get any ideas about escorting me, I stepped

out and waved a quick goodbye, then hurried into Level Six.

Only to find that the place was deserted. All of the desks were empty, all of the offices abandoned, piles of paper left helter-skelter. Where was everyone?

Feeling unsure, I headed to the infirmary where Stokes had been. Surely he was still too sick to move?

As I drew close to the small room, I heard voices. With relief, I recognized one of them as Wigmere's.

When I knocked, the voices stopped abruptly, then Wigmere's bulk filled the doorway, looking large and puffed up, like a cat when it's trying to scare you.

His face relaxed when he saw it was only me. "Theodosia?" His gaze moved past me to the floor, then all the way back to the lift.

When I turned to follow his gaze, I saw a long puddling trail behind me from the water running off my waterproof. "Sorry about that. I'll clean it up later, if you like."

"Never mind," he said. "Come in and let's get you out of your wet things. Then you can tell me what you're doing here." I can't say he sounded particularly happy to see me.

Wigmere stepped back and motioned me into the room. Stokes was sitting up in bed, and a table had been set up next to him, on which there was a large map spread out with lots of little pins stuck in it.

There were a few moments of fumbling as I wriggled out

of my waterproof and Wigmere found someplace to hang it. "So," he said at last. "Only something of great importance could bring you out in this sort of weather. I trust something has happened?"

"No," I began.

His face drooped.

"Something even better than that," I continued before he could get too discouraged.

He perked up again and I must say I quite enjoyed being the one to bring that look to such a long face. I reached into my pocket and pulled out the carefully wrapped bundle. "Here."

He looked from the bundle to my face, then back to the bundle again. "What is this?"

"Open it and you shall see." I was nearly dancing in anticipation. He would be so pleased!

Wigmere took the bundle out of my hand and unwrapped it. Once he had lifted the last of the wrapping away, he turned the velvet pouch upside down.

"Upon my soul!" he gasped. The Heart of Egypt sat in his palm, winking and blinking and glittering in all its malevolent brilliance. "How on earth did you get hold of this?"

"Are you sure you want to know?"

His mustache twitched. "I think I'm up to it. Come, have a seat and tell us your tale."

I made myself comfortable in one of the extra chairs and

relayed my story. It was gratifying to have Wigmere's and Stokes's full attention. They were full of "I says!" and "Good Lords!" The whole time I talked, Wigmere kept turning the Heart of Egypt over and over in his hands.

When I'd finished, Wigmere looked at me, his face deceptively bland. "And just how much did you tell your brother and his friend?"

"Nothing!" I hurried to assure him. "Remember, they knew some of it before we even met you. I just built on that."

His face relaxed. "You do understand how dangerous it was to tackle those men by yourselves, don't you? You or one of your friends could have been injured, or killed. Or worse."

I looked at him in surprise. "What could be worse than being killed?"

He and Stokes exchanged a glance. "Being tortured," Stokes said softly. "To give over secrets, betray your mates or this organization. That type of thing."

My mind immediately flew to the iron maiden and the rack we had in the Inquisition collection at the museum. I gulped.

"Exactly," said Wigmere.

He handed the Heart of Egypt to Stokes, who took a turn admiring it. Then the two men exchanged one of those silent looks that are full of meaning.

Wigmere took the artifact back and ran his finger over it one more time before he looked up at me. "Do your parents know you've found this?"

I shook my head. "I saw no point in telling them since they would just have to give it up again. Besides, then I'd have to explain all about you, and I know you didn't want me to do that."

"Excellent. So only the three of you children know?"

I nodded.

"I'm afraid, Theodosia, I'm going to have to ask you to perform yet another service for your country," Wigmere said gravely.

Feeling very confident, I said, "I'd be happy to." After all, we'd just retrieved the most important artifact Britain had ever discovered. Surely we were up to whatever task Wigmere chose to ask of us.

Much to my shock, he handed the Heart of Egypt back to me.

"I need you to take this back to its rightful resting place."

"I beg your pardon?"

"I need you to return this to Egypt for us. There's no one here to do it. We've sent every one of our operatives to Germany in pursuit of von Braggenschnott. We thought he had the Heart of Egypt. It will take us weeks to get messages to them without breaking their cover."

Well, that certainly explained the deserted offices. But still. "What about one of you?" I asked, looking from Stokes to Wigmere and back again.

There was a moment of silence, then Wigmere spoke. "My dear girl, you can't expect Stokes here to go. Not with a twelve-inch gash in his ribs. He can barely sit up for longer than an hour."

"Well, then. What about you?"

As soon as the words were out of my mouth, I wished them back. A pained expression crossed Wigmere's face and he gave a bark of laughter, the kind with nothing funny about it. "My dear, if only I could!" He motioned to his leg. "Don't you think I'd love to travel to Egypt? To have the honor of returning one of their most precious artifacts to its rightful resting place?" He sniffed loudly and stiffened his spine. "But I can barely get down here without a lift, and they don't have those in Thutmoses's tomb, let me tell you. As much as it pains me to say so, I'm simply not up to the journey."

I squirmed uncomfortably at his words. "B-but how am I to get there?" I asked.

"Using boats and trains," Stokes said. "Like everyone else."

"Yes, but I just can't waltz up to a boat and say, take me, an eleven-year-old girl, to Egypt!"

"No, of course not. You'll need to convince your parents to go and take you along."

"But Mum just got back!"

Lord Wigmere scooted his chair closer to me so that we were eye to eye. "I know this is a lot to ask. But you *are* extraordinary, Theodosia, with enormous personal resources. You've got to do it. For Britain."

I was still reeling at the impact of what he was saying. "But I'm not sure they'll be willing to give it up. Not if they know I've found it."

"Well, there's the rub. You still can't tell them you've found it."

"What? You expect me to talk my parents into going back to Egypt—and taking me with them—without telling them why?"

"And you mustn't mention us," Stokes added.

"Have you lost your buttons?" I said, leaping to my feet. "Of course I'll need to tell them about you. Why else would they be willing to go?"

"You'll have to think of another reason," Wigmere said, exchanging another one of those meaningful glances with Stokes.

I took a step toward them. "Why do you two keep looking at each other like that?"

Wigmere cleared his throat. "It's more important than

ever that you don't tell your mother about returning the Heart of Egypt," he said at last.

I narrowed my eyes. "Why? Why is it so important to keep it from her?"

Wigmere shifted a bit in his seat. "Well, it's hard to explain . . ." His words trailed off, as if he had no intention of trying to explain something that difficult.

"Give it a go," I urged.

"Sometimes, when people work around . . . vile things . . . sometimes the effect of those things can . . . wear off on them."

I cannot tell you how much I did not like the sound of this.

"Egyptian funerary and black magic are very—corrosive. They can eat away at a person's good side, until there isn't much of it left."

I froze in place, my hands fisted at my sides. "What exactly are you trying to say?"

He started to look over at Stokes again. "Don't even think of exchanging another one of those horrid glances with him. You look at me and tell me what is going on. This instant." I was breathing hard and my face was hot. It felt like if I dared to look away from Wigmere, my whole world would crumble.

Wigmere's voice was gentle when he spoke. "We've con-

ducted an inquiry, Theodosia. We believe that the theft of the Heart of Egypt was an inside job. We're afraid your mother might have had something to do with it."

A great, yawning silence appeared in the room, black and dreadful. I was afraid it would swallow me up whole.

Wigmere rushed to continue. "It's not her doing, of course. It's the black magic she's been exposed to for enormous portions of her adult life. Think, Theodosia. She's in the pyramids, month after month, exposed to the artifacts in their most pure, undisturbed state for large portions of time. She can't help but be affected. It's like leaving a pudding out in the rain. Eventually the rain will dissolve the pudding and leave pits and fissures in it. We think that's what's happened to your mother."

I shook my head and couldn't seem to stop shaking it. "No," I said, backing away. "No! No! No! You've got it all wrong! What about you? You all specialize in artifacts infested with black magic. Maybe you've all gone bad and are just trying to trick me!"

There they went, exchanging those glances again. "Stop that!" I fairly shouted.

Stokes spoke this time, his voice gentle, as if he were trying to calm a horse. "We wear protection. At all times. It's ingrained into our very skin. And we take . . . precautions several times a month."

"Let me see this ingrained protection," I demanded. It sounded like a cock and bull story to me.

"May I, sir?"

Wigmere nodded his head. "Yes. Of course. Show her."

Moving carefully, as if it hurt his wound, he unbuttoned the first two buttons of his shirt. I gasped. Sitting just below the base of his throat was a wedjat eye. I leaned in for a closer look. "What did you use to draw it with?"

"It's not drawn on. It's a tattoo. It won't ever come off."

I studied the symbol. It made perfect sense. The base of the throat is very vulnerable to evil magic. That's why the ancient Egyptians wore their amulets around their necks.

As Stokes buttoned his collar, Wigmere leaned forward, as if an idea had just occurred to him. "Does your mother wear protection, Theodosia? Or your father, for that matter?"

"No," I said, miserable. "I've tried and tried to get them to. I've even made them amulets, hoping that they'd wear them just to humor me, but they don't." I stiffened my spine. "But that still doesn't mean they've gone bad!" How could the only adult I'd found that I could trust be so completely and utterly wrong?

"Perhaps," Wigmere conceded. He didn't look convinced. "But it's a chance we can't take. Surely you can see that."

"I can see nothing of the kind," I spat. I stared out at the

deserted room with all the empty desks and chaotic papers. How dare he suggest such a thing about Mother? I don't care if it was his job to protect all of Britain; there was no reason to cast Mum's reputation in such an ugly light. How could I convince them? How could I make them see how very wrong they were?

But of course—Fagenbush! If it *was* an inside job, it had to be him. He had been acting strangely since the moment the statue of Bastet arrived, sneaking around in the middle of the night, spying on me when he thought I had it. He had to be the inside man!

Feeling very smug, I turned to Wigmere. "You've got it all wrong. Yes, there is a mole, but it's not my mother. It's the Second Assistant Curator, Clive Fagenbush," I announced, feeling triumphant.

Wigmere shook his head sadly. "No, it's not Fagenbush. We've checked him out thoroughly. He's not the one."

"How can you be so sure?"

"We have our ways," Stokes said mysteriously.

"Well, your ways are wrong. Fagenbush is up to something. I've known that for weeks."

"Maybe so," conceded Wigmere. "But he's had nothing to do with the Heart of Egypt."

I folded my arms and glared at him. "Very well, then. Let's say my mother is in on this whole thing. Why on earth

would she take me with her back to Egypt then? Surely she'd guess that something was up? If she's in on it and all."

"Well, I must say, I haven't much hope that your parents *will* do it. But it's our best shot. If she won't take you back, then I'll just have to go and hope that I don't botch it too badly."

"So if my mother does take me to Egypt, that will prove she's innocent, right? Then you'll realize what a stupid, idiotic theory you've cooked up?"

Wigmere fingered his mustache. "It will go a long way in her favor, I will say that," he finally conceded.

"Very well, then. We will be leaving for Egypt. Within a fortnight, no less. And you can bet your wedjat eye my mother had nothing, *nothing* to do with any of this." My whole body shook with outrage.

Wigmere took a step toward me, his face creased in worry. "I'm sorry to have upset you, my dear. But it's what we *do* here. It's why there's a Brotherhood—to ferret out exactly this sort of thing."

"I don't know, sir," Stokes said. "Maybe it's asking too much."

Wigmere studied me. "Is it too much to ask, Theodosia? If the burden is too great, we'll certainly understand."

Too disgusted to answer, I snatched the Heart of Egypt off the table, grabbed my waterproof from the back of the chair, and ran out the door.

I was so angry my footsteps nearly cracked the pavement as I strode home. I ignored the cold rain as it fell in fat little drops that practically sizzled when they touched me.

But my steps slowed as my mind began whirring. Mother did know von Braggenschnott. She'd even said he helped her get the Heart of Egypt out of the country.

Which proved nothing! Only that he wanted a British citizen to bring the curses back to British soil.

Even so, Mother hadn't seemed very concerned when I'd pointed out the man following her at the station. That was nothing new, though—grownups never listen to a word I say. Just remembering the look on her face when she discovered the Heart of Egypt was missing should erase all doubts.

However, she always had been a wonderful actress. It was one of the ways she managed Father so well . . . In horror, I realized that Wigmere had got to me. Even *I* was beginning to suspect my own mother!

To Egypt
We Must Go

When I returned to the museum, the first thing I did was search out Fagenbush. It was high time we had a talk. I marched straight down to Receiving, certain he'd be sniffing around the newest artifacts.

Nigel and Stilton stopped what they were doing and stared at me.

"Is something wrong, Theodosia?" Nigel asked after an awkward pause.

I tossed my hair over my shoulder and tried to look casual. "I was just looking for Fagenbush. Have you seen him?"

"H-he was h-here just a moment ago," Stilton said, his

left eye twitching the whole time. "I think he went down to the reading room."

"Thank you. I'll look for him there." Before either of them could say another word, I hurried back up the stairs.

And ran smack into Fagenbush.

The weasel had been lurking at the top of the stairway! He stepped out of the shadows as I reached the top stair, startling me so badly I nearly lost my balance. If he hadn't reached out and grabbed my shoulders, I would have tumbled back down the stairs.

He leaned toward me. "What did you do to it?" he asked. The stench of pickled onions made my nostrils quiver, as if they were looking for escape.

I jerked away from his grip, freeing my shoulders. "To what?" I was supposed to be grilling *him*, not the other way around.

"What did you do to the Bastet statue?"

"What do you mean?"

"I mean you ruined it. You did something to it and it's not . . . the same."

So he *had* known about the curse! And had been planning to use it for his own evil ends. I was right. There was a mole in our museum, and it wasn't Mother!

The best defense is a good offense, or that's what Father says when he's getting ready to face the museum's board of

directors. I squared my shoulders. "And what did you do with the Heart of Egypt?" I asked.

A puzzled look came over his horrid face. "What are you talking about?"

Suddenly I realized I had no idea whether or not Mother and Father had told the other curators the Heart of Egypt was even missing. Maybe that part was still a secret. Well, time to bluff it out. "You know exactly what I mean."

He shoved his face right in front of mine. "What do you think I did with it?"

We stood there nose to nose, fists clenched, neither one of us willing to budge an inch.

A voice from the stairway made us both jump. "I say, you two. What's going on now?" Nigel had just come up the stairs and was staring at us as if we'd just been let out of the zoo.

Fagenbush's eyes slid over to Nigel, then back to me. "Theodosia and I were just discussing some of the newest artifacts, that's all."

"Really? Then why do you look like you're ready to come to blows?" Nigel asked.

Fagenbush blinked, then began to stutter.

Oh, honestly. He was going to get us both in trouble. "We just had a disagreement over provenance," I explained.

Fagenbush whipped his head around to look at me.

"You're arguing over where the artifacts came from?" Nigel asked, incredulous. He looked down his nose at Fagenbush. "I don't think the museum's paying you to get into shouting matches with little girls, Clive. Now move along."

Fagenbush muttered something under his breath before quickly leaving. I would need to be on my toes from now on. Now that I knew about the traitor, I couldn't let him wreak any more havoc.

No sooner had Nigel gone back downstairs (after raising an eyebrow at me) than Henry appeared at my side. "Did you give it to them?" he asked. "What did they say?"

I grabbed him by the arm and pulled him into a dark corner of the foyer.

"Ow!" he said. "That hurts."

"Sorry, but you're talking too loud. You're going to get us both in trouble." I was stalling. What should I tell him? That Wigmere had ordered me to return the Heart of Egypt? But then Henry would fuss and whine and moan and insist on going with us to Cairo, which would almost certainly ruin all of our chances. "Yes, I gave it to them," I finally said, which wasn't exactly a lie.

Henry's face lit up. "Was he impressed? Did he congratulate us? Did you tell him of the part I played?"

He looked so hopeful, it broke my heart that Wigmere

hadn't said anything nice. "Yes! Very impressed. I told him of the part both you and Will played and he said your distraction was sheer genius."

Henry folded his arms over his chest and rocked back on his heels. "I should say."

Having appeased Henry, I scuttled off to my closet to try and think of a plan to get Mother back to Egypt in a hurry. This was not going to be easy. And if Henry ever found out about my deception, he'd never trust me again.

I lifted my chin. That's all right. He'd only just begun to trust me. So it only meant we'd go back to being the way we were. I just wish it didn't feel so awful . . .

That night at dinner I kept glancing up at Mum, trying to see if I could sense any whiff of corrosion. Trouble was, it had been ages since she'd been home and of course she'd changed, but I didn't know if it had anything to do with becoming a traitor or not.

"Theodosia! Why do you keep staring at your mother like that?" Dad snapped.

Startled, I dropped my fork onto my plate, launching a small volley of peas onto the white tablecloth. Father had been in a horrid mood ever since we'd lost the Heart of Egypt. Which made all these secrets that much more painful. But the truth wouldn't make him any happier.

Father stabbed at his mutton so hard it nearly cracked the plate.

"Are you all right, Theodosia dear? You look a bit pale," Mother said.

If she shouldered the same burdens I did, she'd be pale, too. Pale! That was it! She'd just given me my first opening. "Well, I do feel a bit pale," I said. "I feel like I need a rest somewhere warm and dry." There. I'd dropped my first hint.

"I'll get you some chamomile tea before bed," Mum offered. "That will help you rest."

I hate chamomile tea.

I turned my attention back to my plate and cut my mutton up into tiny pieces, hoping I would fool Mum into thinking I'd eaten some. My worries rather squelched my appetite. Even though I had worked out that Clive Fagenbush was the mole, I couldn't help but wonder how to convince Wigmere of Mother's innocence. What would it take to prove it to him? What if I couldn't? Would Mum go to jail? Be found guilty of treason? Would anyone even care that it wasn't her, but the corrosive power of the black magic she came into contact with every day?

Except, I reminded myself, it *wasn't* her. Wigmere had got it all wrong.

After what seemed like hours, Father finally pushed his plate away and sighed in contentment.

Now it was time for my next move. "Mum, when do you think you'll be going back to Egypt?"

"Good heavens, Theodosia!" Father said. "She's only just got back."

I shrugged. "I'm just curious. Trying to plan out my year, you know, that sort of thing."

"Plan out your year? Good grief." Father didn't seem to think my year needed planning out. Henry just looked at me, clearly puzzled.

"Not for a while, surely," Mother said gently.

"But aren't you eager to get back? See what else was in Amenemhab's tomb? I mean, who knows what other marvelous finds might be hiding there? Doesn't that sort of thing get under your skin? Make you itch to get back to it?"

Father stared at me with his mouth open, and Mother frowned slightly. "I'm not sure what you mean, Theodosia. Of course, any sort of intellectual discovery is invigorating, but you make it sound like more of an . . . obsession or something."

Maybe I'd poured it on a bit thick, but I was trying to see if I could detect any hint of the traitorous behavior Wigmere had been talking about. "But aren't the winter months the best time of year to go to Egypt? Isn't the weather milder then?" I asked.

My parents exchanged glances. "Yes," Mum said. "Now *is*

probably the best time to be there. But it's the time when Henry is out of school, and the museum board has its annual meeting. There are many commitments here in London right now."

Convincing them was going to be harder than I thought.

SHABTIS
ON THE MARCH

WHEN I AWOKE THE NEXT MORNING, I felt wretched. Not only had I not talked my parents into returning to Egypt, but I'd dreamed of those revolting little shabtis again. Only this time, one of them was chewing on my ankle. Terrifyingly enough, when I opened my eyes, the sensation didn't go away.

Had the shabtis come to life? I sat bolt upright, only to find that it was just Isis. And she wasn't gnawing on my ankle, but curled up in a warm furry ball, knitting at my feet with her claws. Gently. Which meant . . . the Demon Isis was gone!

I reached down and rubbed her tummy, then scratched behind her ears. And then, I heard my favorite sound in the world.

Isis purred.

And purred and purred. It was like a motor that wouldn't turn off.

The mud bath had worked! Oh how I wanted to stay there all day snuggling with my cat, but I had far too much work to do. Beginning with those filthy shabtis.

I gave Isis one last belly rub, and she gave me one last affectionate swipe with her paw.

Before I tackled the shabtis, I wanted to be sure I was adequately protected. First on my list of things to do was to make more amulets. I'd given one to Stokes and another to Danver. I was running low. Of course, I hadn't realized that both men had their own specially ingrained protection. Although, come to think of it, fat lot of good that had done Stokes. Or Danver. Can't use a tattoo as a tourniquet.

When I reached my study, I dragged the old carpetbag out of the cupboard and pulled Eggbert Archimedes' *The Power of Amulets: A Lost Art* off the shelf and got to work.

The trick with amulets is figuring out exactly which ingredients are needed to protect you against which types of curses. Providing you know what type of curse it is. If you don't, then you must resort to general protection, which

isn't quite as powerful. So, while it might seem like an excess to have seven amulets, it's not. All you have to do is remember Danver and his unfortunate experience to know that.

I decided to regenerate the heart amulet I'd used on Stokes. It worked very well on physical injuries and the way things were going, I had an uneasy feeling there might be more of those.

I carefully scraped all the old wax and linen off the heart-shaped pebble, then rinsed it with purifying water. I cut a new piece of white linen and, using a special ink I'd made out of myrrh, I drew a wedjat eye in the center, then drew a snake around that. The viciousness of the snake would repel danger, and the eye would invoke wholeness and health.

I rummaged through my kit until I found a small sliver of malachite, a green, semiprecious stone used by the ancient Egyptians to invoke regeneration and healthy life. (You'd be surprised how many artifacts, in spite of our best efforts, crumble and disintegrate when handled. When that happens, I scramble to collect the tiny bits and slivers that no one else bothers with. They come in very handy at times like this.)

I placed the sliver of malachite in the center of the wedjat eye and carefully folded the linen over it until it was a tiny little wad. Next, I lit a candle stub and let the wax drip

all over the linen to seal it. While the wax was still warm, I pressed it onto the pebble.

While that was cooling, I grabbed a length of gold-colored wire—to invoke the power of the sun god—out of my bag and began twisting that into the shape of an ankh. Ankhs are the Egyptian symbol for life and wearing one is thought to lengthen one's life. I looped a thin cord through the top of it, then slipped it over my head.

Then as one last means of protection, I took four white threads (purity), four green threads (life and regeneration), four yellow threads (representative of the sun, which was eternal and imperishable), and four red threads (fiery protective power of the Eye of Ra) and plaited them together. I tied it off in a knot, then added six more knots (to form a barrier through which hostile forces cannot pass). It would make a lovely bracelet. Perhaps I could even talk Mother into wearing it.

Now properly armed, I put my supplies away and hurried toward the short-term storage down by the loading dock.

Something felt different as soon as I stepped into the room. It was in the air, as if the elemental particles had been disturbed. It felt as if the invisible threads that wind themselves through the atmosphere had been snarled.

Something had tangled these invisible threads into a twisted mess.

Ignoring the familiar punch of nausea, I went over to the closest box of shabtis.

Once again, they had changed. They were now exquisitely detailed little statues and they lay in their crate in a jumble, not all nicely laid out as we had left them.

Bother. Had the shabtis got up and moved around on their own? Like they had in my dream?

My stomach did a somersault at that thought. It made perfect sense that Amenemhab would have included these small clay figures as part of his curse. He'd included every other possible thing—why not these? Perhaps they were to rise up and help bring the downfall of Thutmose and Amenemhab's enemies from the inside out. Sort of like an Egyptian version of the Trojan horse.

It seemed perfectly logical, in a black magic, revengey sort of way.

I moved on to the next crate and saw a dozen shabtis scattered on the floor around it. Was this the crate Henry had been using for soldiers? Had he carelessly left them out? Or had they climbed out on their own? No, surely one of the curators moved them. Probably Fagenbush had come down here, sniffing around.

Except even Fagenbush treated artifacts with the utmost care. The jumble of nerves in my stomach grew larger.

Looking for answers, I crossed over to the worktable where most of the stele had been laid out. I stood for a bit,

studying the grisly images. The pharaoh's army lined up in endless rows, armed with spears and swords and daggers, grim expressions on their faces. Beheaded enemies lay at the pharaoh's feet, clearly the handiwork of these soldiers. Was that part of the whole plan? Were these shabti figures to rise up, not in the true afterlife like most shabtis, but whenever someone disturbed the tomb?

Words from Amenemhab's *Art of War* came to mind.

But let them remember, to be afraid, even after his death. Let them remember how he smote his enemies in two, renting their skulls asunder as they wished to lay your land. Let them remember that his retribution was swift and terrible, as it will always be through all eternity.

Something touched my shoulder. I jumped, nearly dropping the stele.

"Theo?" Mum's voice sounded above my pounding heart. "Whatever is the matter? You look like you've seen a ghost."

"Nothing, Mother," I said, clutching my heart to make sure it was still in my chest. "I just hadn't heard you come in. That's all."

She eyed me dubiously.

Anxious to get her concerns off of me, I pointed to the stele I'd been studying. "Mum, look here for a moment. You brought home nearly everything pictured in this stele."

"Hm. Yes, I did, didn't I? How clever of you to figure that out."

"But you didn't bring this," I said, pointing to a scepter the pharaoh held in his hand. "The Was scepter, according to the rubbing you gave me. Amenemhab speaks about it quite a lot, actually."

What he said was that whosoever holds the Was scepter in their possession shall be assured wealth and prosperity for their land. I was thinking poor Britain could use a bit of that right now. Plus, if I made it sound enticing enough, Mother might decide it was worth going back to Egypt sooner rather than later.

"Really? I never saw anything like that on our excavation or I would certainly have brought it home. I'll look for it next time, won't I?"

"When do you think that will be?"

"Darling, we just went over this last night. Not for a while yet."

I nearly screamed in frustration. Wigmere had no idea what he was asking. I thought about telling her that the very fate of Britain hung on her decision. That her actions had launched a series of events that could topple the kingdom. I thought about explaining the curse and its repercussions. But in the end, I stumbled upon the *one* thing that would spur her to action.

"When Henry and I were over at the British Museum the other day," I said, glancing out of the corner of my eye

to make sure I had her full attention, "we heard that Snow-thorpe chap talking to one of his flunkies. He was trying to set up an expedition specifically to find this Was scepter. Seemed to think it was nearly as valuable as the Heart of Egypt."

Mother rose up, full of indignation. "But that's our dig! They can't just barge in there because they want something."

Then I played my trump card. "Has that ever stopped them before?"

As she stared at me, I could see the wheels and gears churning inside her head. She glanced over toward the stairs. "Well, I just came to check and see how you were doing down here, darling," she said brightly. "I really must go back upstairs."

To Father's workroom, I hoped.

Where, with any luck, she would soon talk him into a quick jaunt to Cairo.

I spent the rest of the afternoon studying the steles that had been laid out on the table. They told the exact same story that the *Art of War* rubbing told, only in pictures. With vivid detail.

We beseech you, oh gods, that whosoever should take his heart from this land, shall bring upon themselves the agonies of

a thousand deaths. May their actions bring pestilence upon their land, eating away at their bounty as their actions have eaten away at the glory of our land. May famine bring them to their knees, hollowing out their bellies and weakening their bodies. May all the power of the Nile fall from the sky, flooding their lands until all shall float away on a sea of destruction and death.

They showed pictures of emaciated people, who bore an uncanny resemblance to the haunted faces I'd seen in the Seven Dials. One stele showed people with a revolting pox on their faces, writhing on the ground.

Then, oh gods, may plagues rise up to eat away at the people, may pustules and sores erupt over their bodies, marking them for all to see as destroyers of Egypt. May your retribution upon these enemies of Thutmose be swift and terrible, may Sehkmet devour their hearts, and Ammit feast on their heads. May all the lands run red with their blood until they return the Heart of Egypt to its rightful resting place, and lay it back at your feet, so that Thutmose's glory will be whole once more.

I was so absorbed in trying to learn all that I could from the steles, I hadn't realized how late it had gotten. Dusk was falling and the room began to grow dark. Just as I decided I'd better turn up the gaslights, I heard a squeak on the stair.

I froze.

It was the kind of slow, quiet squeak that lets you know

that the person doing the squeaking doesn't wish to be heard.

Frantic, I looked around for some kind of weapon. My eyes fell on the ritual dagger that Mum had brought back. I snatched it up in my hand and tiptoed over to hide behind the wall at the base of the stairs.

As I waited, I tried to take shallow little breaths that couldn't be heard. I pinned my eyes to the base of the stairs, where the intruder would first appear. A shadow rose up on the wall of the staircase, looming tall and black. My heart kicked into a gallop. I raised the dagger.

The shadow stepped off the stairs and into the room. "What are *you* doing here?" I asked, shoving the dagger behind my back.

Lord Wigmere looked a bit surprised, then rather sheepish. "Looking for you, of course."

"Well, why were you sneaking?"

He puffed up at that. "I wasn't *sneaking*. I was just walking quietly."

I sniffed, then returned to the steles I'd been studying, laying the dagger on the worktable. I tapped my toe, impatient for Wigmere to leave. I still hadn't forgiven him his suspicions about Mother.

Wigmere limped farther into the room. "Still angry, are you?"

"I'm afraid I have nothing to say to you," I told him, then strode over to the crates of shabtis.

"Theodosia, look at it this way. I oversee hundreds of museums here in Britain, scores of them in London alone. I can't afford to play favorites, to tell myself that surely nice Mr. or Mrs. So-and-So isn't capable of wrongdoing—I would be negligent in my duties if I did. It would be like you refusing to believe there was a curse on an artifact because the artifact was so pretty."

Well, that little black statue of Bastet *had* been very charming. "Yes, but you can't possibly think I'm going to believe something like that about my own mother."

Wigmere studied me for a moment, pulling on his mustache. "Very well. Pax. I won't insist you see your mother in that light, if you agree that I have a moral obligation to do so. No matter how extraordinary she or her daughter might be." He held his hand out.

I stared at it a moment. He had called pax, after all. And I suppose he was only doing his job. And, since I had every intention of proving him wrong, I suppose I could afford to be gracious. Although, I'd like to know when this gracious stuff becomes fun, because really, it's rather dull if you ask me.

"Oh, all right," I said, putting my hand in his. He *had* called me extraordinary.

His whole face brightened in a smile.

"Besides," I continued. "I'm telling you. The insider is—"

"Your father?" Wigmere asked.

"No!" Just as I started to get worked up, I saw his mustache twitch. "Ha ha. Very funny." I tossed my hair over my shoulder.

Wigmere frowned. "Have you had any luck with your parents?"

"No, but I will. I've only just gotten started on them. They'll be off to Cairo in a matter of weeks. Just you wait and see," I said, hoping it was true.

"Well, the whole reason I came here is," he said, reaching into his pocket. "I have something for you."

He fiddled around a bit, then pulled out a small velvet pouch and handed it to me.

"For me?"

He nodded. I opened it and pulled out a tiny wedjat eye hanging on a thin, golden chain.

"Oh, my," I said, staring at the gold as it spun round in my hand. It was heavily weighted with good magic and protection. I'd never seen any amulet ooze as much protective power as this one.

"Wear it, Theodosia. At all times. Hide it under your collar if you must, but do not take it off. Ever. It is old, very old. It is rumored to have been fashioned by the god Horus

himself, and given to the very first Egyptian king as a sign of the god's favor."

I stared from the artifact back up to Wigmere. "But, the gods are only myths! Aren't they?"

Wigmere put his hands in his pockets and turned to look out the window.

"That's what conventional archaeology says. And what the Brotherhood used to think. But now, after decades and decades of research, and seeing the magic and power that have been wrought into some of these artifacts, we aren't so sure."

"No," I said, shaking my head. "No. That can't be. It simply can't."

Wigmere turned away from the window and looked back at me. He seemed to realize what effect his words had, then shrugged. "As I say, no one knows for certain. All is lost in the shroud of time." He looked out the window again. "That reminds me. I hope you'll be glad to learn that we located that sticky-fingered friend of yours, and I've decided to hire him as an errand boy for the Society."

"You mean Will?"

"Yes. It will keep him out of trouble, and you never know when we might have need of his particular, er, talents."

What a perfect place for him! "I shall feel much better knowing he's working for you."

"Well, my dear," Wigmere said, fidgeting with his cane. "I must be going. You take care of yourself. I have every confidence that you will succeed." He put his hand out for me to shake, but surprising us both, I threw my arms around him and gave him an enormous hug.

Taken aback, he stood awkwardly for a moment, then gave me a few pats on the head. "There now, dear girl. Everything will be all right. You'll see."

I stepped back. "Thank you for coming today. And thank you for this," I said, holding out the wedjat eye. "I'm sure it will come in handy."

"I've no doubt," he muttered under his breath.

VICTORY AT LAST!

HURRAY! VICTORY! This morning at breakfast Mother and Father announced they would be leaving for Cairo aboard the *Rosetta Maru* the day after next—both of them! Father is furious that the British Museum would even think of stealing another find out from under his nose. He considers it a personal affront, one he's intending to address himself. He petitioned the Museum of Legends and Antiquities board of directors for special permission to go to Cairo with Mother. And they granted it! Apparently, they aren't too keen on the British Museum getting the best of them, either.

But despite my best efforts to convince them to take me

along, my parents had the gall to say I wasn't to go. I was too young. Egyptian archaeological expeditions were no place for an eleven-year-old girl. Piffle! And a cavernous old museum *is?*

Then they had the further gall to say they needed me to watch over the museum for them. But they said it in that annoying tone of voice that lets you know they just want you to think you're being useful.

Then, the *coup de grâce* (that's French for "killing blow"). They announced I was to stay with Grandmother Throckmorton while they were away. Not very likely!

And I'd like to know how I'm to keep an eye on the museum when I'm stuck under Grandmother Throckmorton's nose?

Well, I have no choice now. I am bound for Cairo as a stowaway. I just have to work out a plan. Of course, having Father along will complicate things considerably, but I will manage.

And isn't the *Rosetta Maru* a wonderful name? Doesn't it sound like all sorts of adventures and wildly mysterious things could happen aboard a ship with a name like that? Knowing I was going to be smack in the middle of them sent a delicious thrill down my spine.

(Or maybe that was fear. It was hard to tell, as I found myself swinging wildly between the two lately.)

I can't tell you how hard it is to pack for a trip that you're not supposed to be going on. Mum went through my closets and emptied all my winter frocks and coats into a trunk bound for Grandmother's house.

I snuck up to the attic to try and locate a traveling bag I could take to Cairo. I had to pack very different things from what Mum had in mind, let me tell you. Not to mention I didn't have access to any of the things I'd really need once I was in Egypt; lightweight frocks, a parasol, cotton stockings instead of wool. Again, I resorted to the attic and managed to scavenge some old things of Mother's, including one of her old pith helmets. Excited at the find, I tried it on and went to look in one of the cracked mirrors that lived in the attic. I must say, I looked quite dapper and ready for action.

I also nabbed some old woolen stockings with moth holes in them. I was going to need a way to escape from Grandmother Throckmorton's house, after all. They just might come in handy.

I kept a couple of old winter gowns and my favorite coat out on the bed in case Mum or Henry wandered into my room while I was packing. I'd just toss those on top of my satchel, and no one would be the wiser.

Henry was feeling particularly glum, since he was being sent back to school. He's decided he likes the museum, after all, even though I've reminded him a hundred times that adventures like the one we had never happen. He is somewhat mollified by the knowledge that I am being packed off to Grandmother Throckmorton's.

If I didn't know that I was actually going to Cairo with my parents, I think I would simply perish with despair.

GRANDMOTHER THROCKMORTON

WE BADE HENRY GOODBYE at Charing Cross Station and waited on the platform until his train pulled away. I realized I was going to miss the little beast. Either that or I had a bit of coal dust stuck in my eye.

Then Father clapped his hands together and said, "Now, Theodosia. Let's pay your grandmother a visit."

He always tries to make the prospect sound cheerful when both of us know full well it will be dreadful.

Grandmother lives in a very grand house over by St. James Park. It's the kind of house where all the chairs and sofas are covered with frilly covers and she has hundreds of flowery, breakable things crowding every surface imagina-

ble. The whole house is wretchedly uncomfortable and you can't touch a single thing.

When we pulled up in front of the house, a footman came down to greet the cab and carry my bags. He lifted the suitcases and led us up the stairs to the front door, where Grandmother's butler, Beadles, waited for us. Beadles always looked as if he'd just smelled some really nasty fish and was trying to keep his nose as far away from it as possible. Which was really quite horrid because then, if one happened to look up, one could see straight up into his nostrils and practically count his nose hairs.

Wasn't he worried about going cross-eyed staring down his nose like that? I always did, whenever I tried it.

"Master Throckmorton, Mrs. Throckmorton, I shall tell Madam that you are here." He ignored me completely, but then, he always does. He stepped away, leaving us all waiting in the hallway as if we were on a business call. Why does Father put up with this, and what makes him think I am going to?

I heard the rustle of stiff silk over lots of rigid petticoats, then Grandmother Throckmorton was upon us. "Hello, Alistair." She greeted him first, offering up her old, wrinkly cheek for him to kiss.

"Hello, Mother. How are you?" Father asked after he'd given her a quick peck.

She sniffed. "As well as can be expected." She is very

clever, that woman. She said it as if it were somehow Father's fault. I don't know how she does it, but it would be a worthwhile skill to learn.

"Henrietta." She nodded at Mother, but did not offer her a kiss. Lucky Mum, I thought. Then she directed that steely gaze and pinched mouth at me. "And what have we here? Ah, yes. Theodosia. My granddaughter." She sniffed again.

"Are you catching a cold, Grandmother?" I asked.

She drew back as if I had asked what color her garters were, then lifted her monocle from the chain at her neck and peered down at me. She was no doubt trying to see if I was being impudent, but I have spent many hours practicing my most innocent look.

"Hm," she said. "It is well and good that I shall be able to mold you for the next several weeks." Her fierce glare let me know I was in for a miserable time of it. Except, I wasn't. That uplifting secret lay in my heart like the most wonderful of gifts. But I pretended that she had won and looked demurely at the ground.

"Well," Father said, shuffling his feet like a schoolboy. "We really must be going. We've tons of packing to do and last-minute details to see to."

The coward!

Mother and Father gave me a quick kiss, then escaped out the front door. Grandmother Throckmorton and I were

left standing in the hallway, staring at each other. I could hear Father whistling—*whistling,* I tell you—on his way down the front stairs.

I wasn't able to escape Grandmother Throckmorton until well after teatime. No sooner had Father and Mother left than she started in on me. She forced me over to the piano, wanting to hear how my scales were coming along. She quickly learned that they weren't. After wincing her way through my recital, she decided I needed music lessons every day while my parents were gone.

Shortly after that, a seamstress showed up and measured me every which way while Grandmother Throckmorton chose several new lacy, frilly frocks she wanted made up for me. Doesn't she realize how much lace itches?

She prattled on about dancing lessons and comportment (I already know *how* to carry myself, thank you very much!) and—horrors—the painstaking process of finding a new pudding-faced governess!

Then we had to take tea in her stuffy old drawing room, and she made me pour. And of course I didn't just pour, I spilled, too. How could I not when she sat there staring, waiting for me to mess up?

It wasn't my fault. It was those fancy chairs of hers. They

are so stiff and slippery and my feet don't reach the ground. It's like trying to pour tea while perched on the end of a slide.

Anyway, because of my poor showing at tea, Grandmother decided I needed to take my dinner in my room until I was able to handle the tea to her satisfaction. What a relief.

Only twenty-two more hours till I can make my escape. Since I'll be asleep for many of them, I think I can make it.

ESCAPE!

I WONDER IF BEADLES EVER SLEEPS. I'm beginning to think not. I'm also beginning to suspect he has eyes in the back of his head. I could go nowhere in Grandmother Throckmorton's house without him turning up seconds later. Only the knowledge that I'd be escaping soon kept me from despair.

Now, if I could just get through luncheon . . .

Grandmother Throckmorton was waiting for me in the dining room. She watched me like a hawk while I took my seat (checking for *comportment,* she said). Soup was served, and I was certain it was a test, so I ate as carefully as I could

without making any sipping noises. I only spilled one tiny little drop and she scowled as if I'd upped and put the soup tureen on my head. It was time to put an end to this charade.

"Grandmother, I don't feel so well."

She sniffed. "No doubt your poor temperament. I must say I'm not surprised. Well, take to your bed, then. I'll send someone up with a special tonic. You're to drink it all up. A nap wouldn't do you any harm either. You keep appalling hours for a child."

It was difficult not to gloat at how easily she'd stepped into my plan. I walked out of the room (quite meekly, I might add) and headed for my bedroom. Who should be lurking on the landing by my room but Beadles.

"Miss isn't feeling well?" His voice sounded polite enough, but you could tell he was sneering underneath it all.

"No, Beadles. I think I must have eaten some of that bad fish you always look like you've just smelled."

He frowned in puzzlement, and I used the opportunity to slip into my room with no more interrogations. Once I heard him head downstairs, I quietly locked my door.

I had packed my stowaway bag last night. Grabbing it, I went over to the window and looked down; there was no one about. I opened the window, then dropped my satchel to the ground, where it landed with a surprisingly loud thump.

I froze, waiting to see if the sound had drawn anyone's attention, but no one came to investigate. I went to the bed and pulled out all the holey woolen stockings I'd pilfered. Last night, while I was supposed to be asleep, I had tied all the stockings together, rather like a long rope. Now if it would only reach all the way down.

I crossed over to the window and slowly lowered it. It stopped about six feet from the ground. It would have to do.

Next, I tied my end of the woolen stocking rope to the leg of the wardrobe, double-checking that the knot was secure. I glanced at the dresser, where the note I'd left for Grandmother Throckmorton was propped against the mirror. Hopefully they wouldn't come looking for me too soon and I'd have enough of a head start.

Now there was nothing for it but to lower myself down as quickly as possible and hope no one spotted me.

As I sat on the ledge of the windowsill, I found it difficult to actually push off. I reminded myself that the stockings were firmly tied, and it wasn't really all that far down. Before I completely lost my nerve, I grabbed the rope with both hands and slipped off the ledge.

Dangling precariously, I used my feet to gently push away from the house so I wouldn't crash into anything. Slowly, with great concentration and quite a few hasty prayers, I lowered myself to the ground.

When I got to the end of the rope, it was much, much farther a drop to the ground than it had seemed from up above. My arms were quivering under the strain of holding my weight for so long, and there was no possible way I could haul myself back up.

I had to let go.

There was a long sickening second where the ground rushed up at me, then I hit it with a bone-jarring thud, my teeth clanking together. I sat stunned for a moment, then scrambled to my feet. I lifted my hand to my chest, checking to make sure the Heart of Egypt was still securely anchored around my neck. It was. Which meant . . .

I'd done it—I was free!

PART TWO

The *Rosetta Maru*

THE *ROSETTA MARU* WAS ENORMOUS, nearly as big as the *Kaiser Wilhelm der Grosse*. As I stood staring up at the ship, I saw her lifeboats way up on the very top deck. That was my destination.

It wasn't nearly as difficult to sneak onboard as you'd think. First of all, the docks are absolute bedlam and it's all anyone can do to keep track of themselves, let alone anybody else. I was in luck because there were several families traveling. I attached myself to the largest, noisiest one. I think there were seven children, maybe six. It was hard to tell. I trailed at their coattails as they followed their parents

up the ramp. As soon as we'd cleared the boarding area, I scooted off to find myself a lifeboat.

And the ship had lifts—lifts! How grand was that? I made my way to one and punched the button to open the door.

The lift attendant did a bit of a double take, but I did my Lady Throckmorton bit, which worked. He took me to the uppermost deck. I waited till the lift's door had closed, then began working my way forward until I reached the railing.

The entire city of London spread out before me like an enormous map. I stopped to watch all the people moving about, as tiny as ants. The salty breeze picked up, sending a spray of drizzle smack into my face. I looked up at the sky, where clouds like big purple bruises were rolling together. I needed to find cover. And quickly.

I hurried to the lifeboats, giving a small squeak of dismay when I realized they were all up high, like cradles hanging out over the railing. How on earth was I to get up there?

Like a monkey, that's how. And I'd never be able to lug my bag up there. I'd have to find somewhere to stash it down here on the deck where no one would find it.

Well, getting into the lifeboat without taking an unplanned swim was quite a challenge, but I made it, safe and sound. It was a little colder than I thought it would be, but I de-

cided to ignore the chill air and pretend I was quite cozy. It helped to think of it as a little cave I'd built for myself, like Henry and I used to do when we were younger. Thinking of Henry made me feel surprisingly lonely, so I pushed that thought aside. (I seem to be doing a lot of that lately.)

Stowaway

SLEEPING IN A LIFEBOAT is a beastly experience, I must say. They are surprisingly less comfortable than sarcophagi. Odd, you'd think wood would be softer than stone.

And one blanket was barely enough to keep me warm. I had intended to wad up my extra coat and use it as a pillow, but I had to keep it on during the night so I didn't freeze. It's very difficult to move when one is wearing two coats, let alone an Egyptian amulet. (It chafes!) Also, did you know ocean liner motors are very loud? And they vibrate.

In addition to being cold and hungry and bored out of my mind, there was far too much time to think. My mind

had been playing over this solemn task I'd set for myself (or Wigmere set for me, I can't quite remember if I volunteered or he volunteered me) like a cat worrying a mouse. I mean really, the more I think about it the more I think it's a bit much to expect me to save the nation.

It was very difficult to stay hidden in a lifeboat all day. I was all cold and cramped and grubby, but I could hear people wandering about on deck, laughing and talking and having a grand time.

Oh, the conversations! These intriguing bits of "Did you see what that woman did last night at dinner?" or "Has that man no shame?" Just when my curiosity got piqued, they wandered too far out of range and I couldn't hear another word.

And why on earth didn't I think to bring something besides jam sandwiches? I am quite sick of them and can't help but wonder if a person can die from eating too many. That is, if they don't freeze to death first.

I don't know why I ever thought this stowing-away business would be a good idea. I was suffering—and I do mean suffering—from the cold and hunger and sleep deprivation. And what would I get when it was all finished? I'd get to take on von Braggenschnott and his lot while trying to put an ancient artifact back where no one can ever find it again. Not to mention that I was trying to outwit Amenemhab,

one of the Egyptian New Kingdom's most brilliant military minds. Honestly. What kind of fool would even attempt such a thing?

I couldn't stand it a moment longer. I had to get out of there or I would go stark raving mad. Not only that, but I was desperate to find the lavatory!

I waited until dark, when it was cold and everyone had gone in to dinner. Then I crawled out and hobbled around, frantically looking for a lav. (Oh, the relief!) After I took care of my business, I allowed myself a brisk stroll around the deck to work out the kinks in my legs.

Just as I began to crawl back into my lifeboat, clinging to the rigging like a young monkey, I heard a voice say, "Hullo."

I nearly fainted.

I stopped climbing and turned toward the sound of the voice. "Hullo," I answered back. Croaked, really, as my voice was rusty with salt and disuse. A man stood there, dressed in his dinner jacket and sipping something elegant-looking in an odd-shaped glass. He turned to look out over the ocean, shook his head, then turned to look at me again.

"I say," he said, peering at me rather closely. "Are you my pink elephant?"

I dropped down to the deck. Pink elephant? What kind

of nonsense is that? I would have been horribly insulted except he seemed rather fond of pink elephants.

He decided to walk with me while I stretched my legs. We spent a few minutes chatting about the weather (cold gray drizzle) and where he was headed (crocodile hunting on the Nile) and what our favorite refreshment was (his—gin and tonic, mine—lemon tarts.) He didn't ask me what I was doing there or if I was a stowaway or anything like that. And he promised to bring me a bit of dessert tomorrow when he came out for his evening walk.

Now that's the kind of grownup I like!

It was much easier to sleep once I'd taken some exercise. I dreamed of what kind of dessert Mr. Wappingthorne (that was his name) would bring me tomorrow.

The next day, Mr. Wappingthorne brought me two buttered rolls that were still warm and a small raspberry tart from the dessert tray. He also snuck me a small pot of tea—such luxury! I savored the tea, letting its warmth fill me up. I was half-tempted to use part of it to bathe with. Did you know sea air makes one all salty and sticky? I have a dreadful layer of salt clinging to my face and hands.

Only two more days until we pass the halfway mark. Then, when it is too late to turn back, I will announce my presence to my parents.

DISCOVERED!

THAT NIGHT, when Mr. Wappingthorne came for a visit, he brought his fiancée, a Miss Pennington. He wanted to prove to her that I was real.

Then the fat really began to fry, let me tell you. "Why, she's a stowaway!" Miss Pennington said with a sly look, which was very unnerving. I'd hoped all would be well, since Mr. Wappingthorne got her calmed down and swore her to secrecy. Even so, I didn't relax until they left for the evening. Breathing a sigh of relief, I made myself as comfortable as I could in my little nest. Just as I began to get warm again, I heard a footstep on the deck.

Had Mr. Wappingthorne returned? Or the annoying Miss Pennington?

I heard another creak, and then my lifeboat swayed. Someone was climbing up!

Before I could even think what to do, the canvas cover was ripped off the lifeboat and I found myself blinking into the glow of an oil lamp.

"Well, well, what have we here?" a very pompous voice asked.

Bother. The gig was up. Father was going to be furious.

I clambered out of the lifeboat (quite awkward, really, with people watching you). As soon as my feet touched the deck, an ensign, or something—I wasn't sure what his title was but he had a few fancy things dangling about his shoulders and a terse look on his face—stood over me, glowering.

He started to grab me by the ear, until Mr. Wappingthorne called out, "Now see here, that's not really necessary, is it?"

The man grabbed my elbow instead, which I much preferred to my ear, and, holding it at a high, painful angle, he began marching me forward.

To the dining room.

"Shouldn't we wait for your captain in his quarters or on the bridge?" I suggested. "He won't want to interrupt his dinner for this, I'm sure."

The fellow glanced down at me. "He'll want to talk to you right away. Don't think we're going to hide your sins for you. Ship's policy."

Saw right through that, he did.

My stomach grew queasy at the thought of being discovered so publicly. "You're hurting my arm, could you please not twist it so?" I asked.

He looked down at me, threw open a door, and thrust me into the salon, nearly wrenching my arm out of its socket.

All conversation dribbled to a stop as I stumbled into the room. Everyone had finished their dinner and they were enjoying after-dinner drinks and quiet conversation. I wanted to cringe and hide behind this beastly ensign, but I wouldn't give him the satisfaction. I stood tall and proud, as if I were a Luxury First Class passenger and not a grubby little stowaway. (If Grandmother Throckmorton could ever have got her mind past the stowaway part, she would have been very proud of me.)

The fellow marched me straight up to the captain.

"Look what I found, Captain, lurking about in one of the lifeboats. A stowaway."

The captain turned from his conversation and stared at the ensign before turning his attention to me. He had a face that looked like a leather map, all lines and valleys and ravines across his deeply tanned skin. His iron gray mustaches matched his hair and put me in mind of a walrus.

My arm was screaming in agony from its unnatural position, making my eyes water. I was keeping my eyes open as wide as possible so it wouldn't look like I was crying, but I wasn't sure how much longer I could keep it up.

"May I please have my arm back, now, sir? I'm really not going to run away. I give you my word."

"The word of a thieving stowaway!" the ensign said. "And how much would that be worth? About the same as you paid for your ticket, I would imagine."

"May I have permission to speak, sir?" I addressed the captain directly, and the formality took him by surprise.

He blinked. "Yes."

"First of all, I have paid for my ticket. I put the funds in an envelope and if you send someone back to the lifeboat, you will see that it is all there." (My life savings, as it were.)

One of the captain's eyebrows quirked up. "Indeed." He nodded once at the ensign, who released my arm and took off in search of the envelope.

"Why didn't you just pay for your ticket first, like most passengers?" the captain asked.

That's when I heard the familiar bellow "Theodosia Elizabeth Throckmorton!" This was quickly followed by a muttered "Bloody hell."

Bother. I wrinkled my nose. "Well, that's why, sir," I said, nodding my head at my parents, who were hurrying over to

us. "My parents didn't want me to come, but I had to. Really."

Mother reached me first. She clamped her hands on my shoulders. "Theodosia darling, are you all right?" She knelt down so she could see my face.

"Yes, Mother. I'm perfectly fine. Just a bit dirty, is all. And hungry," I added, just in case they hadn't cleared all the dinner dishes away. I risked a glance up at Father, who was glaring down at me.

"Really, Theodosia, you have gone too far this time." He turned to Mother. "I warned you something was not right when we found those things of hers in your trunk."

For being such an absent-minded sort, Father can certainly be perceptive when he wants to be.

He began talking to the captain, and Mother started fussing over me. Quite frankly, I was very happy to be fussed over. I hadn't realized until that moment how exhausted I was. Between sleeping in a lifeboat, the slimmest of rations for the past few days, and living with the constant worry of being found out, I was feeling rather wet-raggish.

Just as Mother started talking about getting me some food, the ensign showed up again, interrupting that precious thought. "Here's the envelope, sir." He tossed a smug look my way. "But there's not nearly enough in there for a full passage."

The captain's mustaches twitched as he took the envelope and opened it. "You forget, she's only to pay a child's portion." He glanced down at the money, then at me. "Well, Miss Throckmorton, it appears you are not a stowaway after all. At least not from us." He looked shrewdly at my parents. "I think I'll leave the three of you to sort this out." He headed off to his other guests after, much to my surprise, winking at me.

"Come along, dear," Mum said. "Let's go get you something to eat and some warm dry clothes."

"And a bath," I added.

Mum smiled. "And a bath."

"Oh, really, Henrietta," Father interrupted. "Don't coddle her. She's just stowed away for heaven's sake!" He turned to me. "What I want to know is what is so bloody important that you thought you had to stow away on this trip?"

His furious glare drove all the good excuses right out of my head. "I really wanted to see Egypt? And I thought you could use my help diverting the British Museum's attention while you went after the Was scepter?"

Thankfully, Mum shushed Father at that point and kept him from interrogating me any further. I was soon bundled away, warm and snug in their cabin, sipping hot chocolate and telling Mother of my exploits. (Father still wasn't speaking to me.) Soon, however, I was yawning into my

cup, so Mum took it away and tucked me in for the night.

Just as we were all drifting off to sleep, Father sat bolt upright in bed. "Bloody hell, Theodosia! Do you know how dangerous that was?"

I winced. "Sorry, Father," I said in a small voice.

He harrumphed, then lay back down. I decided that now was probably not a good time to ask what a pink elephant was.

A WELCOMING GIFT

A FEW MORNINGS LATER, I stood on the deck of the *Rosetta Maru* as we approached Alexandria. The city rose up in the distance, its towers and turrets and flags outlined against the sharp brilliant blue of the sky.

Oh, the sun! I cannot tell you how marvelous it was to have it shine in my face and feel its warmth against my shoulders. It had been absolutely ages since I'd seen a single ray of sunshine.

I did finally manage to point my face away from the sun long enough to look out over the deep blue water of Alexandria Harbor. Alexandria. The name alone conjured up feelings of mystery and the ancients.

This was the land of Antony and Cleopatra. Where the Lighthouse of Pharos had stood for hundreds of years, one of the Seven Wonders of the Ancient World. I couldn't help but think of the lovely ancient library at Alexandria that had burned to the ground centuries ago. Oh how I wish it still stood. I bet they had loads of fascinating scrolls and texts on ancient Egyptian magic and curses.

The *Rosetta Maru* nosed her way through the harbor, which was full of more ships than I could even imagine. And the docks—what a huge disappointment. I was expecting something foreign and lovely. Instead they looked exactly like the docks back home. Only, the faces were somewhat darker. And the noise! The jumble of foreign sounds beat upon my ears like an exotic drum.

We were met by one of Mother's contacts, a dragoman, she called him. I must say, it was a comfort to have someone to guide us through the turmoil and confusion.

Our guide herded us up into a carriage, and bustled away just as quickly as you please to the station where we could catch the train to Cairo. It was a hair-raising journey. Alexandria's narrow streets were filled with small, crowded shops and unfortunate beggars everywhere. In some small odd way, it reminded me of the Seven Dials back home. Their mournful pleading for backsheesh was heart-wrenching.

I was relieved when our carriage turned into the large

railway station. Our dragoman once again herded us (I suspect he is a shepherd during the off-season), this time toward our train. With luck, we would be in Cairo by dinnertime.

As we pulled out of the station, I vowed to return to Alexandria some day when I had time to see the sights. But today, I let myself be rushed along. After all, I had a mission to accomplish.

It was a pummeling train ride, as if the tracks had been laid down directly over the sand with no railway ties to anchor them. When I mentioned this to Father, he said, "Well, you wanted to experience the romance of travel, so don't complain now that you have." Funny, I never thought romance would be quite so dusty or jostley.

We arrived at a hotel called Shepheard's, which was very grand. It rose four stories high and took up nearly the whole block. Enormous potted palm trees lined the front terrace. Men in turbans lounged on the front steps. A little brown monkey clung to one of the men's shoulder. The concierge (I don't know the Egyptian word for him) greeted Mother warmly and looked at Father rather dubiously. Whether it was because Father was being so narky (I think his leg was paining him) or for some other reason, I couldn't be sure.

We were all quite tired by then, and only had a bit of time to dress for dinner. Father managed to hang on to his temper long enough for one of the porters to show us to our lodgings. Two men struggled behind with the bulk of the baggage.

As soon as the porter unlocked the door, I rushed in and headed straight for the window. A thrill of excitement ran down my spine. How exciting to be in Cairo at last!

The window looked out over a small garden with a little pond and more tall palm trees bowing their heads gracefully in the purple twilight. One or two stars began to show in the sky. I breathed in deeply and caught the fragrance of dust, dates, and sand, glad to have found a bit of romance and atmosphere at last. As the men hauled the luggage into the room, I heard a faint, dry scratching noise. I tilted my head to listen more carefully, but the men were making too much noise. I frowned at them, but they were busy trying to get the trunks to the ground without breaking them or their backs.

Father came to join me at the window. I looked up at him and smiled. He smiled back and I was struck by the mixture of excitement and longing in his expression. Then the scritching sound started up again, ruining the mood.

He sighed deeply. "Must you make that noise, Theodosia?"

"But it's not me, Father. I noticed it too."

We both stood very still and listened for a moment, then an apologetic look passed over his face. "Well, it's probably nothing. Why don't you go find something to change into for dinn—"

A small dark shape emerged from under the curtain, and I shoved Father back from the window.

"I say," he began.

My eyes were nearly popping out of my head as I pointed to the carpet, right next to where he'd been standing. A large scorpion was scuttling across the floor. I took two giant steps back, then stretched my arm out and gently lifted the curtain away from the wall. A whole nest of scorpions was skulking under the curtains. *That's* what had made the horrid scritching sound.

Father reached out and yanked me away from the wall and began yelling at the porters for putting us in a room with a nest of scorpions. This sent them into a panic as they had no idea their perfectly good room had pests, especially poisonous ones.

Pandemonium ensued. The porters bowed and begged a thousand apologies. The concierge himself rushed up to the room and spent the next half-hour assuring us that nothing like this had ever happened before in their illustrious hotel, and they begged a thousand more pardons.

As they carried on, I used the opportunity to make a quick examination of the room (staying well away from the scorpions, who were in fact not moving very much). I glanced over at the dresser and saw a small figure sitting on it. I snatched it off the dresser just as Father bellowed at me to come out of there.

When I stepped into the hallway, I looked down and slowly opened my hand. In my palm lay a small, thumb-size carving of Selket, the scorpion goddess. These scorpions hadn't been a random nest, but *called* to our room by someone who knew of such things.

Who would have done this? And why?

The only explanation I could come up with was that it must have something to do with the Heart of Egypt. But only Wigmere and Stokes knew that it was here, so that didn't really make any sense. Unless von Braggenschnott and his lot had somehow figured it out, or guessed. But how?

Was it possible that von Braggenschnott discovered the Heart of Egypt was missing before he boarded his ship that day? Could he have guessed that Will pinched it when he bumped into him? Then stayed in London and not returned to Germany with the others?

But that still didn't explain how he would have known it was here in Cairo. Unless he was just following Mum's

movements, assuming she had got it back somehow. Or unless Mum—no! I would not let myself even voice the thought. Perhaps it was part of Amenemhab's original curse. Either way, what did that do to my chances?

We finally got everything settled and moved to a new room. My parents spent quite a long time checking under the beds, behind the curtains, anywhere and everywhere a small scorpion might hide. But I didn't join in. I knew they would find nothing.

Our enemies hadn't known we'd be in this room. I was certain we'd be safe. At least for the night.

My head ached and my stomach was a gnawing pit of emptiness by the time we made it down to dinner. We didn't have time to dress, which was quite mortifying as all the other diners looked us over the minute we stepped into the dining room. Mum assured me that this happened often, as travelers arrived at the hotel at all hours and not always with their dinner clothes to hand. Still, I would have liked to have made a more grand appearance for my first night in Egypt.

THE STREET BAZAAR

EARLY THE NEXT MORNING, my parents were up and off to the Antiquities Services or some such in order to speak to the proper officials about gaining access to Mum's dig.

Luckily, Mum left her dragoman, Nabir, with me. They expected us to stay around the hotel, explore the gardens, that sort of thing—but of course, I had other plans. Tomorrow we were leaving for Thebes, which meant I had exactly one day to see all of Cairo. I wasn't going to waste it in a silly hotel. Not with mosques and palaces and bazaars and marketplaces and all sorts of things to experience.

It took a bit of doing to get Nabir to agree to any of it.

He just kept shaking his head and pretending like he didn't understand me. Eventually I gave up trying to reason with him, and slammed a loathsome straw hat on my head so I wouldn't get burned to a crisp in the hot Egyptian sun. Then I marched toward the door.

What could the poor man do but follow? Once he realized I was going with or without him, he began muttering something about "into the hands of Allah" and shaking his head.

I stepped outside into the bright yellow light of the morning, surprised at how different the air in Cairo *feels*. It's not just hotter or brighter or drier, but also older somehow. The ancientness of the city pressed against my skin, drawing me into its age-old mysteries, begging me to explore its secrets.

Once Nabir had finished praying to Allah for assistance, he became much more helpful and steered me to the bazaar. I was dying to see all the Turkish carpets and fancy Eastern goods. Besides, I needed something to get my poor mind off worrying over who had set the scorpion trap. I wasn't terribly anxious to wait around the hotel until they happened to show up again. Who knew what they'd try next time? Cobras? Asps? I had a feeling that scorpions were only the beginning.

The streets of Cairo were bustling with activity. Dark-skinned men were everywhere, some in funny little red felt

hats and others cloaked in layers and layers of white cloth. Donkeys and camels shared the streets with carriages driven by half-naked natives. Swarms of people filled the narrow lanes, speaking more languages than you could imagine. It was almost as if the Tower of Babel had come to life! I was very glad to have Nabir at my elbow.

As the jumble of other languages floated by, I vowed to keep an ear out for German. I was betting it was the Germans who had set the trap last night, although I hadn't the foggiest notion of how they would have learned I was in Cairo.

I followed Nabir as he led me through the maze of streets. High, close buildings loomed on either side and most of the windows were covered with a wooden trellis kind of thing. The skyline was pierced by scores of minarets that topped the many mosques peppering the city. I sighed in contentment. It all felt very foreign and adventurous. There were veiled women carrying jars on their heads and a shopkeeper working out of a doorway. I tried not to stare at the beggars running alongside the carriages pleading for baksheesh or sleeping on the nearby steps.

I had expected the dirt streets to be dusty, but they weren't. They were muddy. Nabir explained that the streets were watered to keep the dust down. I couldn't help but wonder why they felt dust was worse than mud. Personally, I think I would have preferred the dust.

When we finally reached the bazaar district, I gaped in amazement. The shops were tiny, and so crowded together they looked like cupboards, or maybe closets. There were pipe bowls and brass urns, saddles, and colorful Moroccan slippers hanging from poles. I was quite taken with an embroidered red pair with cheerful turned-up toes and wished I hadn't spent all my money on the passage on the *Rosetta Maru*. The old shopkeeper saw me eyeing the slippers and gave me a toothless smile. He took one of them off the pole, then thrust it at me, saying something I couldn't understand.

"He says little miss should try it on," Nabir translated. "These finest of slippers will suit your bright-as-the-sun self."

I smiled at the shopkeeper. I did rather fancy myself a turned-up-at-the-toes sort of person, and I was pleased he'd noticed. But I had to shake my head. "I've no money, Nabir," I explained. "But tell him his slippers are as beautiful as, as . . ." I struggled for an appropriately grand compliment. "A thousand lotus blossoms."

Instead of frowning and shooing me away like the shopkeepers in London would have, the kind man just gave me another grin and put the shoe back on the pole. He folded his hands inside his billowing black sleeves, content to let me browse.

Next we passed sweetmeats, then tobacco, then gold and silver trinkets as well as every color of silk imaginable, wrapped in brilliant bolts or hanging in colorful swags.

As we turned the next corner we had to step back sharply in order to avoid being run down by a large lady dressed in violet silk riding a round little donkey. Her dark eyes studied me above her veil, and I nodded my head in greeting.

When she had passed in a jingle of gold bracelets and silver bells, we continued down the street. There seemed to be nothing but carpets everywhere you looked. There were stacks and stacks of them piled higher than my shoulders, some hanging from the walls like curtains, others displayed on tables. And the colors! Every shade imaginable could be found in that street. The shopkeepers sat cross-legged amid their wares, talking among themselves and keeping an eye out for customers.

We turned on to the next street and Nabir grabbed my elbow, trying to get me to hurry past it. I stopped walking and peered down the narrow street to the jumble of stalls. "What's down here, Nabir?"

"No good. Missy not go down there," Nabir said firmly.

"But why?" I looked at him and stuck my chin out. If there was something interesting down there, I wanted to see it.

Nabir stepped forward and lowered his voice. "Artifacts for sale. Black market. Missy mother avoid them. Missy should, too."

A real live black market—but of course I had to explore! I reached out and patted his arm. "It will be just fine,

Nabir. You'll see." I headed down the street, knowing Mum's dragoman would have no choice but to follow. He did, cursing the whole time in very irate Arabic.

The street was crowded, like all the rest, but there were many more Europeans here. Tourists, most likely, all determined to come away from Egypt with some mysterious artifact as a souvenir.

I moved through this street much more slowly than the others. For one thing, with this many Europeans about, I wanted to keep an ear out for Germans. You would think they wouldn't look much different from the British, but they did. I first noticed it back in the Seven Dials when I'd seen them following Stokes. Their posture was a little more rigid through the shoulders, as if they were marching in a military parade.

I took my time in each shop, examining the bits of pottery and stele fragments. They had an unending supply of these, each one claimed to be a long-lost piece of great value. There was also an enormous number of amulets. My hands positively itched to get ahold of them. There was a fetching little statue of Hathor, and quite a few of Isis, who was very popular. I recognized Osiris and Annubis, Thoth and Bastet. One man was selling an old mummified finger, claiming it had belonged to Ramses III.

As I examined the finger, the shopkeeper motioned to a

large round Frenchman standing next to me. The Frenchman stepped closer and the shopkeeper whispered something in his ear. My French is appalling, as I've ignored it
in favor of hieroglyphics, but I was fairly certain he said
something about mummies. Of course! I'd heard that mummies were available on the black market. I inched closer to
see if I could overhear.

The shopkeeper motioned the customer back behind a
draped doorway. I hesitated, dying to follow. Of course, I've
seen plenty of mummies, but never (to my knowledge) a
black-market one.

Just as I went to step inside, I felt a tug on my sash.
"Missy not go back," Nabir said. "Not safe."

"Whatever do you mean?" I asked.

He wouldn't explain further, but he also wouldn't let me
take a step closer, herding me down to the next shop, which
boasted piles and piles of multicolored scarabs. After looking at those for a bit, we headed to the next stall, passing a
stone archway as we went. I gave a start when I saw a
mummy propped up in the doorway, right out in the open.

I leaned in for a closer look. It was hard to tell how old
she was—and it was a she. I could tell that much by the veil
that covered the lower half of her face.

Faster than a striking cobra, her long bony hand reached
out and grabbed my wrist, drawing me closer. I bit back a

scream and tried to pull away, but she was surprisingly strong for a mummy, er, old woman.

Her bright black eyes studied me intently as she said something I couldn't understand. My hand still clenched in hers, I looked over my shoulder at Nabir. "What's she saying?"

"She offering to tell missy fortune," he explained.

"Ask her if she'll let go of my hand first."

Nabir translated this and the old woman cackled and let go of my hand. The motion sent the silver bracelets on her arm to jangling.

"Very well. I wouldn't mind having my fortune told, but tell her I have no money to pay her," I asked Nabir.

Again he translated, and she replied with something that made him frown.

"What?" I asked. "What?"

"She say she will tell missy fortune for free because missy marked by the gods."

Her words gave me a sharp thrill, but I couldn't tell if it was fear or excitement.

The fortuneteller shook a small black bag, then dumped the contents out onto the dirt. There were shells and bits of wood and what looked like bones.

She rocked back and forth murmuring as she studied the objects in front of her. She poked at a bone, watched it

closely as it rolled over, then her eyes glazed and a rapid string of words began flowing out of her mouth in heavily accented English.

"Chaos swirls around you. It dogs your heels like a jackal. But the thumbprint of Isis lays glowing on your forehead. Isis will protect you. Look to the ancients for help. They smile down upon you." Her eyes widened, then she looked up at Nabir. "They are coming," she whispered.

At her words, a sliver of icy fear wormed its way into my heart. My senses had been heightened all morning, but I'd assumed it was because I was in the land of antiquity itself. And while I may have occasionally felt I was being watched, whenever I checked, there was no one there. I had thought it was the merchants being as curious about me as I was about them.

I muttered my thanks and backed away from the door. I looked down the street, half afraid I'd see giant serpents undulating toward me.

Instead, there were three men in billowing black robes, with turbans and scarves wrapped around the lower half of their faces, headed our way. They didn't stop to look at any of the shops, but kept moving relentlessly forward. Something else wasn't quite right.

It was the way they walked. It wasn't fluid and graceful like the other natives I'd seen, but stiff rather.

Then I noticed their coloring.

They were fair-skinned.

"Nabir . . ." I said, beginning to inch away. "She's not joking." I turned on my heel and broke into a run, tearing down the street, weaving my way between the stalls and the milling people. Nabir was close behind.

I dodged a heavily laden donkey and just missed tripping over a rolled-up carpet sticking out of a stall. I sorely missed Will. He would have known exactly what to do in this circumstance. "Nabir!" I called out. "Where can we go that is safe?"

"A mosque!" he shouted back.

A vivid picture of Stokes trying to claim sanctuary at St. Paul's Church came to me. These people didn't believe in sanctuary. "Something else!" I called back.

I turned onto another street and saw a tramway station. There was a whole mob of people waiting to board. "Over here!"

I ran full tilt into the crowd, annoying several people, but I didn't slow down until I was smack in the middle of them, hopefully hidden from my pursuers. The crowd pressed forward and I realized that this was a line to get on the electric tram. I looked frantically for Nabir and found him skirting the edge of the crowd. My pursuers reached the tram station and looked around, puzzled. One of them barked out an order and they separated, spreading out.

Just then, I was swept along by the crowd and found

myself stepping onto the tram. Again, I tried to keep myself to the middle of the pack and breathed a huge sigh of relief when I saw Nabir climb on board.

I was on pins and needles waiting for the tram to start and take me away from danger. I especially wanted to get away before they worked out where I was. Finally, with a lurch, the tram got under way. I was safe. They hadn't seen me.

An Unexpected Jaunt

I QUICKLY DISCOVERED that the tram was taking us to Giza, to the Great Pyramids there. Which was most excellent because I had been hoping to see them while I was in Cairo. Safe for the moment, I gave myself over to the wonder of being in Egypt and watched the three triangles on the horizon grow bigger and bigger the closer we got.

When Nabir and I got off the tram, I found myself almost reluctant to go forward. Standing before such ancient, timeless creations was humbling. Mesmerized, I walked until I reached the edge of the desert. I climbed up a steady, sandy slope, then gaped as the majestic pyramid towered over me.

Like a set of giant stairs, the rich reddish-gold stone rose

up from the base, rugged and uneven. I had to touch it, to lay my hand on the same stone that the ancient Egyptians had worked with their own hands. The rough surface was warm to the touch, and seemed almost alive, almost as if it were breathing. But of course it wasn't. Even so, the palm of my hand tingled lightly, even after I drew it back.

I wanted to climb to the top. To sit perched on the pinnacle and look down over all of Egypt. It seemed sacrilegious somehow, but the other tourists were doing it. Nabir said he would wait for me at the foot of the pyramid, so I began climbing to the top, a long, exhausting process, I must say. Some of those stones were nearly as tall as I was!

Perched on the top of the pyramid, I had the oddest sense of not being alone. As if there were someone there with me. Someone with a kingly presence who looked out at his vast domain as he had for thousands of years. As if the great pharaoh Cheops himself was standing next to me, watching over his land with love and pride. In that moment, I couldn't help but wonder if the archaeologists had got it all wrong. Perhaps Cheops hadn't built the pyramid as a tomb, but so his *ka* would have a place near the heavens to watch over his land.

Except I'm sure he never imagined that he'd be looking down at a motorcar driving across the sand, leaving a cloud of dust in its wake. Really, I hadn't even realized they *had* motorcars in Egypt . . .

A sense of danger flickered inside me. I squinted, trying to see how many people were in the car, but it was too far away to tell. I suddenly felt exposed and vulnerable and hurried down off the top of the pyramid, where I could be easily seen.

At the lower gallery, there were two corridors. One led up and the other down. All the other tourists headed up, so I chose the downward passage. True, it was roped off, but I was sure that was only because the passage was so low it would be hard for an adult to get down there. As it was, I had to duck my head.

It was a bit of a squash, and very, very steep. I was half-tempted to slide down, but that seemed highly disrespectful, so I didn't, even though I knew that Cheops wasn't buried here, but in the upper chamber. (The fickle pharaoh had changed his mind three times while building the pyramid. Can you imagine? Must have driven those poor workers batty.)

The passageway finally opened up into a large, unfinished chamber hewn out of the red stone. It was hard not to think of the tons and tons of stone perched over one's head, pressing down. It was a little difficult to breathe down here as well, as if not quite enough air was making it into the chamber.

I found a charming little crevice in the rock wall and settled myself into it. It was so easy to close my eyes and almost see the workers from four thousand years ago hacking

away at the walls, clearing the chamber with their simple tools. If I tried very hard, I could almost hear the scrape of those tools on the rock walls.

Wait a minute. I opened my eyes. I could *still* hear the sound of scraping. It was coming from the passageway. But who else would venture down a roped-off corridor? I had just talked myself into believing it was another overcurious tourist like myself when I heard the first footstep reach the chamber. Someone whispered.

In German.

I glanced around, looking for options.

There weren't any.

The chamber was a dead end with no good hiding places.

Another voice whispered back. And that second voice sounded familiar! I'd heard it before, but *where?*

I sensed the bodies coming farther into the chamber. I pulled back against the wall as far as possible and looked downward so as not to call attention to myself.

Three shadowy figures passed by. The men from the bazaar crept forward, heading toward a small cavelike enclosure at the back of the chamber.

I readied myself. As soon as they were as far back into the chamber as possible, I would make my move. Oh, how I wished I had one of Henry's diversions!

Slowly, trying to make no noise, I stood up. There was a slight rustle from my skirt. I froze.

"Was war das?" a voice asked in German.

When they heard no further noises, they continued on to the back. When they reached the cave, one man knelt down on the ground while the other two peered over his shoulder.

Now.

Stepping as lightly as I could, I made a mad dash for the passageway.

"Dort ist sie! Ihr nach!"

My heart hiccupped in terror and I forced my feet to go faster. I reached the passageway and tucked my head low and began running up the steep slope. My pursuers would have to nearly double over to make it through the passageway. That should slow them down enough to give me a chance.

My legs soon ached from the steepness of the climb, my calves burning and twitching in annoyance. I was getting a crick in my neck from keeping my head tucked low.

I could hear them behind me, the clatter of their pursuit echoing loudly in the passageway. They were breathing hard, and I could almost feel their hot breath on my neck.

At last. Light ahead. Almost there. I risked a glance backward, pleased at the distance between us.

Finally, I burst out of the shaft at a dead run, startling a half dozen tourists who'd been milling about the lower gallery. I clamped my hand on my hat and flew down the pyramid steps, startling Nabir.

"Come *on*," I called. "They've found us."

Nabir didn't need to be told twice. We both headed for the tram station at a gallop.

I heard a shout as my pursuers cleared the pyramid and spotted us.

We were almost at the tram station now. In dismay, I saw one of the electric trams just beginning to pull away, heading back to Cairo. There wouldn't be another one for ages. Which meant we'd be sitting ducks.

"We've got to get on that tram," I called to Nabir. He nodded and pulled ahead of me. Luckily, electric trams aren't all that fast, especially when they're just getting started. Nabir leaped onto the tram, upsetting quite a lot of people. He turned back and held his hand out to me. I took it and clambered up, apologizing profusely to everyone I saw.

As we pulled away, I got a chance to see my pursuers. I immediately recognized von Braggenschnott. Even if I hadn't seen his picture in the paper, I would have recognized those cold, cruel eyes from St. Paul's churchyard. The second man's face was still covered by his scarf, but I could clearly see the face of the third man. High pale cheekbones, long thin nose slightly crooked at the end, and a conspicuous lack of chin. It was Tetley! From the British Museum!

A Race to Thebes

MOTHER AND FATHER NEVER FOUND OUT about the close call at the pyramid. Nabir is almost as good at keeping secrets as I am.

We were up at the crack of dawn the next day so we could hustle off to catch another beastly train. Imagine spending twenty hours in a hot, dusty oven being bounced like a rubber ball and you'll get the idea.

We arrived in Thebes in the dead of night. Even so, we were immediately greeted by a local official. At first I thought this was a sign of respect for my parents' position. Then, as

my parents became distressed at the official's rapid Arabic, I realized it was something else altogether.

Father could stand it no longer. "Confound it!" he shouted. "When did this happen?"

Following my father's lead, the official switched to English. "Two days ago, most kind sir."

I snuck up close, trying to hear what was being said.

Father ran his hands through his hair. "It's that blasted Snowthorpe, I know it."

Mum put her hand out to try to calm him. "Alistair, I truly doubt he would have gone so far as to burn our lodgings down around our ears. It could have been an accident. Fires are not unheard of in this part of the country, you know."

But of course, Father had the right of it. Mostly. There was no doubt in my mind that it hadn't been an accident. But it was von Braggenschnott and that traitor Tetley, not the British Museum.

I had *so* hoped I'd lost them at the Great Pyramid. Although really, now that I thought about it, that was rather stupid of me. If they knew where the Heart of Egypt had come from, and they did, they would know where we were headed.

There were quite a lot of explanations given (from the officials), and quite a lot of shouting (from Father), and quite a lot of soothing (by Mother). Finally, everyone calmed

down and we were hustled off to a bungalow that had been hastily arranged for us. We would see about finding new lodgings in the morning.

No sooner had the porters set down our trunks than there was another pounding on our door. Honestly! Does no one ever sleep around here?

"What is it now?" I heard Father ask as Nabir opened the door.

"A telegram for most kind sir," Nabir informed him.

A telegram . . . That didn't bode well.

The man from the telegraph office handed Father a thin envelope. He bowed as Father thanked him, then waited while he opened it.

Mum looked over Father's shoulder and read along with him. She clutched her hand to her throat and let out a gasp. "Oh, no! Alistair!" There was true despair in her voice and the back of my neck prickled uneasily.

Father put his arm around Mum's shoulders. "Don't worry, Henrietta. He's a strong boy. He'll pull through."

Henry! Something had happened to Henry!

"We must get back to him at once," Mother said. "I would never forgive myself if . . ." her voice faltered. "If something happened to him while we were this far away. You know how nasty the influenza has been. I can't bear the thought—"

Her words broke off suddenly as she buried herself in Father's shoulder.

Henry had caught the influenza! I wrapped my arms around myself and hugged tight. Influenza was uncomfortably close to the plague. Try as hard as I might, I couldn't block out Amenemhab's words.

May your retribution upon these enemies of Thutmose be swift and terrible, may Sehkmet devour their hearts, and Ammit feast on their heads. May all the lands run red with their blood until they return the Heart of Egypt to its rightful resting place, and lay it back at your feet, so that Thutmose's glory will be whole once more.

And Mum wanted to go home immediately! Which would be the worst possible thing because I hadn't put the Heart of Egypt *back* yet. If Mum was this distraught at being far away from Henry when he was ill, just think how she'd feel if she found out she was responsible for his illness in the first place.

I'd just run out of time. I had to get the Heart of Egypt back to the tomb as soon as possible.

The Valley
of the Kings

I WAS TRUNDLED OFF TO BED while Mum and Dad stayed up late into the night, trying to make arrangements and inquiries about Henry's health.

They were still sleeping when I snuck out of my room just as dawn broke. I had an appointment with the tomb of Thutmose III.

The hardest part was convincing Nabir that he needed to take me to the Valley of the Kings alone. Luckily, he had sufficient experience with just how single-minded I could be. The argument didn't last long and we soon set off.

The sun quickly turned viciously hot. It felt like my frock

was on fire, and the pack I carried grew terribly heavy. For the first time in my life I was truly grateful for a hat. Mum's old pith helmet kept my brain from frying like a breakfast egg.

We wound our way through a perplexing maze of canyons until at last Nabir led me to a narrow gorge at the very bottom of the Valley of the Kings. I cannot begin to tell you the thrill of finally seeing the necropolis up close, not to mention the tombs of the pharaohs. I have heard about them all my life, dealt daily with their historic finds, and spent hours trying to cipher out their meaning. And now, to finally experience one in its entirety, as it was originally built and conceived, not in crumbled bits and pieces . . . it was as if I stood at the pearly gates of heaven itself.

The tomb of Thutmose III was the very last in the valley. There was a single guard on duty. He recognized Nabir, and they exchanged a few words in Egyptian, then he let us pass. Nabir led me to the farthest corner, then stopped at a small cave. He darted inside, then reappeared a moment later carrying a long ladder.

This did not look promising.

He carried the ladder to a fold in the rocky wall. When I looked up, I could see a small opening in the face of the mountain, some ten or fifteen meters up.

Nabir set the ladder at the base of the wall and leaned it

against the mountainside. It was just long enough. Barely. It was obviously meant to bridge a grownup-size gap between the ladder and the opening. Not an eleven-year-old-size one. I sighed.

Nabir motioned me over to the ladder.

"Give me an hour or two," I told him. "I'll be ready to leave then."

Nabir nodded. "Two hours. Nabir wait here."

"Good." I took a steadying breath, placed one foot on the bottom rung of the ladder, and began to climb.

Even with Nabir holding on to the thing, it was a rickety, wobbly climb, and I kept reminding myself to not look down.

Halfway up the ladder I realized Nabir would have a lovely view of my knickers. Blushing furiously at the thought, I glanced down, relieved to find his eyes politely averted.

A good man, our Nabir.

I finally reached the rung that was second from the top, then hesitated. Once I stepped up onto that top rung, there would be nothing to hang on to except the mountain itself.

I eyed the distance from the top rung to the small ledge above. I thought I could reach it. Hopefully.

Taking another steadying breath, I placed a foot on the top rung. My stomach gave a sickening lurch as the whole

ladder gave a nasty wobble and my fingers bit painfully into the rocky scree. I reached up until I grasped the outcropping ledge. Relief poured through me, until I remembered the scorpions in our room at Shepheard's. This hot dry wasteland was much more to their liking.

Cobras and asps, too.

It takes a surprising amount of courage to place one's hand into an unseen area when your mind is thinking about vermin.

Gritting my teeth, I brought my other arm up so that I could hoist myself onto the ledge. I pulled upward with my arms and felt the soles of my boots leave the security of the ladder. My feet scrabbled for purchase, trying to gain an additional boost up.

I strained and pulled, wishing mightily that I had stronger arm muscles. (I made a note to myself to take up boxing when I returned to London, or possibly arm wrestling with Henry.)

With a long, sharp scrape across my midsection, I finally managed to haul myself up onto the ledge. I lay on my stomach, my feet still hanging out into thin air, panting and letting my weak, trembling arms recover.

"Is miss all right?" Nabir called up.

I quickly scooted away from the edge and turned around so he could see my face (instead of my knickers; I made an-

other note to myself: trousers would be nice). "Yes, Nabir. I'm fine. Thank you." I held up two fingers. "Two hours."

Nabir smiled, toddled over to a bit of shade, and made himself comfortable.

When I stood at the mouth of the cavern, a strange prickling sensation ran over me, and every hair on my body stood on end. The air was so thick with *ka* and *heka*, I was half afraid I would choke on it.

The daylight barely penetrated the darkness of the shaft, so I stopped long enough to pull a torch out of my pack and light it. There was an ancient, crumbling stairway leading downward, and I could only hope I wouldn't slip and break my neck.

Stepping onto the first stair, I tested it to see if it would hold my weight. When it didn't collapse, I held my pitiful light up to the walls and proceeded cautiously.

Figures in bas relief danced in the flickering light thrown off by my torch, but I couldn't make out what they were. I dragged my gaze away and pushed onward, promising myself that once I had returned the Heart of Egypt, I would study these more closely.

I reached the first corridor (where the walls were covered with more stunning carvings), which led to a second set of

crumbling stairs, also leading downward. At the end of the second stairs was a deep shaft. I stared into the yawning blackness at my feet. Why on earth was it here? Did it have some earthly purpose, such as diverting water in case of flooding? Or was there a ritual magic purpose, such as catching falling spirits, perhaps?

Luckily, Mother's workers had fashioned a plank bridge to cross the chasm. I went forward, placing each foot very carefully, horribly aware of the great darkness gaping beneath me.

Once safely across, I found myself in a larger chamber. I took another step, then tripped over a pile of something long and thin—bones, was my immediate thought. I cringed at the incredible racket they made, and the phrase "loud enough to wake the dead" came painfully to mind.

I swung the light around, relieved to discover it was only a pile of torches. Well done, Mum! Of course she would leave some means of lighting her way.

I quickly lit another torch and saw that Mother's team had rigged holders in the walls. I placed one of the lit torches in it, then lit enough to fill all the holders scattered around the chamber.

It's amazing what a little light can do for one's morale.

Most of the chamber walls were covered with carvings. The east wall was covered with hieroglyphs. It looked to be the complete text of *The Egyptian Book of the Dead*. The

next wall showed Thutmose III being taken by the hand by Anubis. In Anubis's other hand was . . . the Was scepter! Hesitant, I reached out with my hand and ran my finger over Anubis, marveling that nearly four thousand years ago, some ancient Egyptian worker had cut this image into the stone.

Enough! I scolded myself. I was never going to get the Heart of Egypt to its final resting place and restore the fate of Britain at this rate.

Resolute, I crossed over to the doorway that loomed darkly on the far wall. Holding the torch firmly in my hand and shoving back a sense of trepidation, I crossed the threshold.

A whispering noise rushed by me, as if a thousand ancient voices in long-forgotten tongues fluttered past my ears, invoking gods and curses and blessings. The thickness of the magic and power swarming around gave me goosebumps.

As I made my way down the stairs, the ancient magic was so powerful it felt like swimming against a current. The thousand voices rose slightly and moaned, whether in warning or resignation I couldn't be sure. I found myself whispering back, *Don't worry. I've come to return something that belongs to you.*

The whispering quieted a bit and the resistance in the air around me grew weaker. Fascinating!

I squared my shoulders and came off the last step into

an even larger chamber, gasping at the sheer force and weight of the magic in the room. It pressed down heavily on me, so much so that I feared my knees would buckle. How could Mum and her team bear this? It was like trying to breathe under water.

I ignored the sensation as best I could and held my torch up high. The burial chamber of Thutmose III glowed eerily around me. An enormous red sarcophagus sat on the other side of the chamber.

Wouldn't it be lovely if all I had to do was lay the Heart of Egypt in the sarcophagus and be on my merry way? But of course that wouldn't work. The first person to come in here after me would find it and the wretched curse would begin all over again.

I walked past an image of Osiris waiting patiently while Anubis weighed Thutmoses's heart—the Devourer sat with his wide, gaping crocodile jaws, hoping for a nice snack—and moved on to the eastern annex, the one that led toward Mum's most recent discovery: the Minister of War's tomb.

The air in this corridor was even worse. The magic that hung in the air was different; heavier, blacker, smelling slightly of sulfur. I ignored the feeling of a whole battalion of icy-footed beetles storming down my spine. Luckily there was a fresh supply of torches in this chamber, so I lit a few and set them in the holders on the walls.

I could see that Mum had barely touched the surface of Amenemhab's cache. Piles and piles of artifacts were scattered on the ground. Only the most rudimentary sorting had begun. At first glance, I saw nothing that looked remotely like the Was scepter. But there was loads of stuff to look through. It could take hours.

Hours I didn't have.

Hoping the paintings on the wall might tell me something about the Heart of Egypt and what I had to do to put it back, I turned my attention to them, then stepped back with a gasp.

These walls were covered with war scenes, grisly and terrifying. Thutmose III stood out, towering over his enemies, his feet crushing their heads, his spear piercing their breasts. Slain bodies lay at his feet, detached heads all in a nearby pile. The tomb artists had given themselves over to a garish job with the red paint. It spilled everywhere on the walls, as if the artisans had truly wanted to indicate the bloody nature of Thutmose's reign.

As I studied the carvings, I heard a shuffle of feet on the sandstone steps. I froze. "Nabir? Is that you?"

There was no answer. It was possible that the noise was just the tomb shifting and settling. But if that was the case, why were all the fine hairs at the back of my neck standing straight up?

I glanced wildly around the burial chamber, looking for a hiding place that wouldn't end up being my tomb.

Not the altar. The cupboard underneath it would hold me, but would most likely be the first place they looked. (Plus, that's usually where the Canopic jars were kept, and I really didn't want to hide next to Amenemhab's entrails. My nerves were skittish enough.)

I thrust the torch into one of the holders on the wall and hurried over to wedge myself into a small space between two large statues of Anubis. No sooner had I ducked out of sight than a footstep crunched on the gritty floor of the chamber itself.

Then I heard something that confirmed my worst fears.

"Come out, come out wherever you are, little girl," a singsongy voice called out in a thick German accent.

Von Braggenschnott! Or one of his henchmen.

Hearing that dreadful voice in such a twisted version of a nursery game made me want to stick my fingers in my ears and start humming. Instead, I grasped my amulet in my hand and tossed out as many prayers as I could think of to anyone who was listening.

What on earth was I going to do? I'm only an eleven-year-old girl, not a secret agent! Even if I am rather cleverer than most, I *do* still have some limitations. And I think I'd just run smack into one.

Unwelcome Company

I HEARD ANOTHER STEP COME INTO THE CHAMBER, then another. Three of them! How was I to get by *three* of them? And how did they get past Nabir?

A hideous thought struck me. Had they harmed Nabir? Guilt rose up in my throat and I almost retched. I had cajoled and pleaded with him to bring me here. If he was hurt, it would be my fault.

Von Braggenschnott started up his little song again. "Come out, come out wherever you are. You have something that doesn't belong to you and I want it back."

The footsteps echoed loudly in the silent chamber as the

others fanned out and began searching for me. There was a scrape of something heavy as they dragged things around, trying to peer into every nook and cranny.

I shrank back against the walls. As my moist palms pressed into the rough wall behind me, a piece of magic lore from *Ancient Egyptian Magical Thought and Procedures* by Cyril Profundicus popped into my head. Ancient Egyptians believed that dust scraped off the carvings in tombs had magical properties. If ever I needed an extra magical advantage, it was now.

Using my fingernails, I began scraping at the rough sandstone, trying to collect some dust.

I kept my attention on the searchers and ignored the jagged ripping of my nails against the wall. The sandstone was soft with age and it didn't take long before I had a small amount of dust in each of my hands. I carefully transferred all the dust into my right hand, then thrust it into my pocket and hoped the ancient Egyptians hadn't been pulling old Profundicus's leg.

Von Braggenschnott barked out an order in German and there was a low, rumbled reply.

Perhaps they were only guessing that I had the Heart of Egypt. There was no way they could be absolutely sure. Perhaps I could bluff my way out.

"There really is no point in hiding, fräulein," von Brag-

genschnott continued. "There are three of us and only one of you. You will not get away, and you only risk making us angry." His voice rose up harshly on the last word.

I glanced around furiously, looking for something other than dust to defend myself with. I stared at the altar, practically willing something to appear. But the only thing there was a collection of small wax and clay figures. I started to turn away, then remembered something from Nectanebus. Hoping against hope, I picked up one of the figures. Bits of hair stuck out of the wax along with a piece of ancient papyrus with writing on it. Yes—an execration figure! (The Egyptian version of voodoo dolls.) With luck, I could tap into their magic and use them to smite my enemies. Or at least slow them down.

Shadows loomed on the walls as the men drew closer. They were unnervingly quiet as they steadily worked their way to my spot.

I quickly began to carve new symbols into the wax with one of my jagged fingernails. I carved the symbol to invoke power, then another symbol for smiting my enemies. Then I paused. This part was tricky because I had to guess the men's names correctly or the magic would be useless. I was almost positive the one doing all the talking was von Braggenschnott, and nearly as sure one of the men was Tetley. But I needed to be certain.

"I am getting tired of these games," von Braggenschnott called out. "If you don't cooperate with us, I will have my men seal you up in a sarcophagus until you learn some manners."

I took a deep breath. "Ha! I spit on your threats," I called out. "I'm not afraid of a sarcophagus. Honestly, I've slept in those things before and there's nothing to them."

"Perhaps." Von Braggenschnott chuckled, a truly horrid sound. "But I'm guessing there wasn't a mummy in yours. And there is in the one I have in mind."

My heart began racing in my chest and my palms grew clammy. To be shut up in a sarcophagus with a mummy? My knees nearly gave out at the thought. "You're bluffing! Mother didn't find any mummies here!"

"Tcht! Surely you don't think this is the only excavation we pay attention to? No. We keep our eyes on all of them. However," he said, his voice quite menacing, "if you really make me angry, we shall pull your brains out through your nose like the ancients used to do. Only you shall be alive to witness it firsthand, yah? Won't that be an interesting thing for someone as curious as you?"

I gulped. There was a sound just off to my left. I looked up to see one of the men leaning over the Anubis statue, grinning at me. It *was* Tetley! Well, now I had one name I was sure of.

Playing for an extra moment or two, I duck-walked around one of the Anubis statues to the far side of the funerary chariot leaning up against the wall. As I carved Tetley's name into the wax figure, I began whispering the execration rites. Just as I finished the final hieroglyph, Tetley's ugly head reappeared, so close I could have reached out and tweaked his nose.

There was only one escape route open to me now. I would be out in plain sight, but at least I would have room to maneuver on either side and wouldn't be caught like a rat in a trap.

I shoved to my feet and made a mad dash to the back wall.

The tomb fell deathly silent as all three of them turned to watch me.

I stood with the tomb wall firm against my back, the exe-cration figure hidden along the side of my skirts, glaring at my pursuers. I recognized von Braggenschnott immedi-ately. And Tetley. And—I gasped. "You!"

"Yes, me," Nigel Bollingsworth said. "Who did you think, Theo?"

Finally, I found my voice. "I-I was sure Clive Fagenbush was the traitor!" A deep wave of relief swept over me. *At least it wasn't Mother.*

Nigel laughed. "Fagenbush. I knew he'd come in handy. No, I'm afraid he's not the traitor, merely a convenient diversion. Which is why I encouraged your father to hire him. He is so perfectly suspicious-looking that I knew all eyes would be turned to him if anything ever went wrong."

"But why are you working for the Germans?" I asked. "You're British!"

A slow, twisted smile drew across his face. "Haven't you worked it out yet in that clever head of yours, Theo? I'm not working for the Germans. I'm working for the Serpents of Chaos."

"The forces of chaos have risen once more," I whispered.

"Ach," von Braggenschnott interrupted. "So you know of our little group."

"I've heard of it. Once. From the man you tried to murder in the churchyard."

"Clumsy business, that. Normally we make no such mistakes."

"It seems to me you've made several over the last few weeks," I replied.

Von Braggenschnott shook his finger at me. "You are in no position to throw insults at us, fräulein. In fact, a little groveling might do you some good."

I stretched myself to my full height, lifted my chin in the air, and pulled off my best Grandmother Throckmorton look. "I will never grovel."

Von Braggenschnott narrowed his eyes and took a step forward. "You will regret your insolence."

Playing madly for more time, I asked, "Why are the Serpents of Chaos working for Germany? Surely Britain could pay you just as much."

Von Braggenschnott laughed, a wicked, grating sound that made me flinch. "But don't you see? We aren't working *for* Germany. We are letting Germany work for *us*. Right now it suits us to go along with Kaiser Wilhelm. His enormous ego and grand ideas for his country are perfect for our purposes."

I was afraid to ask the next question, but even more afraid to *not* ask it. "And what exactly are your purposes?"

That smile again. "Why, I thought you understood. Total chaos, fräulein. We want Germany at Great Britain's throat. We want Britain on the defensive, making stupid, hasty decisions she wouldn't normally make. Then Austria will step in to back up Germany. Then Serbia will feel threatened, and rightfully so. France, of course, will have to stand by its good friend, Britain, and then of course Russia will need to toss its hat onto the pile as well. Finally, Italy will have no choice but to join in. All of Europe will be barking and snapping at each other's necks like rabid jackals.

"While that is happening, we shall slip in, unobserved, and seize the tattered reins of world power."

"You're insane," I said, rather less firmly than I meant to.

"You're talking about an entire world at war with each other. Of bringing total—"

"Chaos. Exactly. And what better place to find the powers we need than in ancient Egypt, where chaos is merely a curse or two away? The plagues of Thutmose III and Amenemhab have already fallen upon Britain. She has begun to weaken. In days she will be forced to sign a treaty that will play perfectly into Germany's ambitions. And ours. Such a brilliant plan, don't you think? All that was required of us was that we let your mother do what she was going to do in the first place."

"Well, not exactly. You stole the Heart of Egypt from her so she couldn't return it."

He cocked his head to the side. "Ah, but would she have returned it, do you think?"

"Of course she would have! If she knew the whole story!"

He ignored me. "Egypt has been the seat of magical power since the beginning of time, but few people have had the courage to bend its powers to their will. Until us."

"So you learned Egyptian magic?" I scoffed. "That's not such a very grand thing. Lots of people know about that."

"Like you," von Braggenschnott said softly. He tilted his head and studied me. "Yes, your powers are very interesting. Which is the only reason you are still alive, fräulein. We are anxious to explore all that you know. And we will."

I fought down a shudder at the thought of von Braggen-schnott and his men trying to extract my magical knowledge from me. "There are others, you know. It's not just me."

"Bah!" Von Braggenschnott dismissed that threat. "That inept Brotherhood doesn't concern me. They are nothing! Weak and stupid men who are afraid to grasp the power right under their noses. Now, enough of this!" von Braggen-schnott called out. "Tetley. It is time to atone for your mistakes."

Tetley came out from behind the funerary chariot and headed straight for me, a very unpleasant smile on his face. He was clearly unhappy that I'd got him into so much trouble.

Out of options, I grasped the small wax figure in my hands. I could only hope I hadn't fudged the magic too badly.

I waited until Tetley had taken two more steps, then wrapped my hand around the wax figure's left leg. Chanting the ancient words of power, I broke the leg clean off the statue with a soft *snap*.

Tetley screamed and clutched his left leg as it folded beneath him. Not stopping to think, I snapped again, this time the right leg. Tetley howled once, then crumpled to the floor.

Bollingsworth started toward me, but von Braggen-schnott waved him back. "So you are not afraid to use the

ancient magic for your own ends, eh, fräulein? And you have bested Tetley once again." His voice cold and hard, he turned to the man lying unconscious on the floor. "That is twice he's failed me. There will not be a third time."

Von Braggenschnott turned his attention back to me and I fought the urge to cower. "Are you sure you're not one of us, fräulein?" he said in a soft, seductive voice. "In fact, I will make you a rare offer. Come work for us. Someone with your skills could go far."

"And abandon my parents? I think not," I said, indignant.

"If your parents really loved you, would they allow you to face the Serpents of Chaos alone? Would they allow someone of your immense natural talent to clatter around an old wreck of a museum, alone? Come with us. We will treat you as you deserve to be treated. We have great appreciation for talents such as yours. Your skills, your cleverness, see how you are not afraid to bend the magic to your will? At heart, you are one of us. We will teach you how to increase this power until no one can stand in your path."

One of them. I would belong to perhaps the most powerful group in the world. "I wouldn't have your organization on a platter," I spat.

"Ach, fräulein. Do not pass up this opportunity out of a misguided sense of loyalty. Those parents of yours don't truly appreciate you. If they did, would they ignore you so much? Pay you so little attention? Allow you to battle

ancient Egyptian magic on your own? They scarcely *see* you, let alone care for you."

"That's not true!" I shouted. "They're just busy! They have important things on their minds. Museums to run. Great discoveries to be made."

Von Braggenschnott continued. "You threaten them. They cannot admit your power, because then you'll be greater than they."

"That's not how my parents think!" I yelled, my hands clenched into fists at my side. My parents loved me. Surely they did. And yet . . . all of what von Braggenschnott said made sense in a horrible, twisted way.

I heard a noise off to my right. As I glanced in that direction, I reached into my right pocket and closed my hand around the dust just before Bollingsworth plowed into me, knocking us both into the wall, narrowly missing the burning torch. He grabbed me from behind, neatly pinning my arms under his.

Holding me so tight that it was difficult to breathe, he leaned down and whispered in my ear. "Your parents don't appreciate you like we would, Theo. Think of all we could accomplish together. Think of the power we can have!" He lowered his voice even further, so only I could hear. "We'll answer to no one." He glanced over at von Braggenschnott. "No one."

I fought against his hold. "You're as mad as he is."

"Don't play hard to get now." His voice was teasing. "I have it on good authority that you'd planned on marrying me when you grew up." He laughed softly.

A deep wave of mortification swept over me and a sense of betrayal sliced through me, so deep I thought I should die from it. Oh, how I writhed, my face boiling hot with shame and humiliation. To have one's innermost secrets discussed and thrown about as if they were a joke! To have Father have so little regard for my confidences, to shatter my trust. Perhaps von Braggenschnott and Bollingsworth were right. Perhaps . . .

No. Father may have betrayed me, but he would never betray his country. Nor would I. My desire to sink to the floor and weep with humiliation quickly turned into something else entirely.

Rage.

How dare they?

I twisted my neck around so I could see his face. How could I ever have thought him handsome? Was there ever a time when he had truly been kind? Now he was only a vile worm to be ground beneath my boot heel.

Quickly, without giving myself time to lose my nerve, I jerked my arms up hard against his and flung the sandstone dust at him.

The effect was immediate and heart-stopping.

He screamed in agony, releasing me immediately as he stumbled forward and grabbed for his face.

Still clinging to the wall, I took a few steps away from him in case he tried to grab me again.

But he was in too much pain. Much more so than mere sand in his eyes would cause.

Still screaming, he pulled his hands away from his face.

I gasped. The sandstone had eaten into his skin like burning acid. Small pits and lines were etched into his flesh. His eyes were screwed shut, and I could see the flecks of sandstone burning into the skin around his left eye.

He roared, then lunged blindly in my direction. I threw myself backward and slammed into the wall with such force, it gave way. Suddenly there was nothing behind me and I was falling through a black nothingness.

I tumbled end over teakettle down a long, narrow shaft. I let all my muscles go loose, like Uncle Andrew had shown me after my first nasty spill off his horse. When I finally hit bottom (on something quite hard, I might add) I landed like a rag doll. Only I'm sure no rag doll has ever felt as dizzy and disoriented as I did.

I heard surprised shouts from up above, which meant that, for a few minutes, I had the advantage. Hopefully, with Tetley crippled and Bollingsworth half blind, I would have only von Braggenschnott to deal with.

I leaped to my feet and grabbed the torch that had landed just a few feet away from me. I appeared to be in a narrow corridor that went on for about ten feet, then opened up into an old junky closet. But that wasn't right. Egyptian tombs didn't have closets. Certainly not junk ones. Which meant . . . which meant . . . I clutched my hand to my throat as I realized what it meant.

I had just discovered a previously unknown annex to Amenemhab's tomb! I'd just landed my first discovery!

Now, if only I could live to tell about it.

"Quickly," I heard von Braggenschnott call out. "Get Tetley out of sight in case someone comes. I'll follow the girl." I glanced around the dusty artifacts in the room. Nothing big enough to hide in. I checked to see if there was another doorway like the one I'd just fallen through. Nothing but pictures of people dying in hunger, and more dying of disease, while even more lay beheaded at Thutmose's feet.

I stopped when I reached Thutmose's picture. The image was even more terrifying than in the previous paintings. Thutmose's face was gaunt and his expression terrible. He looked like retribution personified. Heartless retribution, and there was a gaping hole in his chest, where his heart should have been, to prove it.

The noises coming from the corridor grew louder. It wouldn't take them long to get down here. I needed to come up with a plan.

Desperate now, I turned and hammered on the wall, hoping it too might crumble and offer me an escape route. But it was solid, and I tore a gash in my hand on the sharp edge of the hole in the wall carving. I stared at the sharply cut indentation as awareness shot through me.

It was the exact shape of the Heart of Egypt. Suddenly, I *knew*.

Before I had time to act on that knowledge, I heard a sound close behind me. I whirled around to find von Braggenschnott standing just ten feet away, a slightly insane frenzy in his pale blue eyes. I glanced to the left, then the right, but it was hopeless. There was no place to go.

Von Braggenschnott's cold blue eyes traveled down to my neck.

The Heart of Egypt had come out from under my collar sometime during my struggles. Von Braggenschnott stepped closer, then ever so slowly reached out to hook his finger under the chain.

Quickly, I yanked the chain from my neck, whirled round, and shoved the Heart of Egypt toward the wall.

Von Braggenschnott launched himself at my knees, knocking me to the ground. I struggled and kicked, trying

to get back up. My foot made sharp contact with something. I heard a crunching sound and prayed it was his nose. Von Braggenschnott yelled and loosened his grip. I scrambled to my feet, threw myself at the wall, and thrust the Heart of Egypt into the indentation.

"*Nooooo!*" von Braggenschnott screamed. He grabbed my arm and viciously wrenched me away from the wall. Ferocious pain ripped through my shoulder and my vision blurred. I tried to move my arm but nearly fainted at the fresh wave of pain.

I stumbled back, clutching my useless left arm. The pain was so great I could barely think. I watched von Braggenschnott, blood streaming down from his nose, scrabble at the Heart of Egypt, trying to pull it from the wall.

I held my breath and hoped that I had found the one place that would prevent anyone from ever taking it again.

As he struggled, I noticed a swirling in the air, a thickening of the magic around us. It joined together in little eddies, and the smell of frankincense rose up in the chamber. The Heart of Egypt began to glow, as if lit by a warm, inner light. It lasted only a second, then the wall turned back to the way it had been. Except now the Heart of Egypt sat where only a gaping hole had been. And von Braggenschnott's hand was stuck to it.

"What have you done, you stupid girl?" he yelled at me.

Saved Britain, I thought to myself. And Henry.

Then von Braggenschnott began to scream in earnest. "My hand! It's stuck! It's joined to the Heart. Help me get it free!"

I stared in horrified fascination at von Braggenschnott's hand, which did seem to be stuck smack in the middle of the wall.

Realizing that this was my chance for escape, I turned toward the corridor, screaming when I saw Bollingsworth leaning against the doorway, one side of his face nearly eaten away.

I groped around behind me, looking for something to defend myself with. My right hand closed around a long, thick truncheon. I picked it up, shocked at how heavy it was. Perfect. The heavier the wood, the more solid the hit when I bashed him.

"Don't let her get away!" von Braggenschnott called out, still stuck to the wall. Ignoring him, I held the stick loosely in my right hand and focused on Bollingsworth, gritting my teeth at the pain coming from my left shoulder.

Bollingsworth sneered. "You think you can stop me with that? I think not." A sharp, nasty-looking dagger appeared in his left hand. Then he held it out in front of him, ready to strike.

I hefted the stick and, with as much force as I could

muster, swung clumsily upward. It crashed into the knife, knocking it from Bollingsworth's hand. Not stopping to think lest I lose my nerve, on the return swing I brought the stick down on Bollingsworth's skull. There was a loud crack, like the sound of a breaking melon. My stomach heaved, and I was afraid I was going to be sick.

As Bollingsworth dropped like a ninepin, my vision went black and stars danced in my head as another wave of pain rolled through my shoulder. "You killed him, you wretched girl!" von Braggenschnott called out.

I struggled to the nearest wall, my knees no longer able to support me. "I did not!" Please let him not be dead. Please.

I leaned my head back against the cool stone, closed my eyes, and waited for my heart to quit galloping. Realizing I still held the stick in my hand, I flung it from me, as if *it* had attacked Bollingsworth, not I.

As it hit the ground, the wood shattered, falling off in large chunks and bits. I looked down and saw the glitter of gold shining through.

Using the toe of my boot, I kicked the rest of the wood casing off. Within minutes I had uncovered a long staff made of gold. The Was scepter.

The sheer good fortune of it nearly overwhelmed me. I looked from Bollingsworth's still body to the back wall where von Braggenschnott still struggled to free his hand.

Maybe that old fortuneteller *had* been right. Perhaps the Ancients *were* smiling down on me. Really. There was no other explanation for it.

There was a soft click. I turned and found von Braggenschnott pointing a gun straight at me. Fear rose up in the back of my throat.

"I was reluctant to use this when you were wearing the Heart of Egypt for fear I would destroy it. But that is no longer a problem," he said.

Before I could say anything, I heard the faint sound of someone calling my name.

Von Braggenschnott swung his gun toward the doorway. "If they find me, I will shoot them. Do you understand? The minute they walk through that door, they are dead."

I swallowed, then said, "I understand." I grabbed the Was scepter and stumbled out into the corridor, then hurried over to the bottom of the shaft.

"Miss Theo? Are you here?" Nabir! He was unhurt!

"Theo? Theo darling, where are you?" Mum's voice drifted down the shaft to me. Mum! Nabir must have gone back to get help. And if Mother was here, that meant—

"Theodosia Elizabeth Throckmorton!" Father bellowed. "Where in the blazes are you? Confound it all! Where is that girl? I'm telling you Nabir, if she is hurt or harmed in any way—"

"I'm down here," I called up the shaft as my throat sud-

denly tightened. "I've discovered another chamber!" And wounded two men and possibly killed another, but I kept that part to myself. I didn't want my parents wandering straight into von Braggenschnott's trap.

"Have you really, darling?" Mother's voice was closer now. A second later I saw her head, her lovely, familiar head, as she peered down the shaft at me.

Suddenly Father's head appeared next to Mum's. He surveyed the shaft and the long way down, then scowled. "What were you thinking, Theodosia? You could have been killed!"

His booming voice echoed down the shaft and reverberated throughout the tomb. An unfamiliar warmth spread through me. Father *did* care. In fact, the angrier he sounded, the more worried he was. Von Braggenschnott had got it all wrong.

I smiled. I couldn't help myself. Father's anger was like a balm to my soul. "Yes, I know," I called back. The little shard of betrayal that had been lodged in my heart began to dissolve.

It took them a bit to work out how to get down to where I was and still have a way to get back up again. I kept glancing worriedly over my shoulder, but no sounds came from the chamber. Von Braggenschnott wanted to remain hidden as much as I wanted to keep my parents alive.

Eventually Nabir had the brilliant idea of pulling the ladder up into the tomb and placing it down the shaft.

Father insisted on being the first one down, although I know climbing ladders can't be good for his leg.

When he reached the bottom of the shaft, he never even glanced at the tomb around him. His eyes locked on mine and he stared at me as if I were the most precious artifact he'd ever encountered. I must confess, all that direct scrutiny made me a tad uncomfortable.

He took a step closer. "What happened to you? Are you all right?"

Funny how a little bit of sympathy can make a person positively weepy. I blinked back a few tears and found that I wanted to throw myself into his arms and sob out the whole horrid story. About how close I'd come to being killed, about how we'd had a traitor in our midst the whole time. About how even now von Braggenschnott had a gun that he would use on any of us in a heartbeat.

"Oh, Father. I'm fine. Really." Except, my voice broke horribly and suddenly Father threw his arms around me and drew me into a fierce hug.

Pain surged through my shoulder, burning so brightly that it brought fresh tears to my eyes. But I didn't mind because right that minute, in Father's arms, my world was safe and warm again. The adults in my life were back in charge and I'd let them stay there.

For a bit, anyway.

I pulled away a little and narrowed my eyes. "Father, did

you ever tell Nigel Bollingsworth that I wanted to marry him?"

"Good gracious, no! And embarrass all of us? I think not. Why do you ask?"

My knees grew rubbery with relief. Father *hadn't* betrayed me. Bollingsworth must have been spying on us and overheard. "Never mind. But you should know I don't want to marry him anymore."

"I should say not." He patted me on the shoulder. I squeaked as a jolt of pain crashed through me.

Father frowned. "What's the matter? Are you hurt?"

"Well, yes. I think maybe a little."

Just then Mum reached the bottom of the ladder. "Theo, darling!" She hurried over and grabbed my face in her hands and kissed both of my cheeks, and I had to be careful I didn't accidentally bean her with the Was scepter I'd forgotten I was holding.

"I say," Father said. "What is that thing you're waving around?"

"Why," Mother gasped, her hand flying to her throat, "it's the Was scepter!"

At last Father turned his attention to something other than me and had a good look at the scepter. "Very well done, Theo!" he said. Then he looked back at me. "Now show me where you're injured."

"Don't worry about my shoulder," I said. "You need to come back here." I shoved the scepter at Mother, grabbed his hand with my good arm, and began to pull him toward the chamber where Bollingsworth and von Braggenschnott lay.

"Your shoulder, Theodosia. Now."

"You are a bit pale, dear," Mum said. "You should let your father have a look."

Very gently, he touched my shoulder in a place or two and I nearly screamed.

"It's dislocated," he said. "Easy to fix, but painful. You'll need to be very brave," Father warned.

Brave! If he only knew . . . I nodded, sure that after what I'd been through, I could handle anything.

"Brace yourself," he said, just before he twisted and shoved, sending the most blinding pain crashing through my shoulder.

Then I did what any brave person would do under the circumstances.

I fainted.

Homeward Bound

I DIDN'T BECOME AWARE of my surroundings again until I awoke in a deliciously soft bed with my left arm tightly bound to my side. There was a cool breeze coming in through the curtain and nothing hurt anymore. Delightful.

I breathed deeply and smelled dust and figs and Egypt's own special fragrance. And a faint whiff of lilacs.

I turned my head to find Mum sitting on the chair next to me.

"How do you feel, dear?"

"Much better, thank you." Then, with a start, I remembered. I tried to push myself up to a sitting position, wincing when my shoulder screamed in protest.

"Easy, darling. Easy. You must rest. Father's booked us passage back to England so we can get to Henry as quickly as possible. We'd like to try and leave first thing in the morning. Do you think you'll be up to it?"

I thought of the jostley train ride and grimaced.

"Father's arranging for a steam ship to take us to Cairo," Mum hastened to add. "You're not well enough to travel by train."

"Very well," I said. "But Henry's going to be all right. I promise you."

Mother's eyes were sad and worried. "Let's hope you're right."

"I am," I said, and she looked at me queerly.

"But Mother, what of the men in the tomb? What did you do with them?"

Mother frowned, clearly puzzled. My heart sank. "What men, dear?"

"There were three men in Amenemhab's tomb! One of them was Bollingsworth. He's a spy, working for the Serp—Germans! They were the ones who stole the Heart of Egypt from you." It saddened me that even now I couldn't tell her the whole story.

"Calm down, dear. Calm down. You've had quite a shock with your injury. Besides, our first priority was getting you out safely. When we went back, there was no one there."

Which, of course, meant they'd got clean away. Then I

realized what she'd said. "You didn't take a moment to peek at the new section I discovered?" My parents had passed up the opportunity to explore a previously undiscovered tomb? For me?

"No. Not even a peek. We needed to get you out and find the proper medical treatment. Were there others down there?" she asked. She leaned forward. "Were they from the British Museum?"

I shook my head. "No. I told you. They were Germans. Er, looking for things to sell on the black market."

She clucked her tongue in disgust. A wave of deep exhaustion swept over me. Since there was nothing more to be done, I decided to give up for the moment and let sleep claim me.

Henry and Grandmother Throckmorton were waiting for us at the train station. Henry looked wonderfully alive and well, but he kept giving me accusing looks, as if he were slightly put out about something. Grandmother Throckmorton, on the other hand, was so angry over my running away, she was barely speaking to me. I decided I rather liked this silent treatment of hers.

As we headed back to Grandmother's carriage, I pulled my brother aside. "Look, Henry. I'm sorry I couldn't tell you I was going to Egypt, but I—"

"I thought you trusted me," he said. "We were supposed to be partners from now on." He shoved his hands in his pockets and looked away. "Or so I thought."

Oh, dear. I sorted through all the excuses I could give him, but none of them felt right. In the end, I settled for the truth. "Henry, for years you weren't interested in anything to do with the museum. Now all of a sudden, you are. You have to understand, it will take some getting used to. I'm so accustomed to going it alone . . ."

Henry shrugged and kicked at a leaf. His cheeks grew quite pink. "It wasn't that the museum was so interesting this time around. It's just that you finally quit treating me like a squashed bug you wished someone would put in the dustbin."

"Oh, Henry!" Is that what he'd thought? Had he wanted my attention this whole time, just like I'd wanted Mother's and Father's? "I'm so sorry. Besides, it *was* Wigmere's idea. Orders, really. And he swore me to secrecy."

Henry's head jerked around, his eyes wide. "Really? Wigmere? So are you working for him now, like Will?"

"Sort of. Sometimes, I suppose."

"I say, Theo. That's prime!" Admiration shone in his eyes, and I felt myself relax a bit.

A slight shift in the crowd right behind Grandmother Throckmorton drew my attention as a grimy little hand reached out for her reticule. I opened my mouth to say

something, then clamped it shut. What was it she had said when I got off the train? That I was nothing better than a street urchin. Well, perhaps she ought to have a taste of a *real* street urchin's antics.

Will looked up and caught my eye. He winked, then slipped back into the crowd.

"Theodosia?" Father said, turning around. "What *are* you doing back there?" he asked, scowling. "We've gone to a rather lot of trouble over you, and I don't want to lose you so close to home." Then he put out his hand for me to take. "Come along."

A warm, syrupy feeling ran through me as I put my hand in Father's. Then, hesitatingly, I put my other hand out to Henry. He looked at it, then rolled his eyes. "Girls," he muttered, but he took it all the same. Then we all headed for home.

SAFE—FOR NOW

WE'VE BEEN HOME NEARLY A WEEK NOW and today is the first day I've been allowed back at the museum. Honestly! All this hovering is getting sorely on my nerves. Father, the dear, even brought Isis home to keep me company (and he was sporting a rather vicious scratch on his left cheek for his efforts).

Mum and Dad have decided the Was scepter will be a focal point of our new exhibit, and they are listing me as the person who discovered it! Can you imagine? Me, an eleven-year-old girl, will have my name listed on the museum exhibit. I was quite speechless with joy (which doesn't happen very often).

As I sat in my workroom, trying to draw a diagram of my newly discovered tomb from memory, I heard a loud squeak outside my door. I froze. Fagenbush, maybe? Even though he wasn't a spy, I still didn't trust him.

Before I had time to get well and truly worried, there was a light rap on the door. Visitors who mean you ill rarely knock.

"Come in," I called out. The door opened a crack and Lord Wigmere peeked in. "Are you up for a visitor, Miss Theodosia?"

"Oh, yes! Do come in. I've so much to tell you."

"Yes," he said as he closed the door. "I rather imagine you have."

He limped to my desk and lowered himself into the extra chair. "How did you get in here?" I asked.

He lifted one of his bushy eyebrows at me. "My dear, I am the head of a clandestine society of the most highly trained operatives in the country. I should think I could safely make my way to your . . ." —he glanced around the room— "office."

I leaned forward eagerly. "Did you use the spell Mordecai Quirke talks about in *Black Magic of the Pharaohs*? The one that allows you to pass by people undetected?"

"No. I told the watchman—Flimp, was it?—I was a doctor your parents had consulted." He smiled rather sheepishly. "Now, then. Tell me all about your adventures."

So I did. He listened with rapt attention the whole time, until the end.

"Blast it all!" he said, thumping his cane on the floor in his agitation. "They got clean away?"

"Well, I can't imagine how, what with being stuck to the wall, and broken legs and such. But yes, they did. I'm sorry," I said, hating the bitter taste of failure.

"Oh, I'm sure they had help. Probably had backup nearby. But even so, my dear girl, you've nothing to be sorry about! You served your country in a time of great need. You saved us all. It's just a shame we don't know where they are. It just means we'll have to keep an eye out for them."

"Yes, but you do realize it's not just the Germans they're helping, don't you? Germany is only the beginning. The Serpents of Chaos are intending to reduce the entire world to chaos and then step in and dominate everyone. If we're not careful, the whole world will be at war with itself."

Wigmere sighed deeply. "I knew they had a grand design; I just didn't know what it was. This information will be invaluable as we go forward. How indebted we are to you, I cannot even begin to say. Here. I have something for you." He reached into his coat pocket and fiddled about, then pulled out a tiny silk pouch and handed it to me.

Nearly beside myself with curiosity, I opened the pouch. A stunning gold and lapis beveled ring fell into my hand. "It's just like the one you and Stokes wear!"

"It is. We all felt you earned the right to become an honorary member of the Brotherhood of the Chosen Keepers. You've certainly played your part."

"It's lovely." I sighed in satisfaction as I tried it on. It was small enough so that it fit me perfectly. I looked up at Wigmere. "If I'm an honorary member of the Brotherhood, does that mean I can have one of those tattoos?"

"On a young girl?" Wigmere looked startled, then began to chuckle. "I think not!"

Bother.